THE
DECLARATION

THE
DECLARATION

GEMMA MALLEY

BLOOMSBURY

First published in Great Britain by Bloomsbury Publishing Plc
Published in the United States by Bloomsbury U.S.A. Children's Books
175 Fifth Avenue, New York, NY 10010
Distributed to the trade by Holtzbrinck Publishers

Library of Congress Cataloging-in-Publication Data
Malley, G. R. (Gemma R.)
The Declaration / by Gemma Malley. — 1st U.S. ed.
p.   cm.
Summary: In 2140 England, where drugs enable people to live forever and
children are illegal, teenaged Anna, an obedient "Surplus" training to become
a house servant, discovers that her birth parents are trying to find her.
ISBN-13: 978-1-59990-119-0 • ISBN-10: 1-59990-119-6
[1. Aging—Fiction. 2. Immortality—Fiction. 3. Children—Fiction. 4. England—
Fiction. 5. Science fiction.] I. Title.
PZ7.M2953De 2007   [Fic]—dc22   2006102138

First U.S. Edition 2007
Typeset by Dorchester Typesetting Group Ltd
Printed in the U.S.A. by Quebecor World Fairfield
2 4 6 8 10 9 7 5 3 1

All papers used by Bloomsbury U.S.A. are natural, recyclable products
made from wood grown in well-managed forests. The manufacturing processes
conform to the environmental regulations of the country of origin.

For Dorie Simmonds

Chapter One

11 January, 2140

My name is Anna.

My name is Anna and I shouldn't be here. I shouldn't exist.

But I do.

It's not my fault I'm here. I didn't ask to be born. But that doesn't make it any better that I was. They caught me early, though, which bodes well. That's what Mrs Pincent says, anyway. She's the lady that runs Grange Hall. We call her House Matron. Grange Hall is where I live. Where people like me are brought up to be Useful – the 'best of a bad situation', Mrs Pincent says.

I don't have another name. Not like Mrs Pincent does. Mrs Pincent's name is Margaret Pincent. Some people call her Margaret, most people call her Mrs

Pincent, and we call her House Matron. Lately I've started to call her Mrs Pincent too, although not to her face – I'm not stupid.

Legal people generally have at least two names, sometimes more.

Not me, though. I'm just Anna. People like me don't need more than one name, Mrs Pincent says. One is quite enough.

Actually, she doesn't even like the name Anna – she told me she tried to change it when I first came here. But I was an obstinate child, she says, and I wouldn't answer to anything else, so in the end she gave up. I'm pleased – I like the name Anna, even though my parents gave me that name.

I hate my parents. They broke the Declaration and didn't care about anyone else but themselves. They're in prison now. I don't know where. None of us knows anything about our parents any more. Which is fine by me – I'd have nothing to say to them anyway.

None of the girls or boys here has more than one name. That's one of the things that makes us different, Mrs Pincent says. Not the most important thing, of course – having one name is really just a detail. But sometimes it doesn't feel like a detail. Sometimes I long for a second name, even a horrible one – I wouldn't care what it was. One time I even asked Mrs Pincent if I could be Anna Pincent, to have her name after mine. But that made her really angry and she hit me hard across the head and took me off hot meals for a whole week. Mrs Larson, our Sewing Instructor, explained later that it had been an insult to suggest that someone like me could have Mrs Pincent's name. As if she could be related to me.

Actually I do sort of have another name, but it's a pre-name, not an after-name. And everyone here has got the same one, so it doesn't really feel like a name. On the list that Mrs Pincent carries around with her, I'm down as:

Surplus Anna.

But really, it's more of a description than a name. We're all Surpluses at Grange Hall. Surplus to requirements. Surplus to capacity.

I'm very lucky to be here, actually. I've got a chance to redeem my Parents' Sins, if I work hard enough and become employable. Not everyone gets that kind of chance, Mrs Pincent says. In some countries Surpluses are killed, put down like animals.

They'd never do that here, of course. In England they help Surpluses be Useful to other people, so it isn't quite so bad we were born. Here they set up Grange Hall because of the staffing requirements of Legal people, and that's why we have to work so hard – to show our gratitude.

But you can't have Surplus Halls all over the world for every Surplus that's born. It's like straws on a camel's back, Mrs Pincent says. Each and every Surplus could be the final straw that breaks the camel's back. Probably, being put down is the best thing for everyone – who would want to be the straw that broke the back of Mother Nature? That's why I hate my parents. It's their fault I'm here. They didn't think about anyone except themselves.

I sometimes wonder about the children who are put down. I wonder how the Authorities do it and whether it hurts. And I wonder what they do for maids and housekeepers in those countries. Or handymen. My friend Sheila says that they do sometimes put children down here too. But I don't believe her. Mrs Pincent says Sheila's imagination is far too active and that it's going to be her downfall. I don't know if her imagination is too active, but I do think she makes things up, like when she arrived and she swore to me that her parents hadn't signed the Declaration, that she was Legal and that it had been a big mistake because her parents had Opted Out of Longevity. She insisted over and over again that they'd be coming to collect her once they'd sorted it all out.

They never did, of course.

There're five hundred of us here at Grange Hall. I'm one of the eldest and I've been here the longest too.

I've lived here since I was two and a half – that's how old I was when they found me. I was being kept in an attic – can you believe that? The neighbours heard me crying, apparently. They knew there weren't meant to be any children in the house and called the Authorities. I owe those neighbours a great deal, Mrs Pincent says. Children have a way of knowing the truth, she says, and I was probably crying because I wanted to be found. What else was I going to do – spend my life in an attic?

I can't remember anything about the attic or my parents. I used to, I think – but I'm not really sure. It could have been dreams I was remembering. Why would anyone break the Declaration and have a baby just to keep it in an attic? It's just plain stupid.

I can't remember much about arriving at Grange Hall either, but that's hardly surprising – I mean, who remembers being two and a half? I remember feeling cold, remember screaming out for my parents until my throat was hoarse because back then I didn't realise how selfish and stupid they were. I also remember getting into trouble no matter what I did. But that's all, really.

I don't get into trouble any more. I've learnt about responsibility, Mrs Pincent says, and am set to be a Valuable Asset.

Valuable Asset Anna. I like that a lot more than Surplus.

The reason I'm set to be a Valuable Asset is that I'm a fast learner. I can cook fifty dishes to top standard, and another forty to satisfactory. I'm not as good with fish as I am with meat. But I'm a good seamstress and am going to make someone a very solid housekeeper according to my last appraisal. If my attention to detail improves, I'll get an even better report next time. Which means that in six months, when I leave Grange Hall, I might go to one of the better houses. In six months it's my fifteenth birthday. It'll be time to fend for myself then, Mrs Pincent says. I'm lucky to have had such good training because I Know My Place, and people in the nicest houses like that.

I don't know how I feel about leaving Grange Hall. Excited, I think, but scared too. The furthest I've ever been is to a house in the village, where I did an internship for three weeks when the owner's own housekeeper was ill. Mrs Kean, the Cooking Instructor, walked me down there one Friday night and then she brought me back when it was over. Both times it was dark so I didn't see much of the village at all.

The house I was working in was beautiful, though. It was nothing like Grange Hall – the rooms were painted in bright, warm colours, with thick carpet on the floor that you could kneel on without it killing your knees, and huge big sofas that made you want to curl up and sleep for ever.

It had a big garden that you could see out of all the windows, and it was filled with beautiful flowers. At the back of the garden was something called an Allotment where Mrs Sharpe grew vegetables sometimes, although there weren't any growing when I was there. She said that flowers were an Indulgence and frowned upon by the Authorities. Now that food couldn't be flown around the world, everyone had to grow their own. She said she thought that flowers were important too, but that the Authorities didn't agree. I think she's right – I think flowers can be just as important as food, sometimes. I think it depends what you're hungry for.

In the house, Mrs Sharpe had her radiators on sometimes, so it was never cold. And she was the nicest, kindest woman – once when I was cleaning her bedroom she offered to let me try on some lipstick. I said no, because I thought she might tell Mrs Pincent, but I regretted it later. Mrs Sharpe talked to me almost like I wasn't a Surplus. She said it was nice to have a young face about the place again.

I loved working there – mainly because of Mrs Sharpe being so nice, but also because I loved looking at the photos she had all over her walls of incredible-looking places. In each photo, there was Mrs Sharpe, smiling, holding a drink or standing in front of a beautiful building or monument. She said that the photographs were mementos of each of her holidays. She went on an international holiday three times a year at least, she told me. She said that she used to go by aeroplane but now energy tariffs meant that she had to go by boat or train instead, but she still went because you have to see the world, otherwise what's the point? I wanted to ask 'The point of what?' but I didn't because you're not meant to ask questions, it's not polite. She said she'd been to a hundred and fifty different countries, some more than twice, and I tried to stop my mouth dropping open because I didn't want her to know that I hadn't even known there were that many countries in the world. We don't learn about countries at Grange Hall.

Mrs Sharpe has probably been to four hundred and fifty-three countries now, because it was a whole a year ago that I was at her house. I wish I were still her housekeeper. She didn't hit me even once.

It must be amazing to travel to foreign countries. Mrs Sharpe showed me a map of the world and showed me where England is. She told me about the deserts in the Middle East, about the mountains in India and about the sea. I think my favourite place would be the desert because apparently there are no people there at all. It would be hard to be Surplus in the desert – even if you knew you were one really, there wouldn't be anyone else around to remind you.

I'll probably never see any desert, though. Mrs Pincent says it's all disappearing fast because they can *build on it now. Desert is a luxury this world can't afford, she says. And I should be worrying about the state of my ironing, not thinking of places I'll never be able to go to. I'm not sure she's exactly right about that, although I'd never say that to her. Mrs Sharpe said she had a housekeeper once who used to go with her travelling around the world, doing her packing and organising tickets and things like that. She had her for forty years, she told me, and she was very sad to see her go because her new housekeeper can't take the hot temperatures, so she has to leave her behind when she goes away. If I could get a job with a lady who travels a lot, I don't think I'd mind the hot temperatures. The desert's the hottest place of all and I'm sure I'd love it there.*

'Anna! Anna, will you come here this minute!'

Anna looked up from the small journal Mrs Sharpe had given her as a parting gift and quickly returned it, and her pen, to its hiding place.

'Yes, Mrs Pincent,' she called hurriedly, and rushed out of Female Bathroom 2 and down the corridor, her face flushed. How long had Mrs Pincent been calling her? How had she not heard her call?

The truth was that she'd never realised how absorbing it could be to write. She'd had Mrs Sharpe's journal for a year now. It was a small, fat book covered in pale pink suede and filled with thick, creamy pages that looked so beautiful she couldn't ever imagine ruining them by making a single mark on that lovely paper. Every so often she'd taken it out to look at it. She would turn it over in her hands, guiltily enjoying the soft texture of the suede against her skin before secreting it away again. But she'd never written in it – not until today, that is. Today, for some reason, she had taken it out, picked up a pen, and without even thinking had started to write. And once she'd started, she found she didn't want to stop. Thoughts and feelings that usually lay hidden beneath worries and exhaustion suddenly came flooding to the surface as if gasping for air.

Which was all very well, but if it was discovered, she would be beaten. Number one, she wasn't allowed to accept gifts from anyone. And number two, journals and writing were forbidden at Grange Hall. Surpluses were not there to read and write; they were there to learn and work, Mrs Pincent told them regularly. She said that things would be much easier if they didn't have to teach them to read and write in the first place, because reading and writing were a dangerous business; they made you think, and Surpluses who thought too much were useless and difficult. But people wanted maids and housekeepers who were literate, so Mrs Pincent didn't have a choice.

If she were truly Valuable Asset material, she would get rid of the journal completely, Anna knew that. Temptation was a test, Mrs Pincent often said. She'd already failed it twice – first by accepting the gift and now by writing in it. A true Valuable Asset wouldn't succumb to temptation like that, would they? A Valuable Asset simply wouldn't break the rules.

But Anna, who never broke any rules, who believed that regulations existed to be followed to the letter, had finally found a temptation that she could not resist. Now that the journal bore her writing, she knew that the stakes had been raised, and yet she could not bear to lose it, whatever the cost.

She would simply have to ensure it was never found, she resolved as she raced towards Mrs Pincent's office. If no one knew her guilty secret, then perhaps she could bury her feelings along with the journal and convince herself that she wasn't evil after all, that the little fragment of peace she had carved out for herself at Grange Hall was not really in jeopardy.

Before she turned the corner, Anna took a quick look at herself and smoothed down her overalls. Surpluses had to look neat and orderly at all times, and the last thing Anna wanted was to irk Mrs Pincent unnecessarily. She was a Prefect now, which meant she got second helpings at supper when there was food left over, and an extra blanket that meant the difference between a good night's sleep and one spent shivering from the cold. No, the last thing she wanted was any trouble.

Taking a deep breath, and focusing herself so that she would appear to Mrs Pincent the usual calm and organised Anna, she turned the corner and knocked on the House Matron's open door.

Mrs Pincent's office was a cold, dark room with a wooden floor, yellowing walls covered in peeling paint and a harsh overhead light that seemed to highlight all the dust in the air. Even though she was nearly fifteen now, Anna had been in that room enough times for a beating or some other punishment to feel an instinctive fear every time she crossed its threshold.

'Anna, there you are,' Mrs Pincent said, her voice irritable. 'Please don't keep me waiting like that in future. I want you to prepare a bed for a new boy.'

Anna nodded. 'Yes, House Matron,' she said, deferentially. 'Small?'

The incumbents at Grange Hall were classified as Small, Middle and Pending. Small was the usual entrant size – anything from babies and toddlers up to five-year-olds. You always knew when a new Small had arrived because of the crying and screaming which went on for days as they acclimatised to their new surroundings – which was why the Small's dormitories were tucked away on the top floor where they wouldn't disturb everyone else. That was the idea, anyway; in reality, you could never get away from the crying completely. It pervaded everything – both the wailing of the new Smalls and the memories the sound invoked in everyone else; years of crying which hung in the air like a ghost with unfinished business. Few ever truly forgot their first few weeks and months in the new, harsh surroundings of Grange Hall; few enjoyed the memory of being wrenched from desperate parents and transported in the dead of night to their new, stark and regimented home. Every time a new Small arrived, the others did their best to close their ears and ignore the memories that inevitably found their way into their consciousness. No one felt sorry for them – if anything, they felt resentment and anger. One more Surplus, ruining things for everyone else.

Middles were the six-year-olds up to about eleven or twelve. Some new Middles arrived from time to time, and they tended to be quiet and withdrawn rather than cry. Middles learnt faster how institutional life worked, figured out that tears and tantrums were not tolerated and were not worth the beating. But whilst they were easier to manage than the Smalls, they brought their own set of problems. Because they arrived late, because they had spent so long with their parents, they often had some very bad ideas about things. Some would make challenges in Science and Nature classes; others, like Sheila, secretly held on to the belief that their parents would come for them. Middles could be really idiotic sometimes, refusing to accept that they were lucky to be at Grange Hall.

Anna herself was a Pending. Pending employment. Pending was when the training really started in earnest and you were expected to learn everything you'd need for your future employers. Pending was also when they started testing you, starting up discussions on things like Longevity drugs and parents and

Surpluses, just to see whether you Knew Your Place or not, whether you were fit for the outside world. Anna was far too clever for that trick. She wasn't going to be one of the stupid ones who leapt on the first opportunity to speak their mind and started to criticise the Declaration. They got their two minutes of glory and then they got shipped out to a detention centre. Hard labour was what Mrs Pincent called it. Anna shuddered at the thought. Anyway, she did Know Her Place and didn't want to argue against science and nature and the Authorities. She felt bad enough about existing without becoming a trouble-maker to boot.

Mrs Pincent frowned. 'No, not Small. Make the bed up in the Pending dormitory.'

Anna's eyes opened wide. No one had ever joined Grange Hall as a Pending. It had to be a mistake. Unless he'd been trained somewhere else, of course.

'Has . . . has he come from another Surplus Hall?' she asked before she could stop herself. Mrs Pincent didn't approve of asking questions unless they involved clarification of a specific task.

Mrs Pincent's eyes narrowed slightly. 'That is all, Anna,' she said with a cursory nod. 'You'll have it ready in an hour.'

Anna nodded silently and turned to leave, trying not to betray the intense curiosity she was feeling. A Pending Surplus would be at least thirteen. Who was he? Where had he been all this time? And why was he coming here now?

Chapter Two

Peter didn't appear until a week later. He turned up in the middle of Science and Nature, and Anna tried not to even look at him because that's what everyone was doing and she didn't want him to know she was curious. No doubt he'd think he was something special and she wasn't having that.

Anyway, she knew something that no one else knew. She knew that he hadn't arrived that week; he'd arrived the week before, just like Mrs Pincent said he would. Only he had arrived late at night, and they must have taken him away somewhere because his bed hadn't been slept in when she looked the next day.

It had been about midnight that she'd heard him arrive seven days before. Everyone else had been asleep, but Anna had been up on Floor 2, scribbling in her journal before hiding it away in the one place that she was sure it would never be found. The whole of Grange Hall had been silent except for a few dripping taps and the usual faint crying from the top floor, which suited Anna perfectly because it meant she was safe, that no one would interrupt her.

On her way back from Mrs Pincent's office earlier that evening, she had told herself that she would throw the journal away, ashamed that she'd succumbed to temptation so easily.

But the thought of losing it made her wince with pain and longing, and immediately arguments for keeping it flooded her head, the most convincing of which was that it would get found if she threw it away. There was no way a beautiful pink suede journal would sit in a dustbin unnoticed, and even if she wrapped it up with old newspaper, someone would find it at some point, and when they did they'd find her writing in it.

No, she'd decided, it was much safer hidden, and Female Bathroom 2 was the only place she could think of. Female Bathroom 2 was situated on Floor 2, and it had contained a secret long before Anna's journal entered Grange Hall – a little cavity behind one of the baths. Anna had discovered it years before when she'd dropped her soap down the side of the bath by mistake. Knowing she'd get beaten if she lost it – soap had to last four months and being Wasteful was considered a form of subversion that merited night working as a punishment – she'd managed to squirm into a position from which her arm could reach down where the soap had fallen, and had found it sitting on a little ledge which was completely hidden from view unless you knew what you were looking for.

At the time, she hadn't really thought much about

it – she was so relieved to have got the soap back, she'd just finished her wash quickly and raced back to the dormitory for Evening Vows. But later on, she'd realised that she'd found a little hiding place, and it made her feel both anxious and excited all at once. It was her little secret. And although she couldn't pick it up and take it with her, it was, apart from her Grange Hall overalls, toothbrush and facecloth, the first thing she'd ever owned.

Surpluses weren't allowed possessions; they had no right to own things in a world that they'd gate-crashed, Mrs Pincent said. And although Anna didn't think that a secret cavity really constituted a possession, in the weeks afterwards, as if encouraged by this one first step on the ownership ladder, she'd begun to acquire things that were more tangible assets. Like a magpie, she had alighted upon a scrap of fabric that had been torn off a skirt from the laundry and a tea-spoon that had been left by someone in the House Room, both of which she put in her secret hiding place, delirious in the knowledge that she knew some-thing that no one else did. Of course, that had been a long time ago. She had grown out of that childish game years before.

At least she'd thought she had. Had hoped she had.

Either way, the journal was waiting for her the night that the new Surplus arrived. Anna had gone to Female Bathroom 2 for a late-night wash, just to check that it was safe, just to hold it in her hands one more time and see for herself the words that she had created, that she had made her mark with. It had been a long day, what with training, Cookery Practical and then having to make up the bed for the new Surplus in the Pending boys' dormitory. She had completed all her chores, and meticulously made up the new Surplus's bed with one sheet and one blanket, and had placed a facecloth, toothbrush, soap and tube of toothpaste on top of it, just as Mrs Pincent had asked her to.

As she had sat shivering in the cold bath (Surpluses weren't allowed hot baths – they weren't allowed to use any more of the world's resources than was absolutely necessary), Anna, the Prefect, found her arm gingerly easing its way down the side of the tub, her reward for good behaviour. Anna had known it was wrong, but its hold on her was too strong to resist, and, as she had pulled it out, she could feel herself tremble with excitement. The soft pink between her fingers and the news that there was a new Surplus coming had created surges of adrenaline that zipped around her body, causing her toes to clench and her stomach to leap. A Pending Surplus from the Outside – he'd know what the world was like, he'd be untrained. He'd be . . . Anna had shuddered with anticipation as she'd begun to write. The truth was that she'd had no idea what he'd be like – dangerous and difficult, probably – but she had known that things would be different when he arrived. How could they fail to be?

As these thoughts had rushed around her head,

she'd looked at the clock on the wall and noted with a sigh that it was five minutes to twelve. Grange Hall still had clocks in lots of the rooms, even though Surpluses didn't need to refer to them. They were fixed to the wall, she'd heard Mrs Pincent tell one of the Instructors, and anyway, they reminded Mrs Pincent of a 'better time'. Anna wasn't sure whether Mrs Pincent meant a time long ago, or whether it was time itself that was better on a clock, but either way, she loved watching the hands slowly moving around the large, round clock faces and had convinced Mrs Dawson, one of the Instructors, to teach her how to read them, even though she didn't need to. Surpluses had time embedded in their wrists; Surplus time-keeping was in digital. Embedded Time had been one of the New Ideas for Surpluses, when Surplus Halls were still new. Time wasn't on a Surplus's side, Mrs Pincent said. Time was just one of the things that Surpluses didn't deserve. Legals owned time, but Surpluses were slaves to it, as every piercing bell announcing feeding, morning or bedtime at Grange Hall reminded them.

Embedded Time was one of the only New Ideas that actually took off, Mrs Kean had said once, talking to Mrs Dawson when she didn't know Anna was listening. New Ideas didn't tend to surface much any more, she'd said, because everyone was complacent. No one could be bothered to come up with new things because it was too much like hard work. And Mrs Dawson had nodded and said, 'What a relief,' and Mrs Kean had looked at her for a moment, as if she wanted to say something, but instead, she just nodded and that was the end of that.

Embedded Time sat under the skin, on the wrist, and every movement the Surplus made kept the mechanism going so that it wasn't Wasteful or resource intensive. And with time ever-present, the Authorities argued, no Surplus could ever be late, no Surplus could ever leave their chores early. Anna couldn't remember not having Embedded Time, couldn't imagine why everyone wouldn't have it. But Legal people like Instructors didn't; they wore watches, which did the same thing, only on the outside of the wrist.

Anna had glanced down and confirmed that in spite of the Authorities' best efforts, she was indeed late, if only for sleep. She needed to get out of the bath, to calm herself so she could fall into a deep slumber. Otherwise, tomorrow would be torture. She was safe now that the journal was hidden, and there was no point thinking about the new Surplus. No reason for her to still be feeling jumpy.

Quickly getting out of the tub, she had taken a small towel from the rail in front of her and dried herself mechanically, the rough, dry cotton welcome after the cold, soapy water. And right then, she'd heard him arrive. The sounds were muffled and at one point she'd thought she could hear the anguished yelps of an injured dog, but then she'd realised it was probably a gag. They used gags sometimes, if Surpluses were particularly noisy. The driving unions had insisted on it, Mrs Pincent said – their members were getting upset. It was bad enough Surpluses existing, she said, without also causing mayhem and hurting Legal people.

Then Anna had heard something break and, a few seconds after that, a crack and a noise that had sounded like something heavy but soft hitting the floor. Then some more muffled voices, and a minute or so later, silence.

She'd crept out of the bathroom and held her breath for a few minutes, listening for something else – perhaps the sound of the Surplus being taken up the stairs to the Pending boys' dormitory, but eventually she'd given up. He must have gone to Mrs Pincent's office, she decided. She'd find out tomorrow, anyway. Right now it was time to go to bed.

But in the morning, when she'd taken a detour to breakfast in order to have a look at the new incumbent and perhaps to introduce herself, she'd found that the new Surplus's bed hadn't been slept in after all. The other Pending boys had simply shrugged when she'd asked them about him; Mrs Pincent hadn't even told them someone new was coming and they certainly weren't going to trouble themselves over an empty bed. An empty bed meant an extra blanket and no one was going to complain about that.

When there was no sign of him the next day, nor the day after that, Anna had begun to think that they must have taken him to a different Surplus Hall, or maybe to a detention centre; perhaps they'd decided that Pending was too late to arrive at Grange Hall.

But then, a week later, he'd turned up again.

He arrived, dressed in regulation navy overalls, the same overalls that every other Surplus wore – shapeless, sturdy and practical – just when Mr Sargent was telling the story of Longevity for about the fiftieth time. Mr Sargent was their Science and Nature teacher and he never got sick of that story, never tired of telling them about the natural scientists who found a way to cure old age. Before they did that, people used to die. All the time. From horrible diseases. And they looked awful too.

Anna knew the story of Longevity very well and, like Mr Sargent, she never got sick of it either. Longevity was how humans fulfilled the ambitions of Nature. Longevity proved that humans were superior in every way. But with superiority came responsibility, Mr Sargent said. You couldn't abuse the trust and bounty of Mother Nature.

Before Longevity, people died from things called cancer, heart disease and Aids. They also got something called disability, sometimes, which meant that something went wrong and couldn't be fixed. Like if someone lost a leg in an accident or something, they had to spend the rest of their life in a chair with wheels on it because they couldn't make new legs back then. Renewal didn't exist and brain exercises weren't invented yet, and everyone died by the time they were seventy, apart from a few lucky people, but they weren't really that lucky; they were tired all the time and couldn't hear properly so they might as well have been dead, really.

Then the natural scientists discovered Renewal, where you could get new, fresh, cells to replace old ones and they mended the rest of your cells too. First they cured cancer. Then they cured heart disease. It took them quite a bit longer to cure Aids, but eventually they cured that too, although it needed more cells.

And then a natural scientist called Dr Fern discovered something else. He found out that Renewal worked against old age too. He took some of the drugs himself to see what happened, and he stopped getting older, just like that. Only he didn't tell anyone about it for a while. And when he did, the Authorities (which used to be called the government) made it illegal to take the drugs if you didn't have Aids or cancer, because they were worried about things called pensions and people being a Burden on the State.

Dr Fern died eventually because he wasn't allowed to take the drugs any more, but a few years later, the Authorities realised that with Longevity, people wouldn't have to stop working. If people didn't get old, and they didn't get ill, the government would save lots of money. By then Longevity drugs were being taken by people anyway, only they were doing it illegally. There were lots of people saying that Longevity drugs should be legalised, and so in 2030 the Prime Minister commissioned a trial. And when he realised that there were no side effects and that people could now live for ever, he decided that this was a breakthrough, and the biggest drug companies in England got together to start producing Longevity drugs for everyone.

That's when dying stopped, first in Europe, America and China and then, gradually, everywhere else. Some countries were late adopters because the drugs were expensive, but then terrorists started to attack England because they wouldn't give everyone the drugs and soon after that the price got lower so everyone could have them.

'And what do you think happened, then?' Mr Sargent always asked, his beady eyes searching out someone in the classroom who would encapsulate the fundamental flaw in the programme.

More times than not, Anna would put up her hand.

'There were too many people,' she would say seriously. 'If no one dies and people have more children, there's nowhere for everyone to go.'

'Exactly,' Mr Sargent would say. And then he would tell them about the Declaration, which was introduced in 2065, and which said that people could only have one baby. If they tried to have another, it would be terminated.

Then, a few years after that, they realised that one baby was still too many. So in 2080 the new Declaration said that no one could have any children at all, unless they Opted Out of Longevity completely. Every country had to sign the Declaration and Surplus Police, or Catchers, as they began to be called, were responsible for tracking down anyone who broke it.

Opting Out meant that you were allowed to have a child. 'One child per Opt Out' or 'A life for a life', as the Declaration put it. But that meant you would get ill and then die, so Opting Out wasn't very popular.

People who Opted Out were regarded with suspicion, Mr Sargent told them. Who would die just to have a child, when you didn't even know if the child would be any good? Of course, there were some selfish, criminal people who didn't Opt Out and still had children to suck up the world's natural resources and ruin things for the Legal people . . . but they all knew about that, didn't they? That was why Grange Hall existed – to give the Surpluses that resulted from such criminality a purpose; to help them learn their responsibilities and to train them to provide a useful service to Legals. Surpluses weren't allowed Longevity drugs either. 'Why prolong the agony?' Mr Sargent said.

And that was the point at which Peter arrived. The door opened, Mrs Pincent walked in, and Peter followed. Anna didn't know he was called Peter then; when she first saw him walk through the door into the Science and Nature lab, she only knew that this, finally, was the Pending Surplus. That he hadn't been taken somewhere else, after all.

Everyone was looking at him, sneakily. Without letting anyone see that she, too, was shooting little looks at him, Anna noted that he was tall and gangly and had very pale skin that had some dark marks on it that could have been bruises but could equally have

basement – Floor 0 housed the training rooms, Central Feeding and Mrs Pincent's office; Floor 1 housed the boys' dormitories with ten large rooms accommodating between ten and twenty occupants each (you could fit more Middles in a dormitory than Pendings, particularly the younger ones) and two bathrooms; Floor 2 housed the girls in a similar way; Floor 3 housed the Smalls and the Domestics, who were Legals that performed any cleaning and cooking tasks that weren't taken care of by the Surpluses, and whose job it was to care for the Smalls, although 'care' didn't come into it much. Every room and corridor was decorated in the same way – pale grey walls, darker grey concrete floors, fluorescent lighting and thin radiators which had been fitted when Grange Hall served a different purpose; now they were permanently turned off because Surpluses, Mrs Pincent said, had no right to central heating. The low ceilings and triple-glazed windows, each covered by a long, grey vertical blind, kept in the heat as well as excluding the Outside; security cameras on the perimeter walls screened every visitor to the Hall and ensured that no one could leave unseen.

When Anna came across Peter, she was on her way to replenish the stock cupboard, one of her jobs as a Prefect, and in her hand she was carrying a detailed list of exactly how many tubes of toothpaste and bars of soap had been used in the past month by the Surpluses in her dormitory. One tube or bar too many, and they would all be made to work extra hours to make up for the squandering of essential resources. Anna's dormitory never went over their quota, though, she made sure of that.

She looked at Peter, narrowing her eyes slightly as she passed him, and it was only when he said her name that she reluctantly stopped.

'Anna,' he said softly. 'Anna Covey.'

She stared at him angrily.

'Surplus Anna,' she corrected him. 'Please don't use words from the Outside in Grange Hall, and please don't pretend that you know my parents, because as far as I'm concerned I don't have any.'

Peter looked at her uncomprehendingly, his eyes making her shift uncomfortably on her feet because she wasn't used to anyone scrutinising her like that.

'So what goes on in here, then?' he asked, looking at the door to the sanatorium.

'Health check,' Anna said curtly. 'You'll be checked for any weaknesses and given vaccinations against diseases. And weighed. Surpluses have a duty to maintain their health so as not to burden the earth further with illness.'

Peter raised his eyebrows. 'I thought Surpluses weren't allowed drugs. I thought they wanted Surpluses to die off as quickly as possible.'

His voice was low and had an edge to it and Anna found herself getting warm.

'Of course Surpluses can't have drugs,' she said crossly. 'Vaccinations are preventative, not curative.'

She found her eyes drawn to Peter, drawn to his

dark, agitated eyes, his pale skin, his defiant chin. Quickly, she forced herself to look away.

'Being Surplus means you have to limit your impact on the earth,' she said, with a sigh. 'They don't want us dead. They just don't want us spreading disease, or being too weak to be Useful.'

'And you're "useful"?' Peter asked softly.

Anna frowned. 'Of course. I'm set to be a Valuable Asset. They're the most Useful Surpluses.'

Peter nodded silently, his eyes cast downwards, then they flickered up to Anna's. 'Do you have computers here? Or a library?'

Anna stared at him. 'Computers?' she asked cautiously. She knew what computers were. Mrs Sharpe turned hers on for two hours a day to watch television programmes and to read about the news, and Mrs Pincent had one, too, but Anna had never actually used one. How could she, when anything that used unnecessary electricity was banished from Grange Hall? She didn't like the idea that this new Surplus might know more than she did. 'We don't need computers,' she said defensively. 'And anyway, they use too much energy. Everyone knows that.'

'Of course they do. Silly me,' Peter said, with a sigh. His foot was tapping the ground beneath it, and once more, Anna felt her eyes pulled to his strong but slender frame. He seemed so full of confidence, energy and curiosity, and it made Anna both intrigued and nervous. Surpluses were trained to be passive, obedient, and just the glint in Peter's eyes made Anna feel like she was looking at something she shouldn't, like she was being drawn into a whirlpool, even though she suspected that the current would be too strong, even though she knew she couldn't swim.

'I have to go now,' she said quickly. 'I have stock to collect.'

She started to walk away, but she stopped again when she heard Peter's voice.

'You . . . you like it here, Anna?' he asked softly, his gaze challenging.

Anna turned and frowned. What kind of question was that? She bit her lip, and found herself reddening as Peter smiled at her, a little twinkle appearing in his eye, which made Anna feel like she was already in the whirlpool and drowning.

'I *am* here,' she said, her voice suddenly slightly hoarse. 'And so are you. Surpluses aren't here to like things, Peter, they're here to do things. Useful things. And the sooner you learn that, the better for everyone.'

Quickly, Anna turned and marched briskly down the corridor, trying to push the picture of that smile out of her head and to focus instead on the number of toothpaste tubes she would need for the following month.

Anna didn't see Peter at any more training sessions that day. The male and female Surpluses shared certain sessions – Science and Nature, Decorum, Laundry and House Maintenance – but the majority were single sex. The classes were held in smallish rooms with the desks packed tightly together and on rare hot summer days it was not uncommon for weaker Surpluses to faint from heat exhaustion. Today, though, it was bitterly cold, and as she listened to the Instructors Anna had been desperately tensing and untensing her leg muscles under her desk, just in order to try and stay warm.

By the time she got to supper that evening, she was so cold and ravenous that she didn't notice Peter slipping silently behind her in the queue for broth. It was only when she had the hot bowl in her hands and was carrying it towards one of the long, narrow tables that filled Central Feeding, that she saw him, and realised that he was about to sit down next to her.

'Usually the boys sit together,' she said tightly, as she put her bowl down and immediately started to spoon the lumpy mixture into her mouth. She felt tired and irritable, and she just wanted to sit quietly and eat her food; the last thing she needed was Peter with his stupid comments and constant questions.

'But not always?' Peter asked, putting his bowl on the table and noisily scraping back the bench so that he could sit down.

Anna ignored him and continued to eat as the table filled up.

'This is disgusting,' Peter said a few moments later. 'What is it? It tastes vile.'

No one said anything, and after a few seconds of silence, Anna reluctantly put her spoon down.

'This is good, nutritious food,' she said wearily.

'What's good and nutritious about it?' Peter demanded. 'This isn't even meat. It's like sawdust.'

Anna swallowed her mouthful. 'It's reconstituted meat,' she said. 'With flour to thicken it. And I think it's delicious.'

'Then you can have mine,' Peter said, pushing his bowl towards her.

Anna stared at him. 'You have to eat your food, Peter. It's our duty to stay strong and . . .'

'Strong and healthy, yeah,' Peter interrupted her. 'Well, I'm not going to be either if I eat this.'

Anna felt her heart begin to quicken in her chest. All the other Surpluses at the table were studiously looking down, but that didn't mean they didn't know what was going on. An offer of extra food was a rare thing, and Anna's eyes were already looking at Peter's bowl greedily. But if Mrs Pincent found out that Peter hadn't eaten, he might be beaten for selfishness.

Looking around furtively, Anna grabbed Peter's bowl and poured half of its contents into her bowl, then pushed it back towards Peter.

'You have to eat the rest,' she said, her voice low. 'You have to eat something.'

Peter shrugged. 'There's worse things than being hungry, you know,' he said softly. 'Don't you agree, Anna?'

She could feel Peter's eyes on her, and she decided to ignore him, gulping down her broth quickly. She wanted to get away from Peter, wanted him to stop talking to her and looking at her as though he thought she was interested in anything he had to say.

But instead of taking her hint, Peter moved his head closer to Anna's. 'Your mother is a wonderful cook, Anna. She makes the most delicious food. Shall I tell you?'

Anna clamped her hands to her ears, knocking her spoon to the ground in the process. 'No,' she hissed. 'No, she doesn't, and no I don't want you to tell me anything.'

She leant down to pick up her spoon, but as she reached for it, a large, heavy foot landed on her fingers and she yelped.

'Dropped something?' a voice asked, and Anna grimaced. It was Surplus Charlie, another Pending, tall like Peter but broad too, his large frame pushing at the seams of his overalls.

'Get off my hand,' Anna said angrily, pushing at his leg with her free hand. 'I'll report you . . .'

'Are you bowing down to me, Surplus Anna?' Charlie asked thinly, his greenish eyes mocking her. 'It looks to me as if you might have finally Learnt Your Place.'

Anna gritted her teeth and tried again to pull her hand away, but before she could do so, Charlie suddenly went tumbling to the floor. She rescued her hand and sat up to see Peter towering over Charlie, his foot pressed into his chest.

'Maybe *you* need to learn your place,' Peter growled. 'Maybe you need to learn some manners.'

He looked at Anna with a little smile. 'What shall I do with him, Anna Covey?' he mouthed silently, and she stared at him fearfully. Fights between Surpluses were tolerated in dormitories, but in Central Feeding Surpluses weren't encouraged to even talk to each other; Peter could have all three of them beaten if any of the Instructors saw what had just happened. What made it worse was that he had pushed Charlie down to defend her, and it made Anna feel vulnerable, the one thing that she'd worked so hard to avoid.

'I don't need a protector, Surplus Peter,' she said angrily. 'And if you don't let Surplus Charlie go right this minute, we'll all end up in Solitary. You might be comfortable down there, but I'm not, thank you very much.'

Peter frowned slightly, then shrugged and moved his foot.

Charlie scrambled to his feet and looked at Peter menacingly. 'You'll regret that, you Outside scum,' he said bitterly.

Charlie walked away to join the food queue, and Peter sat back down next to Anna, making her shift along the bench self-consciously. Everyone was staring at them, and she could feel her heart quickening as she felt Peter's eyes looking towards her.

'I was only trying to help,' he muttered, putting his elbows on the table and hunching over them.

'Surpluses don't help each other; we're here to help Legals,' Anna said tightly. 'And I can handle things on my own, thank you very much.'

'Fine,' Peter said irritably. 'Then I'm sorry I even bothered. I just thought . . .'

'Well don't!' Anna said. Her eyes flickered over to Peter and met his, and they stared at each other for a few seconds, before Anna managed to pull her eyes away.

Chapter Four

The new Surplus is 'difficult'. He thinks he's better than a Surplus, thinks he's better than me. And he's not. He's quite stupid, actually, and he lies all the time. He's already been in Solitary twice, and frankly I think he should be kept down there.

He doesn't Know His Place and he thinks it's OK to whisper things during training sessions when it isn't at all. He said he wasn't Surplus Peter; that he was called Peter Tomlinson, like he was Legal or something. And he told me my name was Anna Covey and that he knows my parents. I mean, how stupid is that? Everyone knows that Surpluses don't have more than one name, and that my parents are in prison where they belong. What – so he grew up in prison with them? Yeah, right. He's a troublemaker, just like I thought he'd be. And he's lying, just to get some attention. Like Sheila did when she first arrived.

It shows what happens when they don't catch

Surpluses early enough. Shows how lucky I am to have come to Grange Hall when I did. The way he walks, you'd really think he was Legal. You'd think the world belongs to him, when the truth is he's got no right to be here, like the rest of us.

There was another boy here once before who didn't fit in either. His name was Patrick and when he arrived he cried all the time, even though he was virtually a Middle and should have been more grown-up than that. He was always in Solitary or getting beaten, because when he wasn't crying he was arguing with the Instructors, telling them that he wanted to go home, that his parents were going to find him and that then Mrs Pincent would be sorry. I tried to talk some sense into him, but he refused to listen. Mrs Pincent says that sometimes Surpluses find it hard to adjust and don't like to 'face facts'. He thought he was better than the rest of us, Mrs Pincent said. He only stayed a few weeks and then they took him away. Mrs Pincent said that he was going to a detention centre, where they could deal with people like Patrick better, where he wouldn't interfere with our training. If Peter isn't careful, he'll end up going there too. Mrs Pincent said that they have to do hard labour all the time in a detention centre. And that the boys don't even get one blanket, even when it's really cold. It was for Patrick's own good that he went there, Mrs Pincent said. If he didn't learn how to be a Surplus, he'd never find employment, and then what would he do?

Yesterday, Peter was put in Solitary because he told Mr Sargent that it was old people who were Surpluses, not us. None of us could believe it when he said that and I've never seen Mr Sargent so angry. He didn't even go red – he went white instead and the vein on his forehead started throbbing. I think he was going to beat him, but then he decided to call Mrs Pincent instead and Peter was taken away to Solitary. The worst thing of all was that he winked at me as they took him out. Like it was really cool to be put in Solitary.

He came out this evening, but I'm not sure it taught him anything, because he still grinned at me stupidly across Central Feeding, like we were friends or something. Peter isn't my friend. I wish Mrs Pincent would send him away so things can get back to normal around here. Or even better I wish Mrs Sharpe would decide that she wants me as her permanent house keeper, to go around the world with her and keep her house spotless and clean. I wish she'd take me a long way from here.

Anna carefully closed her journal and secreted it back on to the ledge behind the bath. Already it felt like a close friend, a confidante. When she'd been little, she and the other Surpluses in her dormitory used to talk to each other, sometimes late into the night, sharing secrets and thoughts. But then Mrs Pincent had appointed her Dormitory Monitor, which meant that she had to report any secrets or wrongdoings of anyone in the dorm. It hadn't taken long for her former friends to stop taking her into their confidence and ever since then she'd become used to walking into a room and seeing groups of people breaking up, whispered conversations halting. She didn't care, she told herself proudly; it was more important to be a good Surplus. Surpluses weren't supposed to spend time whispering to each other, anyway. They were supposed to take orders, to listen to Legals. Anna was determined to be the best Surplus ever. She'd be so good, it would almost make up for her existing in the first place. But it was still quite lonely having no one to talk to, particularly now, with Surplus Peter making her feel agitated and confused. He'd been at Grange Hall for three weeks, and every time she glimpsed him in the corridor, Anna felt herself go red, found herself looking away, only to turn to look at him once he'd passed. He unsettled her, kept trying to talk to her when all she wanted him to do was leave her alone. Anna felt like he was watching her constantly with that slightly mocking smile on his face, making her self-conscious, and confused, and she was determined not to let him know that she'd noticed.

After getting out of the bathtub and drying herself quickly, Anna shot one last look at the bath to make sure that her journal was completely hidden, and made her way back to her dormitory, running through the next day's schedule in her head as she went. Managing Supplies Efficiently was at 8.30 a.m., followed by Decorum at 9.30 a.m., and then they were having a polishing demonstration with some real silver. Mrs Sharpe had had a great deal of silver in her house – cutlery, candlesticks, frames and more – so Anna was confident that she would impress everyone with her ability to create a real shine. 'It's a job you can't rush,' Mrs Sharpe had told her. 'And nor should you want to. Polishing silver is therapeutic.' Anna agreed. Silver was beautiful when it gleamed and she hoped that one day she would work in a house with as much silver as Mrs Sharpe had.

Everyone was asleep by the time Anna got to her dormitory. Quietly, she slipped off her robe and got under the thin sheet and blankets, tucking the edges under herself to keep the warmth in and allowing herself to fall quickly into an exhausted sleep.

She was so tired that when, twenty or so minutes later, she felt a light tap on her shoulder, she nearly slept through it. But the tapping was insistent and wrenched her from her dreamless sleep back into the cold, dark dormitory. She opened her eyes silently, then sat up, her eyes wide with incredulity. It was Peter, crouched down over her bed.

She frowned. 'You . . . How . . . What are you doing here?' she hissed.

She was angry, and she didn't mind him knowing it. It was nearly midnight, and she needed these precious hours of sleep. Peter, sitting in front of her with an anxious look on his face, had broken so many rules coming here that they could both be doing hard labour for weeks, months even. Pending boys never came anywhere near the Pending girls' dormitories.

'What are you doing here?' Anna repeated crossly, before he could respond to her first questions, outraged that Peter should willingly break so many rules, as if somehow they didn't apply to him.

Peter moved his finger to his mouth as if to tell Anna to stay silent, then looked around the dormitory quickly, his eyes darting from bed to bed. He leant over and took her hand.

'Anna Covey, I have to tell you about your parents,' he whispered. 'They wanted me to find you. You've got to get away from that evil Mrs Pincent. I've come to take you home, Anna.'

Anna pushed him away and her eyes narrowed. 'You do not know my parents and I have no home,' she hissed. 'My parents are in prison. My name is Anna. Just Anna. I'm a Surplus. And so are you. Get used to it, and leave me alone.'

Peter frowned slightly, but made no attempt to move.

'You have a birthmark on your stomach,' he whispered softly. 'It looks a bit like a butterfly.'

Anna froze and she felt the hair on the back of her neck stand upright. How did he know that? Who was he? Why was he telling her this?

'I have to get back,' Peter said, before she could say anything.

And then he left, silently slinking out of the dormitory

and disappearing down the corridor. Like a ghost, Anna thought as she lay back down on her bed, a sudden overwhelming desire to cry washing over her. Slowly, she moved her hand down to her stomach, where she felt for the red birthmark just above her belly button. The birthmark that had caused her nothing but shame, the birthmark that she kept hidden at all costs to avoid the taunting and name calling that inevitably started when anyone saw it.

How did Peter know about it? Who had told him it was shaped like a butterfly, she wondered. When Mrs Pincent had first seen it, she'd remarked that it looked like a dead moth and had said that it was Mother Nature's way of branding Anna a pest. Moths ate things that belonged to other people, she'd told her, and abused their hosts. 'How very apt,' she'd said.

And yet, Peter's description stirred something in Anna, almost a memory but not quite; more a vague feeling that at some point she, too, had thought it resembled a butterfly. Anna almost thought she remembered believing, when she was very little, that it was a sign that one day she'd grow wings and fly away from Grange Hall. But Mrs Pincent had been right – it wasn't a butterfly, it was a moth. It was red and ugly and she hated it.

How dare Peter come here and remind her of it? How dare he sneak around the place, confusing her and pretending he knew things that he didn't, telling her that Mrs Pincent was evil? Maybe it was all part of an elaborate test, she thought to herself. Perhaps right now, he was reporting back to Mrs Pincent and working out new ways to trap her into saying something or doing something wrong. Perhaps she should have told him that Mrs Pincent wasn't evil, she thought worriedly, little beads of sweat appearing on her forehead in spite of the cold. But she hadn't had a chance, had she?

Then she shook herself; it was a stupid idea. Mrs Pincent would never use someone like him as a spy. She didn't trust Peter one bit; Anna could tell from the way she never took her eyes from him.

So if he wasn't a spy, there had to be some other explanation. Someone must have told him about her birthmark. They were probably all laughing about it right now.

Not that it mattered. Whoever he said he was, she wasn't going to listen to him. She was a Prefect and that meant not entertaining any nonsense.

Turning over, Anna closed her eyes and forced herself to sleep.

But it was a restless sleep, and throughout the night her dreams were filled with crying children, a woman screaming and a little butterfly, trapped in a cold, grey prison.

Chapter Five

Grange Hall was a Modern-Georgian building, built in 2070. Its design was based on Sutton Park, an old stately home in Yorkshire which had been built in 1730 and had long since crumbled to the ground. Photographs remained, however, and its style was admired very much by the present Authorities, who had decided that all government buildings should be built to resemble it, although in grey, not cream, because that colour withstood the elements better, and with lower ceilings. Lower ceilings meant lower heating requirements in the winter, and with the stringent tariffs for energy the Authorities been forced to impose, high ceilings were a luxury few could afford these days.

Initially, Grange Hall had housed the Revenue and Benefits Department, but it was soon declared too small, and was left empty for several years until the Surplus Act was introduced and the idea of Surplus Halls mooted. The original idea had been to create new, dedicated buildings for Surpluses, with the latest technology and teaching tools to develop an obedient, hard-working and amenable workforce; in the meantime, Grange Hall was hurriedly converted to house the growing number of Surpluses being gathered up around the country. Over the years, plans and papers had been periodically submitted by the Longevity and Surplus Department – usually when someone new had been given the Surplus remit – plans for new buildings, for merging the three UK Surplus Halls into one, for moving to the European model of deportation. But each time, nothing was done, because change carried risks, because change led to instability, because new technology meant using precious energy, and because, at the end of the day, no one really cared. And so, lethargy prevailed and Grange Hall was now the oldest Surplus Hall, its carpets and wall colours unchanged from its time as a government building, the smell of red tape and frustration still lingering in its very fabric.

Margaret Pincent hated the low ceilings of Grange Hall. She'd been brought up by her father to believe that stature directly influenced the height of one's ceilings. Those who could pull enough strings to get hold of extra energy coupons enjoyed the highest ceilings; everyone else was forced to accept lower ceilings, to crouch and bow and scrape just to keep warm. Mrs Pincent's father would bow to no man, he had told her regularly, so why should he be forced to bow by his own house?

Her father had never visited Grange Hall, of course, and had never shown any interest in it. It was hardly surprising; Mrs Pincent and he had not actually spoken for over fourteen years. Not since . . .

Well, not for a long time. Mrs Pincent felt the familiar anger clenching in her stomach and the nauseous feeling welling up her throat as memories she worked so hard to suppress found their way back into her mind. The unfairness. The shame.

But what was the use remembering? No point crying over spilt milk, she thought bitterly. Those were the exact words her father had used when the truth had come out. And when her husband had left her, her father had made it clear that he wouldn't be able to offer her any financial assistance; no assistance of any kind. That she would understand if he didn't see her again.

It had been left to Margaret Pincent to fend for herself, and fend she did. She'd seen the job advertised at Grange Hall and, ignoring the irony of the situation, had applied. Few people were interested in working with Surpluses, it seemed; in spite of her complete lack of qualifications and enthusiasm for the job, it had been offered to her straight away. And here she'd been, ever since, doing her best to break any spirit that the Supluses in her care might be tempted to exhibit; seeing it as her duty to treat the children as harshly as possible without rendering them completely useless. She was not running a holiday camp, and was not here to be a surrogate mother. These children did not deserve to be on this earth, and if they had to exist then they were going to be put to work. They were going to make up for their very presence, were going to carry the weight of their guilt with them everywhere they went. That was Margaret Pincent's promise to herself, and it was one that she had, so far, been able to keep.

Until now, that is. Until Peter arrived. It had been just a week and already she had seen the signs she'd been dreading ever since she took on the role of House Matron. The look of defiance. The refusal to obey her. The lack of respect. Mrs Pincent hated many things, but above all she hated not to be respected.

This is what happened when they didn't find Surpluses early enough, she thought to herself angrily. As far as the Catchers were concerned, it was probably a triumph to find a Surplus at this late stage, when his parents thought they'd got away with it. No doubt there was a publicity campaign being carefully managed right now to celebrate this great success. But what about her? How was Grange Hall supposed to train someone who had been on the Outside for so long? And they didn't tell her anything, of course. A phone call a few hours before he arrived, telling her he was on the way, that was all. Telling her. Not asking if it would be OK, not asking for her advice, oh no. She was to prepare a bed, she was told. This one was likely to need some special treatment, they said. He's been on the Outside rather a long time. He was found in the middle of nowhere and we don't know where he's come from. *We'll want to keep an eye on him.*

'Why do you want to keep an eye on him?' Margaret Pincent had wanted to ask. 'Why did you find him so late? Where do you think he might have been?'

But of course, she didn't ask. And even if she had, she would have been met with silence. After all this time, they still didn't trust her. Not really. And that meant that she didn't trust anyone either. Not one little bit.

Still, for the time being her priority had to be this new Surplus, to prove she could manage him. The trouble was, he didn't react like the other Surpluses. There were always one or two who thought they were something special; one or two who thought that they could get round her, play the system a bit. Surpluses who felt they were better than the rest.

But there were tried and trusted tools and techniques to deal with them. Beatings. Humiliation. Making them feel so wretched that they started hating their parents for putting them in this position, for bringing them into this awful world. You had to get them to hate their parents; that was the key.

That boy Patrick had been the last Surplus to create real problems, but his anger had just been bravado; he'd broken soon enough, once he was really put to work. Funny that Anna, her most obedient Surplus, was desperate to go to the place she'd sent Patrick to be worked to death. Nothing like building in the desert heat to give a rebellious Surplus a bit of perspective. Not that the Authorities knew about that, of course. Selling Surpluses as slave labour wasn't strictly approved of by officials, just as getting involved in black market Longevity drugs wasn't exactly in her job description. But perhaps they should pay her a better wage if they didn't want her supplementing her income from time to time. And anyway, no one had missed him. His file had been lost, and no questions had been asked.

Sometimes the system made mistakes, of course. There had been the situation recently with a Surplus called Sheila who, it turned out, was actually the progeny of two Opt Outs. The fools had gone away for the weekend, leaving the child with its grandparents. Their neighbours had heard the child cry and, assuming it was a Surplus, had called the Catchers to secure their reward. The parents had appealed, of course, but Mrs Pincent had held firm. The grandparents didn't have a licence; technically the Catchers had been well within the law in confiscating Sheila. Technically, during her stay with her grandparents, Sheila was indeed a Surplus.

The fact was that you couldn't start sending children back after every little mistake; there would be no end to it. And if Sheila had been returned to her parents, it would have stirred up the other Surpluses. Given them hope. Hope was the last thing you wanted to encourage in a Surplus. No, she had done the right thing. Five times Sheila's parents had come to see her – not to Grange Hall, of course, but to the London office; no one was allowed within a mile of any Surplus Hall for security reasons. Five times her mother had broken down, clutching at Mrs Pincent's ankles and begging for her little girl back – it had been embarrassing, really. Uncomfortable.

But Mrs Pincent wouldn't give in. Why should she? Sheila was a good age. She could still be a Valuable Asset, no doubt about it at all. More than a Valuable Asset, if Mrs Pincent had her way. Sheila, like all female Surpluses and, to a lesser extent, male Surpluses, had value that her parents knew nothing about. Young stem cells. Youth in every atom of her body, which laboratories were crying out for all around the world. You couldn't explain that to the parents, of course, particularly since they'd Opted Out. But others would be grateful. Renewal was a hungry beast; it needed constant feeding.

Peter, on the other hand, was different. When he arrived, he'd actually looked pleased with himself, the arrogant little twerp. He'd looked her right in the eye, and there was something mocking about his face. It was as if he was saying to her 'I know. I know the truth about you.' But of course, she was just imagining that. She had to be; how could a Surplus know anything? He was just clever, that was all. He had spotted a weakness and was using it to his advantage.

Still, real or not, it made her hate him. And, worse, it made her afraid of letting him leave until the look had gone. Sending him to the desert like that was too dangerous; what if he did know something, however unlikely the prospect was? It didn't look like she'd be able to lose his file either, not if they were *keeping an eye on him*.

The whole situation was intolerable. She would have to deal with him herself. And if he thought that Margaret Pincent was weak, he had another thing coming. If the week of beatings and starvation when he first arrived hadn't done the trick, there were other more interesting methods. Sleep deprivation. More Solitary. Leave him in that cell until he was so desperate for company he cried out her name.

She thought for a moment, then smiled briefly. Perhaps she should attack him with kindness first. That was how you really destroyed a Surplus: make it think you love it before abusing its trust so completely that it could never trust another human being again. Yes, she thought with a satisfied nod, she would break Peter. And when she had broken him completely, then she would get rid of him. The Authorities would have to lump it. It wouldn't be much of a loss – even broken, Peter was unlikely to be of any use to anyone.

Anna sat with her eyes focused on the food in front of her. She didn't want to see Peter. Didn't want to even acknowledge his existence. Although, when a quick scan of Central Feeding revealed that, strangely, Peter wasn't even there, she felt something close to disappointment because that meant he wouldn't have seen how forcefully she'd been ignoring him. Sighing with irritation that even by being absent Peter seemed able to annoy her, Anna finished her porridge and got up to go.

But just as she was about to clear away her breakfast bowl and plastic cup, Peter appeared in the doorway, flanked by Mrs Pincent, his gaunt frame towering over the House Matron's. Mrs Pincent found Anna's eyes and nodded for her to come over.

'I want you to look after Peter,' she said matter-of-factly, as soon as Anna had walked over. 'He has come to us late, and seems to be finding it hard to fit in. I want you to show him the ropes, help him learn. And make sure he has an extra blanket on his bed. Now, Peter, I expect you'll be hungry. Anna, can you make sure Peter has some porridge before training starts this morning?'

Anna's heart sank, but she didn't react, except to nod silently. An extra blanket was unheard of, except for Prefects, and Mrs Pincent's almost familial language – 'show him the ropes, help him learn' – was unfamiliar and strange. But Anna knew better than to say anything. Not while Mrs Pincent was standing so close, anyway.

Once she was gone, that was a different matter. As Mrs Pincent disappeared down the corridor, Anna turned to Peter.

'I don't know what you've done, but Mrs Pincent certainly seems to like you now. Still think she's evil?' she said haughtily.

Peter shrugged, and shivered involuntarily, making Anna soften slightly.

'I'll get you some breakfast,' she said cautiously, 'and I'll show you the ropes. But no more stories. No more sneaking around late at night. I'm a Prefect, and if I'm going to help you you're going to have to Learn Your Place.'

Peter nodded sagely. 'Thank you,' he said under his breath. 'Thank you, Anna Covey.'

Anna sighed irritably. This was going to be a long day.

Chapter Six

Peter proved to be a fast learner. He quickly learnt the layout of Grange Hall and when Anna tested him on the daily schedule she was impressed to find that he'd managed to learn it off by heart within a day. She couldn't be sure whether he was concentrating in the boys-only training sessions, but in the sessions she shared with him, he was well behaved and polite. If it wasn't for his insistence on calling her Anna Covey, he'd be like any other Surplus. He'd even sat through a Science and Nature class without saying anything, although afterwards, when he and Anna had been alone, he had erupted.

'It's all lies. Lies!' he'd muttered, his eyes darting around to check that no one was listening. 'Anna, you have to believe me. This is not what Mother Nature wanted . . .'

Anna had shaken her head. 'You only think that because your parents wanted to have their cake and eat it,' she said firmly. 'You shouldn't be angry with Mr Sargent – be angry with your parents. They're the ones who broke the Declaration. They're the ones who put you here.'

He'd disagreed, of course. He always did. In the corridors, in Central Feeding, whenever they could speak without being overheard, he railed against Grange Hall, against the Instructors, against everything, as far as Anna could tell. Mostly, she told him to be quiet and to show more respect for Mother Nature and the Authorities, but sometimes her curiosity got the better of her and she found herself furtively asking questions about his life before Grange Hall, pretending as she did so that she wasn't really that interested. The truth was that Peter was a window through which Anna could glimpse the world outside, and the temptation to keep looking was quite overwhelming.

Peter lived in London, he told her, in a house in Bloomsbury, a place where famous writers used to live many years ago. That had interested Anna, who was still hiding in Female Bathroom 2 as often as she could to scribble in her journal, relishing those moments in which she tried to make sense of her world and vented her frustrations. The house where Peter had grown up had an underground apartment, which was where he had spent most of his time when he was little. He'd been taught to read, write, use a computer, and to 'question things'. He had read books and newspapers and been encouraged to 'form opinions'. The very idea of being allowed to read stories that weren't at all to do with making you more Useful seemed incredibly exciting to Anna, who had only ever been allowed to read approved text books on Longevity drugs and Housekeeping, along with long, ponderous works like *Surplus Shame* and *The Surplus Burden on Nature: A Treatise*, books which extolled the achievements of Longevity and explained in long, detailed paragraphs the Surplus Problem and the Enlightened Humane Approach, which enabled Surpluses to work in order to cover their Sin of Existence. Anna had read these books again and again, relishing the beautiful words and the cogent, well-structured arguments, which had convinced her, above and beyond anything that Mrs Pincent had told her, that her life was an imposition, that all she could do was to work hard in the hope that she might eventually be so valuable that her Sin of Existence might be forgiven.

Peter, on the other hand, knew nothing of these books, but he made up for it with knowledge of the Outside, of things that Anna had never dreamt of seeing or touching. Once a year, he told her, he'd been smuggled out of the house for a trip to the country, where there was a piece of land so big he could run around without anyone seeing him or hearing him shout. He would scream and yell as loudly as he could on those brief sojourns, knowing that for the rest of the year his life was to be conducted in whispers and furtive movements.

Peter didn't talk much about his parents – not at all, actually – but he said that the adults he knew were all part of an Underground Movement that had been set up to fight the Authorities, to challenge the Declaration. When Anna's parents had got out of prison, they joined the Underground Movement too, and Peter had gone to live with them. He said that they were trying to find out more about the use of Surpluses.

Anna didn't really believe him, and had very little interest in his hatred of the system or tales of her supposed parents. But she treasured the guilty pleasure of listening to him talk about his life Outside, enjoyed the idea of running around a field, shouting and laughing. She thought that she would like that very much.

It was one such tale of the Outside that Peter was whispering to Anna one evening, just over a month after his first arrival at Grange Hall. The two of them had finished clearing up Central Feeding after supper and were sitting at one of the tables drying cutlery.

As they picked up the old, stainless steel forks and knives, drying them methodically with old rags, he described sitting by an open fire in the country, made up of illicitly collected driftwood, toasting marsh-mallows and playing something called a card game. And then he told her about Virginia Woolf, a writer who lived in Bloomsbury many, many years ago and had her first book published in 1915. She wrote all the time, Peter told her, but even her writing couldn't make her happy and in the end she killed herself.

Anna listened in silence as she did her best to scrape the congealed fat from the knife she was holding – washing the cutlery in tepid water rarely achieved more than dislodging large pieces of food, and cleaning fluids weren't considered necessary or affordable by Mrs Pincent. If Virginia Woolf had been a Legal, what could have made her want to die, she wondered. Virginia Woolf could probably have made as much noise as she wanted and wouldn't have had any guilt at all to carry with her. She frowned, and noticed that Peter was staring at her. She still found it disconcerting the way he looked right at people, unashamedly.

'What?' she asked. 'You know, you shouldn't look at people like that. It's rude.'

Peter grinned as if he didn't really care if it was rude or not, then his face turned serious.

'You really hate your parents?' he asked her.

Anna answered without thinking. 'Of course I hate them. It's all their fault.'

'What is?'

Anna sighed. Sometimes Peter could be really dim. 'Me being here. Being responsible. Paying back Mother Nature for their Sins. Whatever you say, the Declaration was introduced for a reason and my parents abused Mother Nature's benevolence. They make me sick.'

'And you seriously believe that they're wrong and the Authorities are right?'

Anna nodded. 'Of course I believe it,' she said flatly. 'It's the truth. Even if you do know them, I don't care. They deserve to go back to prison and stay there for the rest of their lives. Now just shut up about it.'

Peter looked at her then and took her wrists firmly in his hands.

'Your parents love you,' he said in a very low voice. 'You're not surplus to anything, you're Anna Covey, and you should never have been locked away here. Your Mrs Pincent is the person you should hate. She's the one who brainwashed you, the one who beat you and starved you, just like she tried to do to me. Just like she'll do again when she realises she hasn't won. We need to get out of here. We need to get back to London.'

Anna stared at him, her mouth set crossly. 'Brainwash!' she said contemptuously. 'That isn't even a word.'

Peter smiled sarcastically. 'Not a word they'd teach in Grange Hall, I suppose, but it is a word, Anna. It means to indoctrinate. To make you think things that aren't true, to make you believe that you don't deserve to live on the Outside, that you're lucky to live in this prison.'

Anna pulled away, her eyes stinging with tears. Usually she loved to learn new words, treating them as exciting possessions that she could employ as she chose – in her journal, in her conversation – relishing the newness and the beauty of each one. But there was nothing beautiful about the word 'brainwash'. To clean the brain. To strip it bare.

'If anyone's brain needs washing, it's yours,' she

said angrily. 'You don't know anything. You're full of lies, Peter.'

'No,' Peter said urgently, pressing her hand. 'I'm not the one who's lying, Anna. You and I can get out of here. Together. There's a whole world out there, Anna, a whole world for us to explore. And a home, waiting for us in London.'

He was looking at Anna intently, and she felt herself weaken, felt herself wanting to believe him even if just for a moment, but then she forced his hand away. She couldn't listen to him. Shouldn't listen to him. Every paragraph in *Surplus Shame* refuted his arguments, explained in long, detailed prose, exactly why he was wrong.

'I don't want to go to London. And anyway, you're talking rubbish,' she said passionately. 'My parents don't love me. If they loved me, they'd never have had me. And Mrs Pincent's the one who asked me to look after you so I don't know why you hate her so much. She only beats you for your own good, to make you realise the truth . . . '

She felt her voice quiver with emotion and tried to steel herself, wiping her eyes irritably.

'I wish Mrs Pincent had asked someone else to look after you,' she said eventually, her voice soft and low. 'I wish you'd just leave me alone.'

Peter stared at her, his eyes flashing. 'I don't think you mean that, Anna Covey, but if you really want me to, I'll leave you alone,' he said bitterly. 'You're wrong about your parents, though, and you're wrong about Grange Hall and Mrs Pincent. I'm going to get out of here somehow and you have to come with me. It's not safe here.'

Anna looked at him with contempt. 'Of course it's safe here,' she said. 'Safer than trying to escape to the Outside when they'd only send the Catchers after you and put you in a hard labour camp. Your problem is that you think you're better than other Surpluses, think the rules don't apply to you. Well they do, and I'm sick of you talking about my parents and stuff. I don't want to hear any more. And don't expect me to keep watching out for you either.'

Peter shrugged, but his dark eyes belied his casual stance, staring deep into Anna's and making her shift uncomfortably. 'Fine, suit yourself,' he said evenly. 'Stay here and turn yourself into a good little house servant. Let Mrs Pincent and the rest of them tell you what to do, what to think – or, rather, what not to think. See if I care. I mean, I got caught just so that I could find you, so that I could bring you back to your parents, but don't worry about it. I'm sure you'll be very happy, Anna Covey.'

'Don't call me that!' Anna cried, putting her hands to her ears. 'And I didn't ask you to come . . .'

'No, you didn't, you're right,' Peter said slowly. He looked away and folded his arms defensively. 'You know, tracking you down to Grange Hall wasn't easy. And I knew that being here was going to be hard. But I never thought *you'd* be so difficult. I thought you'd be pleased I came.'

'I am pleased you came,' Anna said quickly, surprising herself with the words. 'But you're wrong about everything. You're better off here, really you are. Can't you be my friend and stay?'

Peter shook his head and Anna rolled her eyes in irritation.

'Look, I could get in trouble just talking to you about this,' she said. 'The fact is that Mrs Pincent seems to quite like you now. You could be OK here, instead of having to spend your life hiding.'

'I can assure you that Mrs Pincent doesn't like me,' Peter said sarcastically. 'She doesn't like any of us. Anyone who can beat someone the way she beat me isn't capable of that emotion.'

Anna looked down at the floor. She'd suspected as much.

'You don't get beaten if you don't break the rules,' she said quietly.

'You really have fallen for all her crap, haven't you?' Peter said with a sigh. 'You believe every single word that woman feeds you. Well I don't. Anna, we've got as much right to be on this planet as the Mrs Pincents of this world. More right. They're the ones who have outstayed their welcome by living for ever and they're blaming us for it.'

Peter's eyes were flashing and Anna looked at him with terror. What he'd just said was blasphemous. He'd be flogged if anyone heard him. She would too, just for listening.

'Look,' he said with a sigh, 'I'm getting out of here,

and if you're not going to come with me then that's your business. But I can't wait for ever. You have to decide, Anna Covey. You have to decide whether you're going to live a life of slavery or not.'

Anna stared at Peter, then stood up, only to discover that her legs were shaking. How dare Peter tell her she was a slave? Putting a hand on the table to steady herself, she took a deep breath and forced herself to look him directly in the eye.

'I've already decided,' she hissed. 'You're the one that believes crap, Peter. I'm a Prefect. A *Prefect*. In six months I'm going to be a Valuable Asset. You can ruin your own life, but you're not ruining mine. Try and escape if you want, but I don't want anything to do with it. I don't want anything to do with you either.'

And with that, she turned and left, leaving Peter alone in the vast hall that was Central Feeding. She walked without thinking out of the door, across the covered courtyard that separated the feeding hall from the main building, then walked more quickly towards the stairs. It was only when she got to Floor 2 that she realised where she was going, and was soon running towards Female Bathroom 2. Once there, having made sure it was empty and safely shut the door behind her, she finally allowed her tears to fall freely as she collapsed on the floor in a heap of sobs.

'I am not Anna Covey,' she said to herself as she wept. 'I am not Anna Covey. I am Surplus Anna. I am. I know I am. Please let things get back to normal. Please let everything be OK again.'

Chapter Seven

3 March, 2140

Peter says I'm a slave and that I should stand up for myself. He makes me so angry. I'm not a slave. I'm a good Surplus. It's not like I chose to be one - it's just the way things are and I don't see why Peter has to make me feel bad about it.

He says he's my friend and then he gets me upset and I feel like I can't breathe properly because he talks about the Outside and he gets me imagining what it would be like, when it doesn't matter because I'm a Surplus so Outside doesn't belong to me.

If he was really my friend, would he say stupid, horrible things like that?

Peter isn't afraid like the rest of us. And that makes him dangerous. It feels dangerous being with him because I never know what he's going to say next, and whatever he does say, he'd never be able to say in front of Mrs Pincent. But sometimes he says nice things, or he looks at me and it doesn't feel

*dangerous, it feels exciting, even though they're prob-
ably the same thing. And I worry that it's because
underneath it all I'm not really Valuable Asset material, I'm just a Surplus, and however much I work and
try my best I will always end up 'letting myself down'
by liking things I shouldn't and doing things
I shouldn't. I shouldn't be writing right now. I
shouldn't have a journal. Maybe I'm really no better
than Peter. Maybe it's me that's dangerous, after all.*

The sexes at Grange Hall were segregated in a
number of ways: firstly by the location of their dormitories, which were on separate floors; secondly by the
timetable of their training sessions – at least half of
the training sessions each day were single sex, focusing exclusively on the skills and expertise each would
be expected to bring to their future employer; and
thirdly by the ways in which they approached their
confinement, the methods they employed to make
their lives seem more bearable, their prospects less
bleak.

The girls, with only one or two exceptions, got
through each day by competing with one another
over who was going to be most valuable, who could
prove their genuine worth to Mother Nature. And
whilst, on the surface, there appeared to be some
camaraderie between the girls; whilst they would
sometimes, in stolen moments, confide in each other
and whisper forbidden thoughts about the Outside,
about what it must be like to be born Legal, to have

life stretched out ahead of you like a beautiful, soft carpet full of pleasure and expectations, in reality there was little friendship. Pity, sympathy and empathy were qualities that the female Surpluses could not afford the luxury of feeling; pity or sympathy extended to another could only highlight their own failings, their own destiny. And so, instead, the girls lived side by side, never letting their guard down fully, nearly always suppressing their instincts and questions, and constantly watching each other for the smallest transgression, even in stolen moments of leisure and recreation. In the hour or so before bedtime when, on the rare occasion that all chores had been completed satisfactorily for the day and the girls in Anna's dorm had some free time, they would always play the same game. It was called Legal-Surplus, and would see one of the girls anointed 'Legal' for the duration of the game, and one other as her Surplus. The 'Legal' girl could ask her Surplus to do anything, from cleaning the floor with her tongue to eating faeces. The more creative and inventive the Legal could be in finding ways to humiliate and abuse her Surplus, the more the other girls would applaud and laugh until Lights Out were announced and the game's Surplus would be allowed to escape her tormentor.

The boys, on the other hand, did not let their minds stray too far into the future, did not allow their thoughts to rest too long on the short life of servitude that lay before them. Instead, they coped with their frustration and restlessness by engaging in more physical activity. The rules of engagement in their game were similar to those employed in the female Surpluses' game – one against one, with the other Surpluses acting as the audience, but in the boys' version, the victim and bully were not chosen according to strict rotation; rather, the same boy or boys would be picked on and attacked by the same bullies, the others watching, vicariously feeling the pleasure of each kick, imagining the powerful feeling that would come from mastering another completely. The game would continue until the watching Surpluses could no longer control themselves and would throw themselves into the fray, kicking and punching the victim or anyone they considered to be weaker than them. Doing this allowed them, for a short time at least, to feel invincible, to feel as though they were no longer Surplus; the blood pumping around their body made everything outside the dormitory meaningless – their past, their present, their future.

Mrs Pincent and the Instructors knew of both these games and intervened rarely. In fact, Anna had seen Mrs Pincent smile and say that in these games the Surpluses were doing her job for her; the girls were learning to submit themselves fully to their Legal masters, whilst the boys were sorting out the weak from the strong, and taking their aggression out on each other, containing it so that no Legal ever need feel the brunt of it. Surplus boys were often employed in groups of two or three, with a weaker boy attached to two stronger ones, enabling this dynamic to continue until the boys were men and they were no longer gripped with the need to fight, to dominate. Hormone trials had been conducted years before to try and quell the Surplus boys' appetite and need for aggression, but they were found to diminish their strength and brute force, so were soon abandoned.

Anna no longer engaged in the games in her dormitory. She was, after all, a Prefect now and was too old for such things. But the truth was that being a Prefect was not the reason for her looking the other way when one or other Surplus girl was forced to experience new, fresh, horrors, the result of feverish planning by whoever was playing the game's 'Legal'. The real reason that Anna could not bear to watch the tormentor or tormented was that recently, she had begun to lose her appetite for the infliction of pain; she no longer felt comforted by watching another being bullied or, indeed, by tormenting another Surplus herself; no longer enjoyed the brutality and desensitisation that went with it. The shrieks of delight as the chosen Surplus was subjected to some new, horrible punishment used to make her feel elated and relieved, because whatever horrors lay ahead in her life could never be this bad, could never devastate her as the 'Legal' was devastating her slave for the night. But recently, Anna had begun to realise that the horror she faced in the life that lay before her was not in beatings, or humiliation. It was the horror of what they all were, what she was. Surplus. Unwanted. A

Burden. Better off dead. And no amount of pain, no amount of desensitisation could take that away, or even make it matter slightly less.

That evening, when Anna returned from Female Bathroom 2, she found the game in full flow, with Sheila the Surplus and Tania her master. The sight immediately made her stomach clench with apprehension. Tania was a year younger than Anna, and a year older than Sheila. She had been at Grange Hall almost since birth and was a tall, large-boned girl with dark brown hair and even darker eyes. She towered above Sheila, who was so slight she looked as though a gust of wind might blow her over at any minute.

Sheila's hair was a pale orange colour, the same colour as the freckles which covered her fragile, almost bluish skin. This, combined with her fragile frame and watery blue eyes, made her an easy target for bullying and insults; her steely determination and refusal to acquiesce to her bullies' demands had only made humiliating her more attractive to her attackers. Until a couple of years before, when Anna had reluctantly begun to protect her, prompted mainly by the fact that Sheila had begun to follow her around, making her fights Anna's fights, Sheila had been target practice for every bully at Grange Hall.

As Anna walked past, she averted her eyes, refusing the various invitations to watch, and trying to convince herself that the game was nothing to do with her. But as she reached her bed, she could hear the cries and taunts emanating from the other side of the dormitory getting louder, and reluctantly she turned to look. Then she frowned. To her surprise, Sheila was not face down on the floor with Tania's foot on the back of her head, or completing some humiliating task. Rather, she was simply standing beside Tania's bed, tears streaming down her face and her body trembling as she shook her head.

Anna looked away, but the noise from the watching Surpluses was becoming deafening, and eventually Anna turned round again. Sheila was still standing in front of Tania, now with red marks on her cheeks, no doubt the result of a slap or two. Other than that, she could see no other physical damage.

Biting her lip, she walked back towards the cluster of Surpluses. Tania was towering over Sheila, her eyes boring into hers, saying over and over again in a low voice, 'Say it. Say it. Say it.' Sheila, meanwhile, was shaking her head, her hands drawn into little fists.

Anna watched them for a few seconds. 'It's time for bed,' she said. 'You can stop the game now.'

A few of the Surpluses turned to her with strange looks in their eyes, and Tania, without moving her eyes from Sheila's, shook her head. 'She hasn't done what I told her to do yet. The game can't stop until she's done it.'

Anna's eyes shifted to Sheila. 'Come on, Sheila,' she urged, 'just do what she said, then we'll all go to bed.'

'No, I won't.' Sheila's voice was soft, and low, but it was also determined, and Anna felt her stomach sink. You weren't allowed to say no. That was the rule. You had to do what the Legal told you; that was the whole point. No one ever said no. Why did Sheila have to be so defiant?

'Sheila, it's a game. You have to do what she says,' Anna said, feeling the electricity around her as the other Surpluses stared in excitement at the scene unfolding before them.

'I won't,' Sheila said simply. 'I won't.'

Anna looked at Tania. 'What did you ask her to do?' she asked. 'Because if it involved leaving the dormitory or saying something to Mrs Pincent then you know that's not allowed.'

Tania smiled icily. 'I just asked her to say something, that's all. And she won't do it. So until she does, the game isn't ending. OK?'

'Say something?' Anna asked uncertainly. 'Is that all?'

She looked at Sheila. 'Sheila, come on. Just say it. Whatever it is.'

Sheila shook her head. Her face was white with fury or fear – Anna couldn't tell which.

'What did you ask her to say?' she asked Tania.

'I told her to tell me that she hates her parents. That her parents are criminal scum and that they deserve to die,' Tania said triumphantly.

'I'll never say it,' Sheila said softly. 'I don't care what you do to me, I won't say it.'

'You have to say it,' Tania said angrily. 'I am your master. You have to do as I tell you, otherwise we are all going to beat you. And if you still won't say it, then I'll tell Mrs Pincent you don't Know Your Place.'

As Anna watched Sheila standing bravely before Tania, her little back stiff and her eyelashes heavy with salty tears, she found herself thinking of Peter, hearing his words echoing around her head: 'Your parents love you, Anna Covey. They love you.'

Then she braced herself. 'Sheila, you have to say it,' she said flatly. 'It's true, after all.'

Sheila's eyes narrowed and she shook her head fiercely. 'It isn't true,' she said in a low voice. 'And I won't say it.'

Tania was getting red in the face. 'She will bend to my authority,' she said hotly. 'I am her master now. She will do whatever I tell her to.'

'You are not my master,' Sheila said suddenly. 'No one is my master. I'm not a Surplus. My parents love me and I'm Legal, and I hate you. I hate you all.'

Tania stared at her, her mouth wide open, then she drew her hand back and slapped her hard around the face again. Then she pushed Sheila to the floor and started to kick her.

'You do not talk to your master like that,' she screamed. 'You will learn some respect. You are a Surplus, Sheila. Do you hear? You are scum. You don't deserve to breathe the same air as me. You don't deserve to be in the same room as me. You're scum, Sheila, you're worthless.' Tania looked around, her eyes flashing. 'You're all worthless,' she said angrily. 'You're all scum. All of you.'

Charlotte, a short, stocky Pending who slept in the

next but one bed to Anna, muscled forward at this point.

'If anyone's scum, you are,' she said, folding her arms and looking at Tania menacingly. 'You can't even cook properly. You're scum and useless and no one's ever going to want to employ you and you're going to end up being put down because there won't be anything else to do with you.'

'I can cook,' Tania said, drawing herself up to her full height and taking her eyes off Sheila to glare at Charlotte. 'And I can sew better than you too. No one will want to employ *you* because you're too ugly to have in a nice house. No one would want to look at you all day, even if you learn Decorum and make yourself invisible. You'll still be ugly.'

Anna glanced to the floor and watched Sheila inch away from Tania, wincing slightly from the pain, but her face still defiant. Charlotte wasn't inching anywhere, though. Instead, she hurled herself at Tania, grabbing her by the hair and forcing her to the ground.

'Useless . . . little . . . Surplus,' she spat as she slapped Tania around the face. Tania wriggled on to her side and managed to aim a kick at Charlotte, who fell away, crying out with the pain. But before Tania could get up, Sheila appeared from nowhere, hurling herself on to Tania and punching her with little fists.

'Stop,' screamed Anna fiercely. 'The game is over. It's time for bed.'

'I don't want to go to bed,' Charlotte said, looking Anna directly in the eye. 'I don't feel like it.'

Anna's eyes narrowed. 'Surplus Charlotte, Know Your Place,' she growled. 'I say it's time for bed, and you will do as I say.'

Tania pushed Sheila off her and stood up. 'And what if we don't?' she asked, her voice challenging. 'Then what?'

'Then you'll be punished,' Anna said fiercely. 'I am a Prefect.'

'I am a Prefect,' Tania mocked, and a couple of the Surpluses laughed. 'Well Prefects have to Learn Their Place too,' she said, pulling herself up to her full height and looking to the other Surpluses for moral support. 'Maybe it's time you played the game, Anna. Maybe it's time you stopped being so high and mighty and remembered who you are. What you are. Just a Surplus, like the rest of us.'

Anna stared at her. 'I know I'm a Surplus,' she said angrily. 'I Know My Place. I think it's you who doesn't.'

'Really? Well, maybe you're right. Maybe *My Place* isn't in this dormitory,' Tania said, her eyes flashing. 'Maybe *My Place* is in another dormitory. Or on the corridor. Or on the Outside. Maybe *My Place* is somewhere completely different. What then?'

She stared at Anna for a moment, then tossed her head back and charged towards the door, opening it and motioning for the other Surpluses to join her. Charlotte followed cautiously, and Anna pulled Sheila back.

'You stay here,' she ordered. 'You stay right here.'

Slowly, she marched out into the corridor to survey the scene. Tania and Charlotte were running down the corridor, knocking on dormitory doors and screaming out 'Know Your Place, Surpluses, Know Your Place.' One or two doors opened and nervous-looking female Surpluses poked their heads out; they were soon dragged into the corridor by Charlotte or Tania.

Anna slammed her own dormitory door to get their attention.

'You will get back inside,' she shouted, 'and you will all go to bed. Now.'

Tania looked at her and laughed. 'Or what, Surplus Anna? Or you'll tell us off? Run to Mrs Pincent?'

'Or I'll beat you myself,' Anna said fiercely. 'You are Surplus, Tania, and you are to behave as a Surplus, to follow the rules and do as you are told. You have no right to exist, Surplus Tania, and if you can't behave properly, then . . .'

'Then what?' Tania asked. Her eyes were wild and she looked dizzy with exhilaration.

'Then you will be sent to Solitary.'

Silence fell along the corridor and Tania's face went white as Mrs Pincent suddenly appeared.

'And beaten,' Mrs Pincent continued, walking towards Anna, her face impenetrable. 'Anna, I heard you offer to beat Tania yourself. I would be most obliged.'

Anna looked at Mrs Pincent uncertainly. She had never been asked to beat a Surplus before. Surpluses weren't supposed to raise their fist to anyone, not outside the strictures of the game.

'Now,' Mrs Pincent said forcefully. 'So that everyone can see what happens to a Surplus who thinks they are above the rules, who thinks that they can do as they please and insult Mother Nature and humankind's generosity in keeping them alive.'

Anna moved hesitantly towards Tania, who looked at her defiantly.

'Hit her,' ordered Mrs Pincent, who was now walking towards her. 'Make her know her Sins. Help her to learn from her mistakes and to understand what being a Surplus means. Make her see that she is unwanted, a burden; that every step she takes along these corridors are steps that she has stolen. Make her see that she is worthless, that if she dies no one will care, that in fact the world will be better off with her not trespassing on it. Make her understand all that, Anna.'

Mrs Pincent's voice was low and menacing, and Anna found herself trembling. Tania had to understand, she told herself. Tania had to learn, for her own sake. For all their sakes.

Slowly, she drew her hand back to swipe Tania across the face. Tania looked at her for a moment, then her eyes flicked up to Mrs Pincent and back again. And then she smiled at Anna, a mocking smile full of hatred and contempt.

Anna held her gaze for a second or so, and pulled her hand back again. Frustration and anger were bubbling up inside her and she wanted to vent her rage, but somehow she couldn't do it. However much she wanted Tania to Learn Her Place, she couldn't hit her. And the realisation frightened her, particularly as another smile began to wend its way across Tania's face.

'Hit me then,' Tania hissed. 'Go on. Or aren't you as tough as you think, Surplus Anna?'

Anna stared at her, but still she found herself paralysed.

'Thank you, Anna,' Mrs Pincent said eventually. 'Surplus Tania will spend the rest of the night in Solitary, as will Surplus Charlotte, after spending some time in my office. The rest of you will forfeit breakfast tomorrow and will have additional chores every evening this week.'

Immediately, the look of insolence in Tania's eyes was replaced by fear, and Anna watched silently as she and Charlotte were taken away and the corridor quickly emptied.

'Go and brush your teeth, and then I want lights out,' she said, on autopilot, as she walked back into her dormitory, trying to work out why she felt so uncomfortable, trying to work out why she hadn't been able to punish Tania. 'Surpluses need good teeth,' she continued, echoing the words she'd heard Mrs Pincent say so many times. 'No one's going to pay for dental treatment for a Surplus.'

Then, slowly, she walked over and checked on Sheila, who was sitting on her bed, hugging her knees to her chest.

'Go and brush your teeth, Surplus Sheila,' Anna said flatly. Then she looked around at the onlookers. 'No more games until I say so. Does everyone understand? We are all Surplus here, and maybe we need to remember that for a few weeks.'

The Surpluses shrugged and nodded and filed out to the bathrooms to brush their teeth. Anna followed, and soon found Sheila standing next to her at the basin.

'You know, Anna, I'm not a Surplus,' Sheila whispered almost silently, wincing at the pain of moving her cheeks. 'And one day they'll realise and I'll be free. And when I am, I'm going to have Surplus Tania as my housekeeper and I'm going to punish her every day. And I'll have you as my housekeeper too, Anna, but I won't punish you at all. Unless you deserve it, that is.'

And with her eyes fixed straight ahead, Sheila picked up her toothbrush and began to clean her teeth.

Chapter Eight

The next day, Tania and Charlotte arrived back from Solitary in time for morning training. Neither acknowledged their fellow Surpluses. Telltale red weals were evident on their cheeks and hands, and Anna suspected that more were hidden by their overalls. Under their eyes they both bore the signs of a sleepless night – dark shadows and drooping eyelids.

Anna, who was feeling tired herself, not to mention hungry from a lack of breakfast, also couldn't help noticing that Peter was missing from the class. Not that she cared. In many ways, she was relieved – he had made her angry with his taunts about her parents, angrier than she'd realised. She wouldn't have been surprised to learn that he, too, had spent the night in Solitary for some misdemeanour. In fact, she'd half expected him to arrive with Charlotte and Tania.

But he didn't turn up. There was no knock at the door; no last minute interruptions.

Once everyone had noted Tania and Charlotte's appearance, the story of last night's games having spread swiftly around the class, the Surpluses soon started whispering about Peter's absence instead, nudging each other and looking meaningfully at the empty desk next to Anna where Peter usually sat. She, though, was far too proud to get involved in their gossiping. Instead, she stared ahead purposefully, trying to ignore her rumbling stomach and listening intently to Mrs Dawson explain how Surpluses had to master Invisibility – the ability to be on hand constantly and yet never have their presence felt. In truth, she decided, it was probably a good thing Peter wasn't there. Mrs Dawson had a firm expression on her face, and Peter never failed to perform badly in this class, never left without some punishment or other being imposed on him.

Where Mrs Pincent was small in height and stature, Mrs Dawson was large – about a hundred and eighty-eight centimetres and with rolls of flesh that wobbled as she moved. Her hair, although pinned up in a chignon like Mrs Pincent's, somehow managed to break free regularly, meaning that she constantly had to sweep it back off her face.

Anna liked Mrs Dawson and was determined to do well in her class. Decorum was very important for Surpluses. Mrs Pincent said that Legals considered Decorum one of the most attractive skills in a Surplus, male or female.

'It should be as if you don't exist at all,' Mrs Dawson said, her voice firm. 'You should blend into the background as you go about your chores, and yet, when you are needed, you should be there immediately. It is a great skill, and one that you will learn with practice . . .'

Anna nodded seriously, and imagined herself in Mrs Sharpe's house, appearing out of the shadows when she was needed, blending into the background when she wasn't. The perfect Surplus. A true Valuable Asset.

'And how might you ensure that your presence is not felt? Tania?'

Anna allowed herself to glance quickly at Tania, who was staring resolutely ahead.

'Keep our eyes lowered,' Tania said, her voice quivering slightly, last night's defiance all but gone from her voice.

'And?' Mrs Dawson asked.

'Not talk, or offer our opinions,' Tania continued quietly. 'Not think or read or do anything that might distract us.'

'That's right,' Mrs Dawson said, looking at Tania thoughtfully. 'What about you, Charlotte? Do you have anything to add?'

Charlotte, who was sporting a black eye and a defeated expression, bit her lip. 'To anticipate the requirements of our Legals,' she said hesitantly. 'To always be thinking about what they might need or want . . .'

Mrs Dawson nodded. 'That's right, Charlotte. To always be thinking about what Legals might want. And what about the things you might want,

Charlotte? What about those?'

Charlotte looked down at the floor. 'We're Surplus,' she said flatly. 'We don't want anything. We don't have the right to desires. We are here to serve.'

'Good,' Mrs Dawson said matter-of-factly. 'Let's see it in practice shall we? One after the other, I want you to cross the room in front of me. Silently, so I can't hear a thing. Anna, you start.'

The Surpluses gathered at the side of the room, and Anna glided across the floor as quietly as she could, followed by Sheila and Tania, all of them prompting nods of approval from Mrs Dawson. Next Surplus Harry made his way across, picking his feet up and frowning in concentration. Harry was a tall boy, with curly hair, large feet and an almost skeletal frame. He had arrived at Grange Hall in the same year as Anna, but he had more in common with Surpluses who had arrived when they were much older – he was quiet, often distracted, and wasn't good at anything as far as Anna could tell.

'I hear you,' Mrs Dawson snapped. 'Go back and do it again.'

Reddening slightly, Harry went back to the side of the training room and started again, staring intently at his large feet as he tried to stop them making a sound.

'No!' Mrs Dawson shouted when he had taken just two steps. 'You clumsy boy. Do it again.'

Harry retreated and he wiped beads of sweat off his forehead as he started again, this time forcing himself on to tiptoes and looking nervously at Mrs Dawson. Halfway across, Mrs Dawson opened her mouth as if to speak. Harry's eyes opened wide in anticipation of another criticism, and as they did so, he lost his balance, grabbing on to a desk as he fell to the ground, and pulling it down with him.

Mrs Dawson stood up.

'Up!' she shrieked. 'Stand up. You useless Surplus.'

Harry pulled himself to his feet, apologising profusely, but Mrs Dawson was deaf to his words. She pulled his hands in front of him, placed them on a chair and then picked up the cane she always carried with her, smashing it down on Harry's fingers. 'Clumsy!' she shouted. 'You will learn not to be clumsy. Now, do it again.'

His face white with pain and shock, Harry made his way back to where his fellow Surpluses were waiting their turn. One of his fingers was bent the wrong way and he seemed disoriented as he started to cross the room for the third time. He made it only a quarter of the way across the room before stumbling again, his entire body clenching with fear as he awaited his inevitable punishment.

Mrs Dawson looked at him in disgust. 'You will go without supper tonight and you will practise walking across this room all night,' she said. 'And if before breakfast you cannot do it silently, then you will miss all meals tomorrow and practise again the following night until you can do it properly. Do you understand?'

Harry nodded and staggered over to where Anna,

Sheila and Tania were standing. He stared at the floor nursing his bleeding hand, as Surplus Charlie's turn was called.

'She only picked on you because Surplus Peter isn't here,' Charlie hissed at Harry when he'd successfully crossed the room a few moments later. Then he looked meaningfully at Anna. 'And Peter's going to pay for it too.'

Anna stared at him, then looked away. She didn't care. All she'd ever wanted was to be a Valuable Asset. And she was determined that she wouldn't care about anything else. If her lip was quivering slightly, if she felt suddenly gripped by fear and uncertainty and a feeling like she was falling, then she was fairly sure it would pass. Things generally did at Grange Hall. Mrs Pincent saw to that.

For the rest of the day, Anna applied herself to her training sessions and chores in a way that would have made Mrs Pincent proud. She polished the floor of her dormitory, and then polished the corridor outside just for good measure. She was at Central Feeding early to help prepare that evening's feed, and didn't even roll her eyes when she was given the meat to prepare. As a Prefect, meat preparation was a job she was well within her rights to delegate to a younger Surplus. It was a lowly job, made harder by the fact that the kitchen knives were so blunt they barely scratched the surface of the rubbery, gristle-filled flesh they were given once a week, offcuts from the local maximarket where Legals bought their food. Instead, she performed a thorough job of boning and chopping, and all the while, she was practising being invisible, keeping her eyes lowered and her feet light. And as she worked, she focused her mind on the task at hand by repeating Evening Vows to herself.

I vow to serve, to pay my dues
And train myself for Legal use.
I vow to bear the Surplus shame
And repay Nature for the same
I vow to listen, not to speak;
To steel myself when I am weak.
I vow to work and most of all
To serve the State if it should call.

Evening Vows were said every night before bedtime. They reminded Surpluses of their Place in life, Mrs Pincent said. Not that Surpluses could have a purpose, not really; that would suggest they had a reason for existing, when they didn't. But it gave them a sense of what they were to do with their lives, of how they were to pay Mother Nature and the State back for looking after them, when really they should have been tossed back where they came from.

Anna could never really understand how that would work; where would they be tossed back to? But she didn't ask, just in case Mrs Pincent decided to show her.

She frowned, and stood up to put the prepared

meat in the large vat for cooking.

But as she did so, she felt someone coming up behind her, and turned suddenly, to see the face of Surplus Charlie just a foot away from hers. Surplus Charlie was also a Prefect, but where Anna exercised her authority through firm words, a belief in rules and a much-talked about closeness with Mrs Pincent, Charlie's authority stemmed primarily from his size. At fifteen, he wasn't particularly tall for his age, but what he lacked in height he made up for in bulk, partly because of a natural muscularity, and partly because he regularly commandeered the food from other boys at his table, who would readily give up their bread or broth in spite of their hollow, aching stomachs because the alternative was far worse than hunger. Charlie could torment a boy until he no longer had bladder control; could dole out such horrific punishments that Solitary seemed a welcome respite.

Today, his face was swollen, something that Anna had registered in Decorum, but hadn't dwelt on. Surpluses regularly sported bruises and cuts – the result of punishments, fights and games. No one asked why a cheek was red or a hand wrapped in a makeshift bandage, and unless the injury was very serious, no treatment was ever sought – or given. Only on very rare occasions was a doctor was sent for. It had only happened twice during Anna's time at Grange Hall, once for a boy who broke his leg in several places during a game, and once when a new Surplus had a fever. Illness was feared by Surpluses.

Without Longevity drugs, they were vulnerable to any number of viruses and ailments, but few admitted their discomfort until it was absolutely necessary; Mrs Pincent had made it clear many times that sickness was a sign of weakness. Illness suggested that Mother Nature didn't think you'd ever be Useful and wanted to 'weed you out early'.

That's what had happened to the new Surplus. She had something called a fever and she died, in the end. Bad genes, Mrs Pincent told Anna a few weeks later. It was 'for the best'.

Anna looked briefly at Charlie. His lip was bloody and his left eye was barely visible, hidden behind the cheek that had inflated protectively around it. It was odd, Anna thought to herself, slightly nervously, how Charlie looked even more threatening when he was injured.

'So now I know who to blame if the meat's ruined,' Charlie said sneeringly as Anna narrowed her eyes at him.

'What do you want, Surplus Charlie? You shouldn't be in the kitchen,' she said, trying her hardest not to shrink back at the mere sight of him. She turned back to the vat and continued to scrape the meat into it, but she could feel his eyes boring into her neck and it made her uncomfortable.

'Your little friend,' he said in a low voice. 'Where is he?'

Anna frowned and looked at him uncertainly. 'I don't know what you mean,' she said evenly.

'I don't have friends, Charlie.'

Charlie moved closer so that Anna could feel his breath on the back of her neck. 'Surplus Peter,' he said coldly. 'Where is he?'

Anna stopped what she was doing. Charlie was in Peter's dormitory. If he didn't know where Peter was, then who did?

Cautiously, she turned round. 'Why do you want to know where Peter is?' she asked.

Charlie smirked. 'I knew it. So, he went running to you, did he?' He shook his head slowly. 'You know that Surplus is trouble, don't you, Anna? You know that he deserves everything he gets. And you do too.'

Anna gripped the knife she was holding.

'I don't know what you mean,' she said flatly, forcing herself to look Charlie in the eye, to show that he didn't intimidate her. He was no threat, she reminded herself. She was a Prefect. She wasn't a weak Surplus ripe for bullying.

Charlie shrugged. 'If he went running to you, it won't make any difference. He had it coming. Needs to learn some respect. Mrs Pincent understands, you know, Anna. She knows that Peter only got what he deserved, so there's no point telling her any different. You think you're her favourite Surplus, but you're not. She pities you.'

Anna felt her stomach clench in anger. 'No one pities me, Surplus Charlie,' she growled.

Charlie smirked, and leant down closer to Anna. 'Everyone pities you, Surplus Anna. Peter especially,' he said, his voice menacing. 'Why do you think he tries to protect you? Because he thinks you're pathetic, that's why.'

Anna stared at him, her eyes wide. 'Protect me?' she asked uncertainly. 'I don't know what you're talking about.'

'I'm talking about this,' Charlie growled, opening his overalls to reveal a large greeny-black bruise stretching across his chest. 'He's a maniac. And all because I said the most useful thing they could do with you is to put you out of your Surplus misery. I meant it too.'

Anna could feel Charlie's breath on her forehead and she jutted out her chin to show him she wasn't scared.

'Wherever he is,' Charlie continued menacingly, 'I'll find him. I kicked his head in because he deserved it and I'll do it again too. I'll kill him if I have to. Mrs Pincent won't care. And I'll be sure to make it look like an accident, don't you worry about that.'

Before Anna could say anything in response, Charlie walked off, just missing a Domestic who had come to check on Anna's work.

'Hurry up,' she shouted angrily, staring at the still raw contents of the vat. 'Get on with it, you lazy Surplus.'

'Yes,' Anna said, her voice level in spite of her racing mind. 'I'm sorry, I'll be quicker now.'

She added boiling water along with a packet of powdered stock to add bulk to the stew, but as she stirred the mixture, all thoughts of Evening Vows had left her head. Instead, all she could think about was Peter. About the trouble he was in. About the conviction, deep down inside of her, that she had to tell him, had to warn him. She knew it was out of the question; knew that it would mean breaking every rule that she had so vigorously upheld for most of her life. But she also knew that she didn't have a choice. Peter was her friend, however much she tried to deny it. And Anna, who had never before allowed her heart's voice to be heard, was now unwillingly and unavoidably in its thrall.

At 1 a.m., Anna lay awake in her bed, contemplating what she was about to do, working out how long it would take her to get to Solitary to see if Peter was there, how likely it was that she would disturb a Surplus in her dorm or, worse, get caught once outside. There were no longer cameras along the corridors of Grange Hall – those that had been installed originally had proved too expensive to run and there was no money for replacements. But Mrs Pincent didn't need cameras to keep the Surpluses at Grange Hall in their beds at night; she preferred to rely on good, old-fashioned fear, preferred to stalk the corridors herself when she couldn't sleep, which was often. If Anna was caught out of bed, she'd be beaten; if she was found making her way to Solitary, she couldn't conceive of a punishment severe enough.

Gingerly, she sat up and looked around the small,

cramped dormitory that had once served as the office to the Director of Operations, Department of Revenue and Benefits. There were ten beds in all, with little space between, each with a steel frame and thin mattress. On nine of them, female Pending Surpluses slept, hair splayed over their pillows and hands curled into little fists, a situation replicated all the way down the hall in all the other dormitories containing all the other Surpluses.

Trying not to think too much about what she was doing, Anna eased herself out of bed and winced as her feet touched the cold, hard floor.

Softly, recalling her Decorum practice, she slipped silently out of the dormitory and down the corridor. Grange Hall was strangely silent – even the Smalls seemed to be asleep. A surge of fear gripped her. She felt so exposed, so utterly vulnerable, alone in the darkness, her toes clenching against the coldness of the floor. With five hundred Surpluses and thirty staff, the Surpluses were rarely alone at Grange Hall; to be so now felt both terrifying and exhilarating at the same time.

Slipping through doors, down the stairs and then along the cold, damp and dark corridor that ran along the basement of the building, Anna finally found herself approaching the Solitary cells. Shivering, she wrapped her arms around herself.

'This better be worth it, Surplus Peter,' she muttered to herself as she turned the corner.

But then she stopped abruptly and slipped back

behind the wall. There, outside one of the three Solitary cells, was Mrs Pincent, with two men, one of whom was carrying Peter through the large, metal door.

Anna frowned, trying to work out what was happening. Was he ill? Where were they bringing him from?

Anna felt her heart beating loudly in her chest, and held her breath, peeking round the corner to see what was happening. She was fairly sure no one had seen her, but if Mrs Pincent and the two men were planning to go back upstairs via Staircase 3, she would be trapped. There would be nowhere she could hide – the stark grey corridor had nothing but the locked doors to store cupboards, and there was no way she could outrun them either; they were just a few metres away.

But to her immense relief, once the men had deposited Peter and locked the door of his cell, they turned and followed Mrs Pincent the other way along the corridor.

'You'll get your money upstairs,' she heard Mrs Pincent say as they walked away. 'And if you say one word about this to anyone, the Authorities will find out about your little black market ventures, do you understand?'

Anna heard the men grunt in reply, and waited until their footsteps could no longer be heard, then stealthily slipped round the corner towards the door of Peter's cell.

'Peter,' she whispered. 'Peter, can you hear me? It's Anna.'

Chapter Nine

It took five minutes of whispering and lightly knocking on the cell door before Anna got any response from Peter, and even then it wasn't much more than a moan.

'Peter, is that you?'

There was a pause, then she heard a shuffle. It sounded like Peter coming closer to the door. She felt scared and relieved and embarrassed all at the same time.

'Anna?'

His voice was muffled and sounded sleepy.

'Yes. I . . . I just wanted to check that you were OK. I didn't know where you were, and then Surplus Charlie . . . I just wanted to check you were here,' Anna said awkwardly. She shivered violently and wished she'd thought to bring her blanket with her now.

'Anna. You're here.'

Anna frowned. 'Are you OK?' she whispered. 'You sound funny. Did Charlie hurt you really badly?'

She heard Peter yawn.

'My head,' she heard him say. 'I feel . . . They gave me something. An injection. I feel woozy. How long have I been here?'

Anna frowned. 'You didn't have an injection, Peter. Surplus Charlie kicked your head. He told me. But why are you in Solitary? Did Mrs Pincent find you?'

'I don't know,' Peter said vaguely. 'I remember the fight. But Mrs Pincent got me out of bed later and brought me down here. At night-time. They gave me an injection . . . What time is it?'

Anna looked at her wrist.

'Half past one,' she said, her heart sinking as she realised just how little sleep she was going to get tonight.

'Look, I can't stay,' she said quickly. 'I just had to warn you about Charlie. He wants to kill you, he said. I didn't know where you were, so –'

'I can handle Charlie,' Peter said, his voice beginning to sound a bit more normal. 'But Anna, don't go. Not yet. Stay and talk to me.'

Anna felt her face flush slightly and bit her lip self-consciously. The floor was freezing and damp under her bare feet, but still she sat down.

'You can't defend me, you know,' she said awkwardly. 'You can't let Surplus Charlie bully you. I can take care of myself. You're in enough trouble as it is.'

'I don't care about trouble,' Peter said flatly.

'You can't say that!' Anna said agitatedly. 'When you get out . . . you have to learn how to behave.'

'If I get out,' Peter said darkly.

Anna sighed. 'Of course you'll get out, Peter. You just have to Learn Your Lesson, that's all.'

'And what lesson's that?' Peter asked, his voice irritable. 'Don't get born? Don't have an opinion? Don't tell Charlie that he's a bully and an oaf?'

Anna's eyes opened wide. 'You said that?'

'Yes, I said that. And he and five others thought they'd use my head as a football. I'm assuming that's why I'm down here. They must have run to Mrs Pincent afterwards and said I started it or something.'

Anna frowned. 'Charlie didn't say anything about telling Mrs Pincent,' she said. 'He didn't know where you were either.'

'What do you mean, he didn't know where I was?'

'None of us did. I mean, I didn't know you were definitely down here. That's why I . . . I mean . . .'

'You came to find me?' His voice was chirpy, almost teasing, and Anna felt herself redden.

'I . . . I just wanted to know where you were,' Anna said quickly. She cleared her throat. 'So what happened? When did you get brought down here?'

There was a pause, then Peter started to speak, his voice low. 'I don't know . . . They came for me last night. Quite late, because I was asleep. And Mrs Pincent kept asking me questions and hitting me when I wouldn't answer. Then I was put in here, and they came and got me again – tonight, I suppose. She was asking questions again but then this man got out a needle and I can't remember much until they were carrying me back again.'

Anna frowned. This didn't sound like a punishment she'd encountered.

In her experience, Mrs Pincent had several ways of 'teaching you a lesson'. There were beatings – usually with a belt, sometimes with a ruler and, very occasionally, with her bare fists; there were reduced rations, from hot food to whole meals to blankets, depending on the crime; there was extra work, often late into the night; and there was Solitary.

'What questions?' she asked. 'Was she asking you why you were bad? Because when she does that you have to say "Because I was stupid and I won't do it again."'

'No, they weren't about that. She kept asking me what I knew. Who I was. Why I was here. They wanted to know where I'd been living. I think they wanted me to tell them about your parents. I didn't, though. I didn't say a thing. I'm far too clever for your Mrs Pincent.'

'She's not my Mrs Pincent,' Anna said defensively. 'And why would she want to know about my parents?'

Anna said the words awkwardly, finding it difficult to say 'my parents', let alone contemplate the reality of them existing, of them being linked in some way to Peter's encounter with Mrs Pincent.

Anna heard something bang against the wall.

'Yes, your parents.'

'What was that noise?' Anna asked. 'And why would she care about my parents? Why would she even think you've met them? They're just criminals . . .'

'They're not just criminals. Your parents love you, Anna. And they're in the Underground Movement.'

Anna heard the bang again.

'Peter, shush, what's that noise?' she said nervously. 'You'll wake someone up.'

'We're two floors below everyone, Anna Covey. I'm not going to wake up anyone. I need to bang my head to wake myself up. They must have drugged me.'

Anna shook her head as her logical response kicked in. 'Surpluses aren't allowed to be given drugs,' she said immediately in an authoritative tone. 'Everyone knows that. It's in the Declaration. And stop calling me Anna Covey.'

'That's your name. Anna Covey. I think it's a nice name. And I don't care if Surpluses are allowed drugs or not – they definitely injected me with something. There's still a mark on my arm.'

Not sure what to say, Anna took one of her feet, which were now feeling like ice blocks, and held it in her hands, trying to encourage the blood to circulate a bit better.

'I've got to go to bed, Peter,' she said anxiously. 'I just wanted to check you're OK, and you seem to be. Don't do anything stupid. Mrs Pincent will let you out soon, I know she will.'

She waited for a reply, but Peter was silent.

'Peter? I said I'm going to bed. I –'

'I don't think she will let me out,' Peter said suddenly. 'Anna, she said something about terminating me. When we were coming down the corridor. She asked one of the men if he was qualified for termination . . .'

Anna shook her head incredulously. 'Don't be stupid, Peter,' she said firmly. 'Charlie's the only one making threats. Anyway, you were asleep when you came down the corridor. You just dreamt it, that's all. You'll probably be out tomorrow. And if you're not, maybe I'll come down again tomorrow night, to see if you're OK . . .'

She regretted saying that as soon as the words had left her mouth, but before she could take them back, Peter said, 'Please come.' His voice sounded so sad and vulnerable.

'I'll try my best,' she promised reluctantly. 'But you mustn't fight with Charlie again. If you get out. I mean . . . when.'

'Thanks Anna. You're . . . you're my best friend.'

Anna flushed.

'You're my friend too,' she said hesitantly, the words feeling strange in her mouth.

'Run away with me, then?'

Anna shook her head. 'Peter, don't be ridiculous. No one's running away. Why don't you just concentrate on getting out of Solitary?'

'Actually I'm better off here,' Peter said sulkily. 'Solitary's where the escape route out is.'

He paused, then spoke again, this time his voice more animated. 'Anna, listen to me, I've seen the plans to Grange Hall and there's a secret tunnel. Comes out near the village. I could go now, if I wanted to – I can see the grate it's hidden behind. But you have to come too. You have to escape with me, Anna Covey.'

Peter's voice was becoming slurred again, but it sounded close and Anna realised he must be pressing against the door, only centimetres away from her. For a moment, she let herself imagine leaving Grange Hall with Peter, imagined leaving Mrs Pincent and Tania and Charlie behind and feeling grass under her feet in some magical, safe place. But even as the thoughts entered her head, she knew they were pure fantasy, and a dangerous one at that.

Once, on a winter afternoon when Anna was meant to be cleaning the big ovens in the kitchen, Mrs Pincent had caught her peeking behind a blind. It was snowing, and the entire landscape was quickly being enveloped in a wonderful new coat, even the tall, grey walls that separated Grange Hall from the Outside, the world beyond it where Legal people lived. She could see Domestics and Instructors through the gates pulling their coats around them more closely as they made their way home. She looked longingly at them, thinking how wonderful it must be to feel the wind and snow in your face. Surpluses were not allowed outside unless it was absolutely necessary. Mrs Pincent said they were easier to manage inside. Anna had pressed her nose against the cold glass in order to admire the swirling snowflakes, mesmerised as she watched them coming directly towards her and billowing on to the window sill, joining others until there was a big mound of delicious, new whiteness covering all the grey and grime. She'd been wondering what it would be like to touch something so magical, to hold it in her hands and feel it melting through her fingers, when Mrs Pincent saw her and dragged her away angrily.

'The snow is not falling for you,' she'd shouted at her as she pulled Anna to her office by the hair, then set her down on the floor as she searched for her belt. 'How dare you even look at it! How dare you spend one moment of your life looking at something beautiful when you should be working. Nothing good in this world exists for you,' she'd screamed as she gave up the search and used her own hands instead to slap her across the face. 'Know Your Place, Anna. Know Your Place. You are nothing. You deserve nothing. You will never feel snow in your hands or the sun on your skin. You are not wanted on this earth and the sooner you can accept that, the better for all of us.'

'I do accept it,' Anna had whimpered as she closed her eyes against the pain. 'I'm sorry, Mrs Pincent. I succumbed to Temptation. It won't happen again. I do Know My Place. I have no Place. I'm nothing . . .'

Pushing the memory out of her head, Anna looked back at the metal door that imprisoned Peter. 'Don't talk about escape,' she said agitatedly. 'Why can't you just accept things? Why can't you just be my friend here, in Grange Hall?'

'Because we don't have much time,' Peter said, his voice beginning to fade. 'We don't have for ever,

Anna. Not like the rest of them. We need to get out, before it's too late.'

Anna stared at the cold, metal door separating her and Peter, and shook her head silently. 'Too late for what?' she wanted to ask. 'What does time matter when every moment is stolen anyway?'

But instead, she stood up and briefly pressed her hand against the door, before forcing her frozen legs to carry her silently back up to her stark, grey dormitory.

The next day, when Anna woke up, her night-time visit felt rather like a dream, like an unreal vision that might even have happened to someone else. There was nothing like the chill of the morning air on your body and the knowledge that you had five minutes to get to breakfast fully dressed to put a bit of perspective on things, she thought to herself, as she pulled on her overalls and regulation knee-length socks. Nothing like the threat of a beating to get rid of dangerous thoughts and expose them for the deceptions they were. She felt guilty now, embarrassed and fearful that someone might have seen her creeping down to Solitary in the middle of the night. She couldn't believe how reckless she'd been, couldn't believe she'd actually told Peter she'd do it again that evening too.

Silently, she led the other Pending girls out of the dormitory and down towards Central Feeding for breakfast, single file as always. As they approached the hall, she stopped them, and inspected their appearance quickly, telling one to pull up her socks properly and another to straighten her hair. Then her eyes were drawn to Sheila's overalls, and she frowned.

Sheila had never really fitted in at Grange Hall, had never really been able to adjust to institutional living. And she wasn't any good at anything either – everything she touched, whether cooking or cleaning or mending, seemed to go wrong and she would look at it helplessly, as if she couldn't understand how she'd ended up with a lopsided pie or the wrong stitch or a floor that was still covered in grease marks. Anna had tried to teach her at first, making her do her work over and over until it was right, but lately she'd begun to cover up for her instead, unable to bear Sheila's haunted expression and ever-present bruises.

Right now, however, Anna wasn't in the mood for Sheila's inadequacies. This was just the excuse she needed to reaffirm her authority – over the Surpluses in her charge, over herself. There was a button hanging off Sheila's overalls, and everyone knew that overalls had to be kept in good repair at all times.

'You've got a loose button,' she said sharply. 'Go and fix it. You can't go into Central Feeding looking like that.'

'I'm sorry Anna, I didn't notice,' Sheila said quietly. The bruises on her face were now a deep purple colour, and Anna could hardly bear to look at them. 'Can I eat first and sew it on later?'

Anna met her eyes and for a brief second, she considered agreeing to Sheila's request; breakfast was the biggest meal of the day where big vats of porridge sat at the top of the hall so that everyone could have at least two helpings. Sheila was thin enough already; a missed meal would make her hollow cheeks positively skeletal.

But then she shook herself. Narrowing her eyes, she looked down at Sheila.

'Do it now,' she snapped. 'If you miss breakfast, that's your own fault. I will not have you let down my dormitory.'

Sheila stared at her silently, then turned and walked back up the stairs, leaving Anna feeling a welcome sense of control. Order was good, she told herself firmly as she approached the vats of porridge. Rules were there to be followed.

But whilst Anna told herself she was fine, she didn't feel particularly fine. Taking her bowl back to her table, she lifted the food to her mouth, but found herself unable to eat. The porridge felt dry, like sawdust, and eventually, having almost gagged on the first mouthful, she gave up.

It was tiredness, she decided. That was all.

'Hurry up, now. Remember that you're on clearing duty this morning. I want Central Feeding clean before training starts.'

Anna looked up to see Mrs Pincent hovering over her, and she nodded quickly.

'Yes, House Matron, I remember. We'll start right away,' she said. 'You can depend on me,' she added unnecessarily, and Mrs Pincent raised an eyebrow.

'Yes, well, I hope I can,' she said frowning slightly

as she swished past, her solid court shoes resonating on the cold, hard floor.

Anna looked up and saw that Sheila was standing nervously in the doorway. The final whistle had just been blown, which meant no more food was to be consumed. And suddenly Anna couldn't bear it.

'Sheila, come in, we're on cleaning duty,' she said loudly, watching closely as Sheila nodded obediently, her eyes surreptitiously moving to the front of the hall where the big vats of porridge were being taken into the kitchens.

Anna picked up her bowl, which was still full of porridge, and walked over to Sheila.

'Here,' she said softly, checking that no one was watching before handing her the bowl. 'Just eat it quickly and don't tell anyone, OK?'

Sheila's face lit up as she took the bowl gratefully. 'Thanks Anna,' she said in her small, soft voice. 'And I'm sorry about the button.'

Anna nodded, and walked away thinking as she did so of Mrs Pincent's take on apologies. *Don't ever say you're sorry to another Surplus*, the House Matron had told her repeatedly when she'd first become a Prefect. *'Sorry' implies a contract, an expected level of behaviour, and Surpluses don't enjoy such a luxury. Surpluses should not ask why, or how – they simply do what they're told, and that's the end of it.* Sometimes she'd pause then, and frown slightly. *Life is very straightforward for a Surplus*, she'd say, almost wistfully. *There's nothing to think about at all.*

Chapter Ten

Later that morning, Anna found herself in Laundry, which that day involved ironing all the clothes they took in for the local houses – the ones that didn't have housekeepers. Grange Hall's income had risen steadily over the years, Mrs Pincent was always proud to point out. They now did laundry regularly for over fifty households and two local hotels and the high quality of the work was often commented upon, something that Anna always heard Mrs Pincent telling people, particularly people who were from the Authorities.

Anna quite liked doing laundry, because she got to see the soft sheets and beautiful clothes that people in the village wore – soft woollen jumpers, wisp-thin silk blouses and beautiful cotton dresses that she some-times liked to imagine wafting around in as if life were nothing more than a wonderful holiday. Not today, though. Today, all she wanted to do was scrub – scrub away dirt, scrub away her wickedness, and scrub away all thoughts of Peter and her appointment later that night. She'd even offered to do under-

garments, which was considered the worst job. They were all hard and full of wire – called 'bones', apparently – and impossible to clean properly.

Anna couldn't understand why anyone would want to wear such uncomfortable undergarments, at least she hadn't until she'd worked for Mrs Sharpe.

'Longevity doesn't cure gravity, unfortunately,' Mrs Sharpe had told her when she'd been caught frowning at a particularly painful-looking thing that she discovered was called an Uplifter. 'Until they develop a drug that renews the skin as well as the body, we're going to need boning to keep everything in place and to hold everything up.'

Anna had just nodded then, even though she didn't really know what Mrs Sharpe meant, but a few days later her employer had called her into the bathroom because she needed a towel. When Anna came in and saw Mrs Sharpe naked, she would have gasped if it hadn't been for all her training, which had taught her never to stare or react to anything except with a nod and, if appropriate, a curtsey.

The truth was that Anna had never seen a body like it. Fully dressed, Mrs Sharpe was so pretty, with golden skin and white blond hair and pretty blue eyeshadow around her eyes, but her naked body was so . . . droopy. That was the only word Anna could find to describe it. Her skin sagged disconsolately aroun her frame, hanging off her flesh as if it were wate logged or had simply lost the will to hold itself up a longer.

Anna had kept her eyes lowered, but Mrs Sharpe must have seen her looking out of the corner of her eye because she looked at her and smiled sadly.

'I just can't bring myself to go under the knife,' she'd said with a little shrug, as Anna blushed furiously at being caught out. 'It's ridiculous, I know, when I could have everything perked up in no time. But every so often, things go wrong on the operating table. And now I know I'll be living for ever, it's made me scared of death. Isn't that silly?'

Miss Humphries took Laundry, and checked every sheet, blouse and towel before it was packed away, because Mrs Pincent had said that every single item had to be ironed to perfection before it could be sent back to its owner.

Anna had partnered with Peter in Laundry for the past few weeks, but today Miss Humphries put her with Sheila, which meant, Anna recognised, that she would have to do most of the load herself if it was going to achieve the high quality expected. She wondered how Sheila would cope on the Outside, whether she would ever prove Useful enough for employment. Anna pushed the thought from her head. Sheila was not her responsibility, she reminded herself. Sheila could look after herself.

Silently, they started to iron the large sheet, folding it into a neat, pressed rectangle as they did so. Then they ironed another, and another, then a duvet cover, then three blouses and a whole load of undergarments

until the entire pile had been turned into a neat, fragrant stack.

'Well doesn't that look nice and pretty.'

Anna looked up to see Tania standing over Sheila, her eyes focused on the laundry sitting in front of her.

She narrowed her eyes in warning, and Tania tossed her hair. 'It's OK,' she said, smiling silkily, 'I'm not going to do anything. But Sheila, I bet your parents would be proud, don't you think? That their dirty worthless Surplus daughter is learning to do her chores?'

Sheila stood up angrily to face Tania, but even standing, the top of her head barely reached Tania's nose.

'At least my parents didn't want to give me up,' Sheila hissed. 'I'm Legal and the Catchers stole me away. But your parents didn't want you, did they, Tania? They just gave you away. I bet you were a really ugly baby. I bet your parents couldn't even bear to look at you. And nor can I.'

Tania's face went red, and Anna stood up quickly. 'Enough,' she said angrily. 'Tania, get back to work.'

Miss Humphries was walking towards them and Tania reluctantly turned, pulling a few strands of Sheila's red hair out of her head as she walked away, forcing tears of pain into Sheila's eyes.

'Why do you do that?' Anna asked, shaking her head. 'You have to learn to ignore her, Sheila, otherwise you're always going to be picked on.'

Sheila smiled benignly. 'I don't mind being picked

on,' she said. 'And I only told the truth. Tania's parents brought her here themselves, didn't they? She wasn't wanted by anyone in the whole wide world. Not like us, Anna. Our parents wanted us. That makes us special.'

Anna looked at Sheila in bewilderment, wondering how she managed to twist the truth so easily. Mrs Pincent said that parents who gave up their Surpluses were honourable; Anna herself had always wished her parents hadn't been so selfish, hiding her away in an attic.

'No Surpluses are special,' she whispered angrily, looking around to check that no one had heard. 'Sheila, don't blaspheme like that.'

But Sheila just smiled secretively.

They didn't talk for the rest of the training session and it was only as they were leaving that she turned conspiratorially to Anna.

'Look,' she said, pulling something out of her pocket. It was pink and silky, and Anna gasped as she recognised it. It was a pair of knickers, but not the sort of knickers that Surpluses wore. They were silk and soft and Anna remembered admiring them as she ironed them. And now they were in Sheila's pocket.

'Put them back,' Anna hissed. 'Put them back or I'll tell Miss Humphries. You'll get beaten, Sheila. Quickly, before she notices . . .'

But Sheila shook her head defiantly. 'I'm Legal, not a Surplus. I should have things like this, Anna. And I like them. I don't want to put them back.'

Anna shook her head in disbelief. 'Sheila,' she said firmly. 'Put them back right now.'

'What, so you're the only one allowed secrets now?'

Anna stared at Sheila uncertainly. 'What do you mean?' she demanded. 'What are you talking about?'

Sheila smiled. 'I woke up last night, Anna, and you weren't there. Where were you?'

Anna felt the blood drain from her face. 'You must have imagined it,' she said firmly. 'You must have been dreaming.'

Sheila shrugged. 'Maybe you're dreaming now, Anna. Maybe I don't have anything in my pocket.'

Anna stared at her, but before she could say anything Miss Humphries arrived at their counter and carefully looked through their work. Anna opened her mouth to tell her of Sheila's transgression, but found herself unable to speak. Instead, she just stared at Sheila, beads of sweat beginning to appear on her forehead.

'Good, good. Well done, you two. You can go now.'

Anna looked at her uncertainly. 'We . . . we can go?' she asked hesitantly.

Miss Humphries frowned. 'Yes, Anna, you can go.'

Sheila was tugging at her sleeve, but still Anna felt rooted to the spot, convinced that if she moved, Mother Nature herself would smite her down.

'Come on, Anna,' Sheila said, smiling thinly. 'We're going to be late for supper.'

'Yes, I suppose we will,' Anna said vaguely, shooting

one last look at Miss Humphries to check that this wasn't a bluff, that she wasn't going to start laughing at them for thinking they'd got away with their crime, that she wasn't going to grab a stick and start beating them on the hands for being dirty little thieves like Mrs Pincent had done years ago when Anna had helped herself to an apple she'd found in the kitchen when she was on cleaning duty.

But it wasn't a bluff. Miss Humphries was now checking the next pair's work, and no one was even looking at them as they left the room.

As they made their way to Central Feeding for supper, Sheila didn't even appear nervous or concerned about her heinous crime, although Anna felt nervous enough for both of them. As she furtively stuffed a roll and hunk of cheese into her pocket for Peter, she wondered whether she was truly slipping deeper and deeper into hell itself. She wondered if Mrs Pincent had been right all along about Surpluses – that they were inherently bad, genetically programmed to leech off the world and do damage. And then, suddenly, a Middle Surplus appeared at her side.

'Mrs Pincent wants to see you in her office at 8 p.m.,' he said breathlessly.

Anna looked at him sharply, her heart thudding heavily in her chest. 'Did she say why?'

The Surplus shrugged and shook his head. It wasn't surprising; after all, Surpluses didn't need reasons, just directions. Anyway, Anna already knew why. Mrs Pincent knew. Mrs Pincent knew everything.

At 8 p.m. on the dot, Anna knocked on Mrs Pincent's door and, when she'd heard the instruction, opened it. Breathing deeply to quieten the butterflies in her stomach and to try and hide the guilt that she had carried with her all day, she walked in and made her way to Mrs Pincent's large desk, where she stood silently, waiting for Mrs Pincent to speak.

The room represented many things to Anna – a confessional, a torture chamber, even a prison – but it was a room she knew, a room that felt familiar and even, in an odd way, reassuring. Mrs Pincent was always quick to punish, but afterwards she would always explain why. As Anna lay shaking on the floor or clutching a hand to her face, Mrs Pincent would smile and say that she hoped the punishment had brought Anna closer to being a good Surplus, had helped her to understand who she was. And Anna would nod, and would think very hard about whatever it was she'd done wrong to make sure it didn't happen again.

'Anna,' Mrs Pincent said eventually, looking up at her with the piercing eyes that Anna had known and feared most of her life. 'Tell me about Peter.'

Anna looked up in alarm and immediately lowered her eyes again in deference. In her pocket, the bread and cheese she'd sneaked out of Central Feeding seemed to burn her leg.

'About Peter?' she asked hesitantly. She swallowed nervously, trying to prepare words in her head, to work out how to explain her visit to Solitary.

'I want to know what he's told you. I want to know where he's come from and why he's here,' Mrs Pincent said evenly.

'Why he's here?' Anna asked nervously. Was this a trick question? 'Because he's a Surplus. Because he was found by the Catchers. Because . . .'

'I know that,' Mrs Pincent interrupted, her voice full of contempt. 'What I want to know is *why* he was found. Why now. And I want to know what he's been saying since he's been here.'

Anna looked down at the floor worriedly. Did Mrs Pincent know that Peter wanted her to escape?

'Anna,' Mrs Pincent continued, her voice now soft and friendly. 'Tell me everything you know. It's for his own good, you know.'

Anna looked up quickly, saw Mrs Pincent looking benevolently at her.

'He . . .' Anna cleared her throat. 'He . . .' she started again, but then stopped.

'He what?' Mrs Pincent demanded, her knuckles whitening visibly as her fingers clenched into fists over her desk. 'What?'

Anna swallowed desperately. She couldn't tell her. For the first time in her life, she couldn't tell Mrs Pincent what she wanted to know.

'He said he got caught in Essex,' she said eventually. 'He said his parents hadn't told him about the Declaration and that he was sick of hiding all the time.'

Her heart was thudding in her chest, but Anna somehow managed to maintain a composed exterior by digging her nails into her palms, which were becoming hotter and wetter by the moment.

'What else did he say?' Mrs Pincent spat out her words. 'He must have told you more than that.'

Anna shook her head, and felt herself slipping deeper into the quicksand. 'He found it hard to settle in,' she said. 'He found it hard to learn the rules. I tried to teach him. I did my best . . .'

Mrs Pincent nodded curtly.

'Did he do something very bad?' Anna reddened as she spoke. Direct questions were a disciplinary offence, particularly those put to Mrs Pincent herself. 'I mean, to go to Solitary, that is,' she continued quickly. 'I just thought, if that's where he is . . .'

She could feel her chest tightening with fear as she spoke – fear, not for herself, but for the truth. In case it was bad. In case Peter really wasn't going to get out.

But instead of shouting at her for her insolence, or telling her that Peter deserved to rot in Solitary, Mrs Pincent frowned, then stood up.

'Peter needs some time to think about his role in this world,' she said thoughtfully.

Anna nodded, and watched as Mrs Pincent walked around her large, mahogany desk and stood in front of it, the light above her creating what looked like a halo of dust over her head.

'Anna, you will find this hard to understand because you are such a good, responsible Surplus,' she said, folding her arms tightly and looking almost fragile, Anna found herself thinking. Mrs Pincent's slender frame and hands clasped around her elbows suddenly lent her the impression of a nervous woman, rather than the aggressive matriarch Anna was used to and it unnerved her.

'You understand your place in the world, you understand the debt that you owe to Mother Nature,' Mrs Pincent continued. 'But Peter does not think of himself as a Surplus. He sees himself as something better, as if he has a rightful place in this world.'

Mrs Pincent paused, and as she did so, Anna noticed the familiar venom creep back into her eyes. Striding back to her chair, Mrs Pincent smacked her hand down on the desk. 'Peter is a danger to the other Surpluses, and a danger to this earth,' she said, her voice now harsher. 'That's why he's in Solitary. I won't allow anyone to mention that boy's name until we rid him of his illicit thoughts. Until I am sure that I have fulfilled my duty and that he understands the truth, I cannot risk him contaminating the rest of you. He is Surplus, Anna. He is lucky to have been given the chance to redeem his Parents' Sins. And he needs to learn that. The hard way, if necessary.'

She paused briefly, then nodded curtly. 'That will be all, Anna. Return to your chores.'

Anna nodded silently and turned to go.

'Oh, and Anna?'

She stopped.

'I understand that a piece of Laundry went missing

during your training session today. Find out who stole it, will you, and send them to me? I want the culprit by tomorrow evening.'

Anna bit her lip. 'Yes, Mrs Pincent.'

She left Mrs Pincent's office and closed the door, but instead of going back to her dormitory, she leant back on the wall just next to Mrs Pincent's door, her hands twisting together anxiously her mind racing.

She took a deep breath, and as she heard Mrs Pincent start talking – presumably into the telephone – she shook her head and turned to walk back to her dormitory. But as she did so she heard Mrs Pincent say her name and looked up in surprise. Mrs Pincent couldn't be calling her, because she wasn't to know she was still outside her office. Curious, Anna moved closer to the door.

'Yes, Anna. Prefect. No, she couldn't tell me a bloody thing. Stupid girl's got no mind of her own, she's been indoctrinated so well. I suppose I should take credit for it, really . . .'

Anna's heart quickened.

'Look, it doesn't matter – what matters is that I want rid of him,' Mrs Pincent spat bitterly. 'I thought we might get some useful information out of him but it's useless. I don't want him here any longer . . . No, I can't send him away. The Authorities seem to see him as a useful experiment – see how a new Pending copes in a Surplus Hall. But I won't have *my* hall used as a laboratory. Well, not that sort, anyway. No, I need your help . . . Yes, exactly. And it's got to look natural. A stress-induced heart attack, maybe. If the little hero dies from an Opt-Out illness, the Authorities can hardly blame us, can they?'

There was a pause, and Anna's eyes widened in fear as she registered what Mrs Pincent had just said. Moments later, her House Matron started talking again.

'Yes, I know . . . I see – not tonight? When, then? Tomorrow?' she said darkly. 'What do you mean, you're working? You work for me, remember that. Well, all right then, it'll have to be early morning. 4 a.m. . . . . Yes, I'll come and get you.'

Her legs feeling like lead weights, Anna forced herself to move away from the door. Her heart was pounding in her chest and she felt as though she might faint, small dots appearing in front of her eyes. There had to be an explanation, she thought to herself desperately. Mrs Pincent would never say those things. She just wouldn't. She couldn't.

But she had. Anna had heard her with her very own ears. Bile was rising up her throat and it was all she could do to stop herself from retching. Mrs Pincent wanted to get rid of Peter. Mrs Pincent was going to kill him.

She closed her eyes briefly, trying to think of some way that she could have misunderstood what Mrs Pincent had said; some way to make things OK again, but she knew it was futile.

And the worst thing, Anna realised – to her shame, because surely nothing could be worse than Mrs

Pincent wanting Peter dead – the thing that hurt most of all, the words that had cut into her like a knife, were the ones Mrs Pincent had used to describe her. She had used the word 'indoctrinated' with vitriol, as if it was a bad thing. As if being a good Surplus, a Valuable Asset, everything that Anna had spent her life trying to be, was something Mrs Pincent held in contempt.

Anna had never known the feeling of hatred before, but now it raged through her body like a rampant cancer, filling her with strength of emotion that she had never known before, and had no capacity to express or handle.

Her head spinning, she found herself walking back towards her dormitory. Then, in a daze, she changed direction and made her way towards Staircase 2. She upped her pace until she was running, oblivious to the looks she was getting from the Middle Surpluses who were stepping out of her way and lowering their eyes in case this most terrifying of Prefects should notice them, and unaware of the slight figure of Sheila, watching her from the shadows.

Mrs Pincent would not get away with it, Anna repeated over and over in her head as she ran. Could not get away with it.

Anna, the stupid girl with no mind of her own, was going to make sure of that if it was the last thing she did.

Chapter Eleven

5 March 2140

Mrs Pincent is evil. Peter was right – Mrs Pincent is the most evil Legal who ever lived. I hate her. I hate her like I never knew I could hate someone before. I hate her so much I don't know what to do with myself. She wants to kill Peter and I didn't believe him. He's got to escape, to get as far away from here as possible.

I don't think I want to stay here any more either. But where else can I go? I can't run away with Peter.

I just can't.

Can I?

At 9 p.m., having splashed her face with copious amounts of cold water so that although her eyes were still red her entire face now matched them, Anna left Female Bathroom 2. As she emerged into the corridor, she studiously ignored the Surpluses who had gathered outside the door, drawn by the sound of muffled crying inside, and made her way back to her dormitory. As she walked in, she noticed that everyone was sitting on two of the beds, huddled together. Once they saw her, they all jumped off, even Tania, and started doing what they were meant to be doing – namely, sweeping the floor and dusting the window ledges before the evening bell and end of day checks – but Anna, who would usually have barked instructions, or told them off for talking, barely looked up. What did it matter if they were cleaning or not? Who cared if the dormitory was dirty? That's how she felt inside – dirty and used.

'Anna? Anna, are you OK?'

Anna hadn't noticed Sheila slipping on to her bed, and she started slightly.

She met Sheila's eyes for a moment.

'I'm fine,' she said abruptly, forcing any emotion out of her voice. 'I got something in my eye, that's all.'

Sheila nodded. 'I thought you might have forgotten about Ramping Duty,' she said, looking at Anna curiously.

Anna started. She had completely forgotten. Ramping Duty involved walking around her floor after the first evening bell, making sure that lights were turned out and that all the Surpluses were in bed. Middles were to be in bed between 9 p.m. and 10 p.m. depending on their age, and Pendings had to be asleep by 11 p.m. After 11 p.m., not a sound was to be heard anywhere – except for the top floor, obviously. Smalls didn't understand instructions and bedtimes yet. They hadn't been here long enough to be indoctrinated, Anna thought to herself bitterly.

'No, no,' she said quickly, her voice brittle. 'Of course I haven't forgotten. And I'm absolutely fine. Which is more than I can say for those window ledges – you can see the dust from here.'

Sheila nodded obediently and slipped away, busying herself with a duster while Anna breathed in deeply and got off her bed. *There's always something to do*, she thought to herself. *And you can always rely on Anna to do it.*

Anna never found Ramping particularly difficult. Some of the Pendings lacked authority and never managed to instil enough fear in the other Surpluses to achieve lights out and silence, but not Anna. The other Surpluses knew how seriously she took her job as a Prefect, knew that she didn't shirk her responsibility to discipline them when necessary and knew that they could get away with nothing when she was on duty. Her eagle eyes noticed everything – Domestics smuggling toys in for favourite Smalls, whispered conversations, last-minute trips to the bathroom that should have taken place ten minutes before – and it was said by many that she was closer to Mrs Pincent than she was to any of the other Surpluses.

That night, though, if any of the Surpluses had

looked closely enough, they would have noticed a list-lessness about her; that her eyes were glassy, rather than focused and that her voice had a tinge of the disinterested about it. She still went into every dormitory and laid down the law, ringing her bell and scolding the Surpluses who were not yet in bed, but there was no energy or urgency about the way she did it. Had anyone disobeyed her or challenged her, she might well have shrugged and walked away rather than ruthlessly punishing them. That particular evening, Anna could not see the point of Ramping. So what if rules were broken? So what if she couldn't have heard a pin drop as she left each dormitory? What did any of it matter?

But luckily, none of the Surpluses did look closely enough, and they fell into line as usual. Several girls were lying on the floor beside their bed, rather than in the bed itself, but that was normal and accepted. When female Surpluses were menstruating, they had to wear a red cloth around their neck to show everyone that they were unclean, that their bodies were dirty, flaunting their fertility which was shameful and evil. Every time a female Surplus reached puberty and discovered the first drop of blood on a tissue or on their knickers, they were sent to Mrs Pincent to be told that they were no longer victims of their Surplus existence, but potential perpetrators; that their bodies were now enemies of Mother Nature and that the pain they felt each month was imposed by Nature to remind them of their Sins. Any Surplus who dared to soil her sheets with the tiniest speck of blood was beaten and scrubbed with a wire brush to wash away these Sins, to make sure that they saw their bodies as hostile, to be despised and controlled. Few had escaped this punishment, and many girls preferred to sleep on the cold, hard floor when they were menstruating to make quite sure that their sheets remained unstained, a situation that Mrs Pincent encouraged because floors were easier to clean than sheets, and the misery of a few sleepless nights was nothing compared with the destruction their bodies were now capable of imposing on the world.

By 11 p.m., everyone was in bed as usual, Grange Hall was silent, and Anna slipped into her own bed, waiting for everyone to fall asleep.

Sleep was the last thing on her mind, however. In spite of her exhaustion, she felt fully alert and at one o'clock in the morning, when she was sure that all the Instructors and Mrs Pincent were in bed, she sat up and looked around. Outside, through the thin blinds, she could see that the wind was billowing, forcing trees to bend so that they looked as if they were performing a macabre dance, their branches resembling gnarled fingers wagging at her. But the triple-glazed windows meant that not a single snap of a twig could be heard inside the dormitory. The only sound was the gentle breathing of the other Pending girls, fast asleep.

Easing herself out of bed and shivering slightly against the cold, Anna wrapped a blanket around herself and made her way slowly into the corridor.

As Anna walked down the hallway that was so familiar to her and yet somehow so different now, late at night, with no one else around, she realised that this was the freest she'd ever felt in Grange Hall. It might be cold and dark, and shadows, cast by the thin rays of moonlight that managed to force their way through the gaps in the doors, might be moving ominously up and down the corridor, but she felt free here on her own. It had been her decision to get out of bed, not an order or demand. And the sheer exhilaration of doing what she wanted to do, even if it could land her in Solitary, made her feel as if she was floating.

She was still scared; she'd have been stupid not to be. But, she realised, she was also, very deep down, more afraid that she might never again have the opportunity to walk around unseen and unaccounted for.

In fact she was so preoccupied with these thoughts that she didn't hear the sound of footsteps behind her until she was halfway down the corridor. But as soon as she did, she froze, barely daring to move a muscle.

Terrified, she gradually turned around to face her pursuer, her slow movement in stark contrast to her mind, which was frantically thinking up excuses for being out of bed as she did so. She couldn't sleep. She needed a glass of water. All rules she wasn't allowed to break, but which sounded a great deal less serious than the truth. Whatever happened, she had to continue her journey down to Solitary. Peter's life depended on it.

But when she looked behind her, she couldn't see anyone. Confused, she looked around, but there was no one to be seen. Had she imagined the sound of feet padding behind her? No, it was impossible. But so was the idea of people disappearing into thin air.

Frowning, and feeling distinctly unsettled, she continued down the corridor, but within a few seconds the footsteps could be heard again, stepping softly after her. Immediately she turned again, and when she saw who was following her, her eyes opened wide.

'Sheila?' she said incredulously, relief washing over her as she realised it wasn't an Instructor. 'Sheila, what are you doing?'

Sheila was so thin and pale that she seemed luminous in the moonlight that lit the corridor.

She looked at Anna fearfully.

'I want to come with you,' she said slowly, her voice small and timid. 'Wherever you're going, I want to come too.'

Anna looked at her uncertainly. 'I'm not going anywhere,' she whispered crossly, hoping to intimidate Sheila into submission. 'Go back to bed.'

'You're going to find Peter,' Sheila said, her voice still nervous, but a little look of defiance that Anna recognised creeping on to her face, making her features seem stronger. 'I know you are.'

Anna's heart nearly stopped, but she managed to shake her head and look surprised. 'I don't know what you're talking about,' she said firmly. 'Go back to bed.'

'If you're not going to find Peter, then where are you going?'

Anna stared at Sheila, then stepped closer and put her hands on her shoulders.

'Sheila, you are to go back to bed now, do you hear me? If you don't, I'm going to make sure you go to Solitary tomorrow, do you understand?'

She stared at Sheila and narrowed her eyes. 'Do you understand?' she repeated.

Sheila nodded miserably.

'I'll go back to bed. But if you and Peter go anywhere, you have to take me with you,' she said, her voice trembling with emotion. 'Please, Anna.'

'To bed,' Anna ordered, her voice firm, but she squeezed Sheila's shoulder as she spoke. 'And don't get caught,' she whispered, then turned around and continued on her path, listening as Sheila padded despondently back to the dormitory.

Peter was wide awake when she finally arrived in the dank confines of Solitary. As soon as she scratched on the door and whispered his name, she heard him jump up and come to the door.

'Anna!' he said, his voice sounding so excited she felt a huge rush of happiness surge through her. She'd never known anyone sound so pleased to hear her voice, anyone speak her name with such elation.

'I knew you'd come,' Peter continued. 'I just knew it.'

Anna smiled, and put her hand against the door.

'Peter, you were right,' she whispered urgently when she'd composed herself. 'About Mrs Pincent. She . . . she wants to get rid of you. You're not safe here. You need to escape.'

'Of course I need to escape,' Peter said immediately. 'But you've got to come with me.'

Anna bit her lip. 'I can't,' she said softly. 'I belong here. I'm not like you.'

'You are like me,' Peter said, his voice choking slightly. 'Anna, you don't belong here. You belong with your parents. With me. You *have* to come with me.'

'I don't know my parents,' Anna said, swallowing furiously as tears began to prick at her eyes. 'How can I belong with people I don't even know? How do I even know they want me?'

'They want you back more than anything,' Peter said, his voice suddenly sad and serious. 'I'll tell you about them. Anna, your parents are really nice people. They took me in and . . .'

He paused.

'They want to see you, Anna,' Peter said gently. 'They love you, more than anything in the world.'

'No one loves me,' Anna said, in a small voice. 'No one. I'm just a Surplus.'

'No,' Peter said fiercely, 'you're not. And when we escape, you'll realise that. You'll see all the amazing things in the world and you'll realise that Grange Hall isn't real. It isn't the world, Anna. It's wrong. Everything about it is wrong.'

Anna said nothing.

'You had a room, Anna. A room full of toys,' Peter said suddenly. 'And so many books to read . . .'

Anna felt a tear pricking at her eye and wiped it away.

'And your parents thought you were the best thing in the whole wide world. They risked everything just to have you, just to give you everything you wanted.'

He paused again, and then Peter began to tell Anna all about them, about the people who seemed to want her back so desperately, about the life that could have been hers – should have been hers, he said. And as he talked, she felt as though she was being lifted up, as if all the pain and treachery of the day was evaporating beneath her. Wrapping herself in her blanket, she closed her eyes and allowed herself to imagine the things that he described. It felt almost as if she was following him up a beautiful mountain; with each word, he was showing her the wonderful views, and the higher they climbed, the more beautiful it became and the fresher the air felt. Cautiously at first, she allowed herself to follow him, but with every step she felt a great fear taking hold. Fear of heights, fear of the unknown, fear that when she finally got to the top and saw for herself how incredible it was, she would find that she was standing on a cliff face and would lose her grip and fall.

But was falling such a bad thing, she wondered. Was it, perhaps, better to see the top of the mountain, even if only for a moment, than never to even try? Or was it as Mrs Pincent would have it – that the higher you allow yourself to climb, the further you have to come crashing down to earth?

Chapter Twelve

6 March, 2140

I am going to leave Grange Hall.

Peter and I are going to run away through a tunnel in Solitary.

He has a Plan.

It's impossible to escape from Grange Hall. The Catchers will come after us, and Mrs Pincent will too. But we have to go. Mrs Pincent was talking about Peter and she wants to get rid of him. She said that I was stupid too. Indoctrinated.

I hate Mrs Pincent. I thought I liked her. I thought Mrs Pincent knew best. I thought she did horrible things for our own good. But she doesn't. She's cruel and mean and she doesn't think I'm Useful at all, even though she told me that I was, even though I've always done everything that she said I should.

I'm scared about leaving Grange Hall, though. I don't know anything about the Outside. On the Outside I won't be a Prefect. I won't be set to be a Valuable Asset either. I don't know what I'll be on the Outside. Just an Illegal, I suppose.

I'd like to run away with Peter to a big field, the one he told me about, where he used to run around and shout. Or I'd like to go to the desert – no one would ever come looking for us there and we'd always be warm.

But Peter says we have to go to London. Peter says we have to go back to my parents. They live in Bloomsbury, in a house which has three storeys. Mrs Sharpe's house was only two storeys. I'll have new clothes, Peter says. And the Underground will protect us and hide us so the Catchers won't be able to find us.

Peter says that in Bloomsbury I won't have to scrub and clean and be Obedient; that my parents will teach me about literature and music and that I can join the Underground Movement.

I don't like it underground. That's where Solitary is. It's dark and dank and scary and you're left on your own for hours and hours and you start imagining things – like noises that sound like screaming and weeping, and footsteps too, in the middle of the night when everyone's asleep and no one's walking around anywhere. And you wonder if maybe you're not even imagining them; maybe they're real.

The route out is in Solitary. Peter knows about it because Grange Hall used to be a government building before and my parents got hold of the floor plans from a neighbour who is 'sympathetic to the cause'. Peter coming to Grange Hall was part of a plan to get me out, he said. I didn't believe him at first – why would anyone go to all that trouble for me? I can't even remember my parents. But Peter says they remember me.

The tunnel was built in case of terrorist attacks. It leads out to the village, past the cameras outside Grange Hall, Peter says.

I don't want to go to Solitary. What if I can't get out? What if I get left there for ever?

I won't, though. I trust Peter. Peter's my friend.

We're going to escape tomorrow night. Tonight, I mean. I suppose it's morning now, even though it's still night really. I should be in bed, but I can't sleep. I've got to do something wrong so they put me in Solitary, and then in the middle of the night, we're going to 'make a run for it'. Peter says the tunnel is hidden behind a grate in the wall. He's loosened it too, he said, so it's all ready. He said that Mrs Pincent would kick herself when she realised she'd put him in exactly the place he wanted to be. He said it like he was enjoying himself in Solitary, but I don't think he is really. It might have a tunnel out, but it's still cold and dark and lonely.

Peter's amazing. He knows everything about everything.

I told Peter that's how I felt in Grange Hall – cold and lonely. He said that he sometimes felt like that too. Even though he was on the Outside. He lived with my parents until he got caught. But only for a while – since he was ten, he said. Before that he lived with some sort-of parents. Lots of different ones.

Peter was Adopted, which means that he's never lived with his real parents. He doesn't know who they are. Parents quite often leave Surplus babies somewhere to die, Peter said. It's so they don't go to prison.

He said his parents didn't want him, that he was a Mistake, so they left him outside a house where some-one from the Underground found him. He didn't have anything with him except a gold ring called a signet ring on a chain that had been put around his neck, and on the inside were two letters, 'AF', which he thinks might be the name of his mother or father, and on the top there was an engraving of a flower. It was taken away when he was caught, though. The Catchers found it, even though he'd hidden it in his mouth, and they told him that the Central Administrators would be very interested in it. They gave it to a man in uniform at the place they took him to before they brought him to Grange Hall. And the man kept asking him questions, and told him they needed more information for his file. Peter wouldn't tell him anything and kept asking for his ring back, but the man wouldn't give it to him. Peter said that when we've escaped, he's going to get the ring back somehow. He said that once he's got it back, he's never going to take it off again.

The people who took him in when he was a baby and all the others who had him after that could have gone to prison for looking after him, he said, or even have been hanged, but they did it anyway because they said that 'children are important' and 'every life matters'. And they made him feel special and loved, while he was with them.

Then when he was ten, the people looking after him got arrested, but the Underground Movement smuggled him out of the house before the Catchers could find him, and my parents said they'd hide him and look after him. He said that's how he knew my parents were the kindest and most wonderful people, because they were 'risking everything' for him and he wasn't even their child. Imagine what they'd do for you, he said.

I can't imagine anything. I can't even imagine having parents.

When we're on the Outside, Peter said he'll take me to the field where we can run around.

I've never seen a real field.

I like the sound if it, though.

Peter said he'd come to the desert with me, if I wanted. He said we could live there.

He said that we belonged together because he was born with a flower and I was born with a butterfly and that flowers and butterflies need each other for survival.

I think I'd like to live in the desert with Peter. I think I'd like . . .

Anna woke with a start, and sat bolt upright. She was on the floor of Female Bathroom 2, her head resting on her beautiful pink suede journal. Quickly, she looked at her wrist and her heart jumped when she realised it was 5.30 a.m. – in just thirty minutes, the morning bell would go. How had she let herself fall asleep? If she got caught now, everything would be ruined.

Or would it? She thought for a moment, her nose wrinkling in concentration. She had to do something bad enough today to go to Solitary. Wouldn't being caught out of bed at 5.30 a.m. be just the thing? But immediately she rejected the idea; being caught out of bed was one thing, but being caught with a journal that clearly described their plans for escape was a pretty stupid idea.

She hadn't even been going to write in the journal but she couldn't help herself. She was bursting with the information Peter had given her, and writing everything down had helped to calm her mind. It had also made it more real. Now she'd written everything down, it had to be true.

Quickly, she stood up and, putting the journal safely back in its hiding place, she tiptoed out of the bathroom, along the corridor and into her dormitory. Everyone was asleep, she noticed with relief, even Sheila, whose little snores could be heard clearly from the corner of the dormitory.

Looking around her cautiously, Anna slipped into bed. Closing her eyes, she found herself picturing the Outside in her head – although the only images she could conjure up were of Mrs Sharpe's house, so she superimposed on to them the things Peter had described. But even as she allowed herself to dream of a new life, she knew how unlikely it was she'd ever really see it for real.

Even if they did get out, they would be fugitives. Surpluses that didn't Know Their Place. And she would never now get the forgiveness of Mother Nature.

Lying in bed and pulling her blanket around her, Anna shivered. Whether it was with cold, fear or anticipation, she wasn't sure; all she knew as she drifted back to sleep was that from today, her life was going to change. Today, for good or ill, *everything* was going to change.

Sheila opened her eyes and watched silently as Anna fell asleep. She'd waited for her in the corridor, waited for over an hour. And then she'd seen Anna's outline coming back up the stairs, but Anna hadn't gone back to the dormitory. So Sheila had slipped after her, so quietly Anna didn't hear a thing. And she'd watched, her brow furrowing with curiosity as Anna softly opened the door to Female Bathroom 2 and went inside.

And now, hours later, she was back. Anna had secrets, Sheila realised, and she wanted to know what they were.

Looking around the dormitory, and satisfying herself that everyone was asleep, Sheila pushed back her covers and slipped lightly out of bed, then padded gently out of the dormitory and down the corridor.

A few moments later, she arrived at Female Bathroom 2, opened the door and closed it behind her.

Then she pursed her lips and frowned, looking around the sparse room, not knowing exactly what she was looking for, but certain, nonetheless that she was in the right place. This wasn't the first time Anna had disappeared into this bathroom. There had to be something in here. Some clue.

She moved over to the scrubbed basins, got down on her hands and knees to survey the floor, and finally sat on the bath and sighed, rubbing her arms with her hands to stay warm.

And then, suddenly, she noticed something. A slight gap between the bath and the wall. Not something that would stand out to anyone who didn't know the value of secrets, but which Sheila instantly recognised as a hiding place. Quickly, she hopped into the bath, taking care to wipe her feet first so that she didn't leave a single speck of dust in it, and carefully slipped her thin, pale arm down the side of the bath. Moments later, she pulled out Anna's journal, the softest, pinkest thing that Sheila had ever seen.

She opened the book and began to read. As she worked her way through the first few pages, her eyes widened with indignation. But she couldn't read it all now. Not when the morning bell was due any moment. Carefully, Sheila put it back in its hiding place and, checking that the coast was clear, she darted back down the corridor to her dormitory and slipped into bed just a few seconds before the violent ringing started, announcing the beginning of another day.

Chapter Thirteen

For the second time that week, Anna found herself not wanting to eat her breakfast. But, feeling Sheila's gaze on her over the table at Central Feeding, she forced herself to swallow spoonful after spoonful of the filling but tasteless porridge. No one must suspect a thing, she kept thinking to herself. Particularly Sheila.

She got through her training sessions that morning without any hiccups; had gone to Female Bathroom 2 to retrieve her journal, which was now burning a hole in her left overall pocket; and had even managed to carve out enough ingredients to make an extra Cornish pasty in Cookery Practical, which she had wrapped up and hidden in her right pocket for Peter, wondering as she did so how she had become so adept at breaking rules. Mrs Pincent had once told her that Surpluses were naturally evil, and Anna had seen it as a challenge – to prove to Mrs Pincent just how not evil she was. But now she knew that Mrs Pincent had been right. And she didn't even care.

When she'd been a Middle, and before she'd been made a Prefect, Anna and the other girls in her dormitory would sometimes find time just before the night bell to tell each other fables and stories about Surpluses who had tried to escape. The tales originated from overheard snatches of conversations, dark warnings given by Domestics and the girls' own feverish imaginations, and each was more horrific than the next. There was Simon, the Surplus who thought he was Legal, and scaled the walls of Grange Hall only to be burned alive by a flame cast down from an angry sun. There was the story of Phillippa, the Valuable Asset, who worked as a housekeeper and gradually forgot that she was Surplus. She started to eat her mistress's food, to sit in her chair and to refuse to take orders, and one day she left the house without permission, stepping into the forbidden Outside alone. The first thing she did was to pick a flower from her mistress's garden, a red rose which she had often admired from inside the house. She brought the rose to her face, smelling its sweet scent and feeling the softness of the petals against her skin. As she brushed it against her cheek, she felt a sudden pain and cried out, but it was too late. The rose had extended its thorns and attacked Phillippa, tearing out her eyes, and ripping up her skin before leaving her, helpless and valueless on the garden path, where she was found by the Catchers and returned to her Surplus Hall. There, she lived out her days blind, in Solitary, begging Mother Nature for forgiveness, and acting as a reminder to the Surpluses of their fate should they Forget Their Place. And then there was the story of Mary and Joseph, who escaped together and had their own Surplus son. The son was born with two heads and it was constantly hungry, constantly demanding more and more until, eventually, unable to control its evil Surplus urges, it ate its two parents, one with each head, then exploded, a victim of its own greed and its Parents' Sins.

Anna hadn't heard these stories for a long time, but she knew them word for word. And a little part of her wondered whether her tale would soon be frightening female Surpluses late at night, the tale of Anna who didn't Know Her Place, who tried to escape. What would the ending of the tale be, she wondered, as she made her way unsteadily to Science and Nature, the training session she'd chosen to be defiant in because Mr Sargent loved sending Surpluses down to Solitary, believed that the dank, dark cold cells beneath Grange Hall taught a Surplus everything they needed to know about their Place on this earth. Would Anna's defiance lead to eternal misery, she thought to herself. Blindness? Or would it be death itself, the only thing that Surpluses had that their Legal masters didn't. For a Surplus's misery was finite; for Surpluses, everything had an end.

As soon as Mr Sargent came into the training room, Anna felt a little surge of anticipation in her stomach, and she was barely able to listen as he started to talk through Longevity drug doses. Surpluses needed to know about drug doses, he explained, because they may administer them in some

148

households. Longevity required a delicate balance of cells and it was important that Surpluses were able to spot the symptoms of under- or over-dosage.

Under-dosage was easy to spot – people got tired, and stiff, and they stopped wanting to go to work or to mow the lawn or anything else. Men might get thinner and women might become forgetful. It was important that the signs were spotted early so they would be addressed before they were irreversible. Longevity meant you stood still, he said, but it couldn't make you younger. Not yet, anyway.

Over-dosage was harder to spot, because there were fewer overt signs, but you could tell if you looked closely, Mr Sargent said. Longevity drugs contained a hormone called thyroxine and if people took too much their eyes might start bulging and they might not sleep well. They might seem agitated, he said, might start to get irritable.

Then he took out the capsules and showed them the different sizes, and how to reduce or increase the dosage in 2.5 mcg units.

Midway through the class, Anna raised her hand, and Mr Sargent, probably expecting a thoughtful and supportive question, because that's what she usually aimed to ask, beamed at her.

'Yes, Anna?'

She smiled nervously and shifted awkwardly in her chair.

'What would happen if a Surplus took Longevity drugs, Mr Sargent?' she asked, her voice small and timid and her eyes apologetic.

He looked at her uncertainly and frowned.

'Surpluses do not take drugs, Anna. You know that. They do not take any drugs. Surpluses are stretching Mother Nature's generosity simply being here in the first place; it is absolutely right that they should live short lives, ending with disease or old age. You know that it would be an abomination to lengthen the life of a Surplus any further than necessary.'

The vein above his eye was twitching slightly, and Anna had to steel herself.

Then she raised her hand again.

Mr Sargent looked at her irritably and nodded.

'But why should Legals get to take the drugs just because they were here first?' she asked. 'Isn't that a bit unfair?'

Mr Sargent was staring at her now, his eyes bulging slightly in their sockets.

'Unfair?' he bellowed. 'Unfair? No, what is *unfair* is that people like you exist. That your selfish, criminal parents thought nothing of the planet and of their fellow countrymen and produced you . . . you *vermin* to feed on our food, drink our water and use our energy.'

Everyone was looking at Anna now, and she realised to her surprise that, now that she had overcome her fear, she was rather enjoying herself. Words and arguments that Peter had used so often when fighting with her now flooded into her head, and she wasn't scared by Mr Sargent's reddening face. This was why so many Pendings failed their readiness test, she realised suddenly. This was her first taste of challenging the doctrine, and it was absolutely delicious.

'But Mother Nature likes new things, doesn't she?' she said boldly, wishing that Mrs Pincent could see *indoctrinated* Anna now. 'I mean, old leaves fall off trees, don't they? Why should the old humans stay and the new ones not be allowed? Is that really what Mother Nature wants?'

Mr Sargent got up slowly and walked over to Anna's table, where he looked down at her and struck her across the head. Then he grabbed her ear. 'You vile creature,' he said, spitting as he spoke. 'You will pay for those words. You will pay for talking to me like that. You will be thrashed and sent to Solitary, my girl. Bit of time to think about what you've just said, that's what you need.'

As Anna heard the words she needed to hear, she found relief flooding through her. She could take a beating; now that she knew she was going to Solitary, she could take anything.

Mr Sargent pulled her up and started to drag her across the room, bashing her into the other desks intentionally as he walked. As she passed Sheila's desk, Anna felt Sheila's gaze boring into her, and, unable to meet her eyes she looked down. She felt something brush against her leg, a touch of friendship, perhaps, and she felt her stomach clench with guilt. Sheila didn't understand, she told herself as she was dragged away. Sheila couldn't understand. Only Peter understood.

'Thank you Mr Sargent. I'll take it from here.'

Mr Sargent stopped abruptly, dropping Anna to the floor. She looked up in shock to see Mrs Pincent standing in the doorway. Immediately, she lowered her eyes, but it was anger, not humiliation, that made her do it.

'Marga— Mrs Pincent,' Mr Sargent said angrily. 'This girl has been saying blasphemous things. She needs to be punished. Beaten and thrown into Solitary.'

'I see. Solitary is not the answer in my opinion,' Mrs Pincent said curtly. 'There is a great deal of cleaning to be done on the Smalls' floor. Perhaps Anna would like to spend a couple of days up there, to . . . think about things.'

Anna's face fell. 'I don't mind going to Solitary,' she said quickly, her voice betraying a slight desperation. 'Really I don't.'

'I will decide the punishment, Anna,' Mrs Pincent said evenly. 'I think, when you are covered in excrement and urine, you may have a different view about your value to Mother Nature. You will be watched around the clock for forty-eight hours and you will be fed just once a day. When you return, your Prefect privileges will be taken away. Now, follow me.'

Mrs Pincent's voice was angry and low and Anna knew that resistance was useless. Feeling sick to her stomach at the realisation that what she'd thought would be her moment of triumph had turned out to be a hollow and pathetic failure, she walked to the front of the room, her legs shaking. Gone was her defiant stance, gone was the elation at finally challenging the Grange Hall doctrine, and back was the familiar feeling of submission and humility.

Listlessly, Anna left the training room and followed Mrs Pincent to the Smalls' floor, where instructions were given to a Domestic to keep her under constant supervision.

It was as if Mrs Pincent knew her plans – as if she somehow knew that this was a far greater punishment than a night in Solitary. There was, Anna acknowledged with a desperate sigh, no way she'd be able to creep down to Solitary this evening. No way she'd even be able to get a message to Peter.

And no way she'd ever be Anna Covey.

Margaret Pincent sat down at her desk angrily. She'd known that Peter would disrupt things. Hadn't she told the Authorities when they announced he was coming that it would mean trouble?

It hadn't even been one of the usual suspects to be corrupted either – it was Anna. Anna, who Mrs Pincent depended on so often to maintain order and root out miscreants. How had it happened, she wondered. How did Peter turn her?

Then she sighed and shook her head. They were teenagers, she supposed. Perhaps Anna had developed a crush on him – or him on her. How remiss of her not to consider that, to have forgotten what it was like to be young.

Well, she would beat any idea of romance out of Anna. And then she would have her transferred as soon as possible. She'd been as useful as she was going to be to Grange Hall, Mrs Pincent realised. Once a Surplus started to ask questions, they never stopped in her experience.

It was a pity she couldn't throw her into Solitary for a few days, really. But she had unfinished business to attend to first. Still, Peter would be dealt with in the early hours of the following morning, she thought to herself with relief. In under two hours she would be on her way to London. She'd return with her old friend Dr Cox before dawn, and once he had 'treated' Peter, the boy would cease to be a problem. In fact, he would cease to be at all, she thought to herself with a little smile.

She might even turn his death into a report for the Authorities that suggested that Surpluses could not be integrated after a certain age – maybe nine should be the cut-off. The stress of change had been too much for Peter, she would tell the Authorities with regret. He couldn't adjust; he'd upset the other Surpluses and he finally succumbed to a stress-induced heart attack. Such a shame, she would say. If only they had taken her advice.

And then? And then, things would return to normality, she supposed. Everyone would fear her again. And love her, of course. Mrs Pincent needed to be loved as much as she wanted to be feared – to her they were two sides of the same coin. Both gave her total control. And when you ran an institution filled with over five hundred unnatural abominations, control was essential just to get you through the day.

Anna stared desultorily at the sink in front of her, which was filled with towelling nappies, each of which contained a day's worth of Small excrement, and each of which she had to scrub with her bare hands. This was the third full sink she'd faced in as many hours, and the job did not get any easier the more you did it.

It was rare for her to be on the Smalls' floor – generally Mrs Pincent forbade them from visiting it, which suited the Surpluses down to the ground because who would want to hang around with a bunch of screaming Smalls? The top floor of Grange Hall, where they were housed, seemed more cramped than the others. It had lots of smaller dormitories instead of ten big ones, and a large room where the older smalls went during the day to learn how to walk and talk, and obey orders and keep their eyes cast downwards.

That was the room that Anna was in now, at one end where a large sink sat surrounded by debris and dirt. All around her was the sound of infants, some screaming, some crying softly and some desperately trying to repeat the words being shouted at them.

But it was the quieter ones that Anna couldn't bear.

The sight of a two-year-old comforting itself by rocking silently on a mat, or a three-year-old gently banging its head against the floor was more than she could stand. She had been that three-year-old, she realised. She had sat in that very spot, trying to make sense of her new surroundings, trying to find a way to regain some control over her life.

And now, she was right back where she had started. If things had seemed bleak when she was three, they seemed so very much worse now.

In truth, she didn't really care that she was faced with the most vile of cleaning jobs, and barely blanched at the stench that emanated from the sink.

All she really cared about was Peter, waiting for her down in Solitary, wondering where she was, wondering why she hadn't come.

As she methodically rinsed the soiled nappies and began to scrub them, Anna found herself wondering what the rest of her life would hold for her. If Mrs Pincent forgave her little outburst, it wouldn't make any difference – she no longer wanted to be a Prefect, was no longer satisfied with the prospect of being Useful. She wanted more. She wanted freedom. She wanted . . .

She wanted Peter, she realised. Wanted to feel once more that wonderful feeling of being accepted fully, for what she was. Wanted to feel the excitement that fluttered through her whenever she even thought of his name.

'You cleanin' them nappies or what? Just 'cause Mrs Pincent's gone to London, don't mean you can stare into space, y'know.'

Anna looked up quickly at Maisie, the young Domestic who was supervising her, and who had looked utterly delighted when Anna had been handed over to her; Domestics rarely got to put their feet up on Floor 3 because Surpluses weren't usually allowed on the Smalls' floor. Had Anna heard correctly? Was Mrs Pincent in London?

Hurriedly, she started to clean again, but her mind was elsewhere. If Mrs Pincent wasn't there, perhaps she had another shot at being sent to Solitary. Surely it was worth a go?

Suddenly, Anna frowned, and let go of the nappy she was holding.

Out of the corner of her eye, Anna watched Maisie picking the dry, calloused skin from her hands, and she had an idea.

Slowly but methodically, she rinsed her hands under the tap, and moved away from the sink. Maisie raised her eyebrows.

'No you don't, missy. You'll stay there till them nappies are clean,' she said, with a little smirk. 'I'm under orders from Mrs Pincent. When she gets back there'll be hell to pay.'

Anna felt a flutter of excitement in her stomach. Mrs Pincent was definitely away.

Emboldened, she smiled sweetly at Maisie. 'Then you can tell Mrs Pincent that I was very badly behaved,' she said, employing her haughtiest voice, the one she used with errant Middles. 'I refuse to clean any more,' she continued. 'It's not my job, anyway. I thought Domestics were employed to clean nappies.'

It was a cheap shot, but, as Anna had hoped, it worked. Being a Domestic at Grange Hall was, according to Mrs Pincent, one of the worst possible jobs on offer to Legals – Anna had heard her say so to Mrs Larson. To be spoken down to by a Surplus was simply too much for Maisie to bear, and before Anna had even finished speaking, she had lashed out, striking Anna across the face.

'You're a Surplus,' she screamed. 'You don't talk to me like that. I'm Legal. Legal, d'you hear? You could be my slave if I wanted you . . .'

'Really? I didn't think Domestics were paid enough to have staff,' Anna continued, wincing slightly at the pain from Maisie's blow, which had caught her on the side of her face.

At this, Maisie drew herself up to her full height and dealt Anna a massive blow across the head, sending her flying to the ground. Then she looked around nervously. Mrs Pincent didn't think much of Domestics and they certainly weren't allowed to hit the Surpluses.

At the sound of Anna falling to the ground, Mrs Larson, who supervised the Domestics from time to time and who had been given the poisoned chalice of looking after things in Mrs Pincent's absence, came looking to see what the commotion was, and cried out, putting her hand over her mouth just in time.

'Maisie, what on earth have you done?' she asked worriedly.

'She was giving me lip,' Maisie said firmly. 'She had it coming.'

'But what will we tell Mrs Pincent?' Mrs Larson continued, rushing over to assess the damage.

'She ought to be in Solitary,' Maisie continued defiantly. 'Like I say, that Surplus had it coming.'

Mrs Larson shook her head in disbelief, then looked around nervously to check that no one else was near.

'Maisie, help me lift her. I think you're right about Solitary. Better to put her down there than have people talk. And one night should teach her how to behave.'

Chapter Fourteen

Anna's right cheek was so swollen from Maisie's blow that she couldn't open the eye above it. Her hair had blood encrusted in it and her bottom lip was bleeding because she had inadvertently bitten it when she'd fallen to the floor. But she had never been so happy in her whole life.

As she came to slowly on the hard, concrete bed, she opened her eyes and sat up to take in her surroundings, then she smiled to herself, ignoring the pain as she did so. She'd made it. She was in Solitary. That one thought made her feel more alive than she could remember feeling before. And powerful. She felt like she could do anything. With Peter, she was invincible.

Looking around to make sure that she was alone, she called out excitedly, her voice soft at first then louder. 'Peter, I'm here. Peter!'

'Anna! You did it! I hoped it was you when I heard them bring someone in, but I didn't dare say anything. What did you do? How did you get them to send you down here?' His voice was coming from the wall behind her, which meant that she was in the cell next to him, she realised to her relief.

'I challenged Mr Sargent,' she said proudly, smiling at the memory of his red face pulsating with shock at her words. 'And then I was rude to a Domestic.'

She heard Peter laugh, and it made her glow with pride.

'So when do we leave?' she asked nervously.

'Tonight,' Peter said, without hesitation. 'Solitary checks are at about midnight and Mrs Pincent said 4 a.m. was when she'd come for me, didn't she?'

Anna made a muffled noise that meant yes. Neither of them particularly wanted to think about Mrs Pincent, or what she was coming back to do.

'So we leave here at two o'clock and go through the tunnel,' Peter continued. 'That way everyone will be asleep. The tunnel comes out in the village, and we need to get as far away as we can before it gets light because the Catchers will be sent out as soon as they realise we've gone. Then we'll find somewhere to hide and tomorrow night we'll start making our way to London.'

Anna smiled, but her heart was pounding in her chest. She couldn't believe they were actually going to escape from Grange Hall. All the windows and doors were alarmed, and there were floodlights which stretched from the building to the gated walls surrounding it. Cameras were fixed to the perimeter walls as an added deterrent. The Catchers always got you in the end, Mrs Pincent said. And when they did, you'd hate your parents even more for having you.

'We'll be fine, Anna, I promise,' Peter said, as if sensing her fear. 'Don't worry.'

'I'm not worried,' Anna said quickly, trying to convince herself as much as anything. The darkness and musty smell of the cell was beginning to get to her, bringing back memories of her last visit to Solitary. She'd been afraid then, imagining that ghosts and ghouls lived down in the cellars, that Mrs Pincent and the others might forget about her and leave her there to die. There had been noises too, late at night when she couldn't sleep. Footsteps, things that sounded like voices but more strangled. Sounds that had filled Anna with such terror that she would have done anything to get out, to never have to come back.

But this time she was here for a reason, she told herself. This time she was here on her own terms.

She looked up at the wall that stood between her cell and Peter's. At the top of it, as with all the other cells in Solitary, there was a gap, about a metre wide and three quarters of a metre high. These holes were the only source of ventilation in the whole of the basement – Mr Sargent had told them so once when Patrick had been sent down there for about the fifth time. Mr Sargent had said that there wasn't much air at all in Solitary. He'd said that if there were more than three Surpluses down there at once, they'd probably run out of air in a few days. The holes were the only thing that kept you alive down in Solitary, Mr Sargent had told them. The hole was also the only way for Anna to get into Peter's cell.

She stood up on the concrete bed to get a closer look, then swallowed uncomfortably. It had seemed like such a great idea when Peter had suggested it, but now she wasn't so sure. The gap was big enough for her to get through, certainly. But she had to get up there first. Standing on the bed, she found that she could reach the bottom of the gap if she went on to her tiptoes. But reaching wasn't enough. She had to be able to get through it.

'The gap,' she called out tentatively. 'The thing is, I'm not sure I can get up there,' she said, trying to keep her voice light. 'Even if I stand on the bed, I won't be able to get high enough.'

'Of course you can,' Peter said immediately. 'If you get hold of the bottom, you can pull yourself through. I tried it myself. Look . . .'

Anna looked up, and sure enough, Peter's face appeared at the gap. Her face lit up and she smiled.

'You look awful,' he said, and Anna immediately turned her face away, embarrassed by her swollen eye and lip.

'Who did that to you?' Peter asked angrily. 'Tell me who did it.'

Anna shrugged. 'No one. I mean, it doesn't matter.'

'It matters to me.'

Anna looked up at Peter curiously.

No one had ever wanted to protect her before. When Mrs Pincent had punished her, sometimes she said it was to 'protect Anna from herself', but that wasn't the same thing at all.

'OK, I'm going to do it,' she said purposefully and stood up again, reaching as high as she could and using her legs to try and scrabble up the wall. She was going to prove herself worthy of Peter. She was going to get up that wall if it took every bit of strength in her body.

But it was no use. Her arm muscles may have been strong enough for laundry, but they simply weren't strong enough to lift her entire weight, and the walls were too flat for her feet to climb up.

After a few minutes of concerted effort, Anna fell back on the hard bed, red-faced.

'I can't get up there, Peter,' she said hotly.

But when she looked up, Peter was at the top of her wall again, and he was grinning. Then he pushed himself through the gap and a second later, he was next to her on the bed. He pulled her to her feet again.

'Put your foot in there,' he said quickly, meshing his hands together to create a foothold. She stared at him.

'Come on, just put your foot on my hands and I'll give you a leg up,' he said, looking at her encouragingly.

Anna's face lit up, and she did as he said. He held her up high as she reached for the gap, and continued to hold her until she had managed to squirm right up the wall, even though she could feel that he was shaking by the end. Then, like a monkey, he scrambled up the wall himself, through the gap, and helped her down the other side.

'See? Easy,' he said, a satisfied grin on his face. 'Any other problems you want to freak out about before we go?'

Anna shook her head and blushed, embarrassed at how quickly she'd given up. Perhaps she wasn't quite as invincible as she'd thought.

'No more problems,' she said gratefully. 'And thanks, Peter. I . . . well, thanks.'

Peter shrugged. 'I said I'd get you out, didn't I? So, you got any food on you?'

Anna nodded happily and took out the Cornish pasty she'd made that morning.

'Did you really come here just to get me?' she asked curiously as she watched Peter eat. 'I mean, did you really let the Catchers find you just for that?'

Peter caught her eye and shrugged again. 'Well I certainly didn't come here for the grub,' he said, his eyes twinkling slightly. Then he put the pasty down on the floor in front of him.

'I . . . I wanted to do my bit for the Underground Movement. Do my bit to help your parents,' he said seriously. Then he swallowed, and looked at her with the darting eyes that she knew so well. 'But I wanted to find you for me, too . . .'

Anna looked at him silently, and he bit his lip, then looked down at the floor.

'I never had any friends, Anna,' he said a few moments later, his voice smaller than it had been. 'Never had parents, or anyone who . . . well, I didn't ever have anyone. And your parents used to talk about you, and how if you weren't in Grange Hall, we'd be friends. You know. And I used to think about that a lot, about you being free, and about us going places, doing things. So that's why I came. I felt like we knew each other. Before we met, I mean.'

He swallowed again, and Anna found her eyes drawn to him, to her friend Peter who, for the first time since she'd met him, wasn't looking defiant or angry, but vulnerable and lost.

'And now?' she asked, her voice almost a whisper. 'Was I like you thought I'd be?'

'I think so,' Peter said, nodding, and his eyes met hers. They were shining, Anna noticed.

'And do you like me?' she asked hesitantly. 'The real me, I mean.'

Peter nodded again slowly. 'I suppose,' he said quietly, attempting a little smile.

Then he took a deep breath and looked down sheepishly.

'I like you quite a lot, actually,' he whispered, his voice so fragile that it barely sounded like Peter. And as soon as the words had left his mouth, he turned away, focusing all his attention on a loose thread hanging from one of the sleeves of his overalls.

Anna stared at him, and for a second she felt like the whole world had stood still, and she had goose-bumps all over her.

Then Peter shrugged and started eating again, and everything suddenly went back to normal. Although not quite normal, because Anna now knew that,

166

whatever happened, she would follow Peter any-where. And that, she knew, could be her salvation – but it could also get her into a whole lot of trouble.

Chapter Fifteen

At two o'clock that morning, Anna woke up and sat bolt upright, shocking Peter, who'd been just about to wake her. She'd gone back to her own cell for the midnight check, and then returned to Peter's right afterwards and since then they had been lying together on the concrete slab that constituted a bed, huddling together for warmth and comfort. Anna wasn't sure quite where Peter's storytelling had finished and her dreams had begun as she gradually fell asleep. She'd been sure she'd never be able to sleep in such a place, with so much anticipation fizzing through her body, but now she was glad she had. She felt sleepy, but she also felt rested and a little calmer.

The vent, behind which their future lay, was the same as the vents found around Grange Hall – rectangular in shape and just about big enough to wriggle through. It was positioned about two and a half metres up the wall, on the opposite side of the cell to Peter's bed. Anna hadn't allowed herself to fully believe that behind it lay a tunnel that would lead them out of Grange Hall until Peter had carefully pulled it off earlier to show her.

'It's small,' he'd said seriously. 'It's not big enough to walk down, only crawl, so we have to go one at a time.'

Anna looked up at the stark, musty tunnel uncertainly, then looked down at Peter. He was pulling a blunt cutlery knife out of his overalls and he met her eyes with a grin.

'Got it a couple of days ago. Lunch, I think it was,' he said, winking. He lifted it up, his forehead creasing in concentration as he used it to unscrew the wire mesh panel. 'Domestic didn't even notice it wasn't on the tray when I gave it back to her. Not that I'm complaining.'

Anna didn't say anything; instead she took one last look around the cell. It was – she thought wryly – quite apt that her last view of the Hall should be of Solitary, the greyest, bleakest area of all. That night she would be leaving this place for ever. She didn't want to contemplate the idea that they might get lost in this small, winding tunnel, to die in the underbelly of her prison.

'I'm going to have to lift you up, so you're going to be going first,' Peter said seriously. 'But I'll be right behind you. OK?'

He was looking at her intently – even in the darkness of the cell, she could see his eyes glinting, looking at her for reassurance that she was all right. She stuck out her chin bravely and nodded. Then, silently, she allowed Peter to hoist her up so that she could wriggle through the opening.

*   *   *

'Will you hurry up!' Mrs Pincent urged Dr Cox irritably. It was late, later than she'd planned to leave London. If they didn't get to Grange Hall by four o'clock, it might be too late. The first checks were at six in the morning, and she wanted the boy dealt with by then.

'All right, I'm just about done,' Dr Cox said, easing the last of the Longevity+ fluid into a small bottle. It was a difficult job, collecting stem cells from unwilling patients, but the rewards more than made up for it.

'The boy,' he said thoughtfully, as he packed up his things. 'I presume I can take what I need from him before I administer the injection?'

Mrs Pincent shrugged. 'Do what you want, but do it quickly. We're going to be pressed for time by the time we get back there.'

Anna expected the small opening to widen slightly once she got through, but to her dismay it didn't. It remained resolutely about fifty centimetres squared, big enough for her to squirm through, but only just, and the dank air and lack of light made her feel like she was journeying into the bowels of the earth.

As she travelled further along the tunnel, the smell got worse and the light all but disappeared. She could hear Peter clamber up behind her, which bolstered her for a while, but it wasn't long before her demons were surfacing again. What if there was a dead end, she found herself worrying. What if they were discovered and instead of being pulled out of the tunnel, Mrs Pincent put the vent back on and left them to die?

'I can't see much at all,' she called back to Peter, not even sure he'd be able to hear her – there seemed to be no space even for sound to travel.

'Just keep going straight ahead,' she heard his muffled reply. 'It's only fifty metres or so.'

'How many metres have we done so far?'

'About ten maybe.'

Anna's heart sank, but she gritted her teeth and continued squirming along the enclosed passageway, half crawling, half wriggling like some oversized worm.

It took them over an hour to travel the short distance the tunnel covered. To her relief it had opened up a little as they continued. Anna's only indication that the tunnel had come to an end was the fact that she squirmed straight into what felt like a brick wall. By now she was hot and sweaty, and covered in foul-smelling slime. Each movement made her squirm. It was absolutely pitch black too and if it hadn't been for the sound of Peter behind her and his stupid jokes she'd have been tempted to give up ages ago.

'Peter, I think we're there,' she said, feeling around for any twist in the tunnel that might explain the sudden wall in front of her. 'But I can't find an opening.'

'Huh. OK, can you feel around for a grate or something?'

Anna felt around again. There wasn't much room to manoeuvre, but slowly and methodically, she felt every centimetre of the wall in front of her, hoping for something – anything – that would indicate the way out.

'I . . . I can't feel anything,' she said eventually.

There was a pause, then Peter said, 'OK, hold still, I'm coming.' Moments later Anna found herself pressed into the slimy ground, her cheek forced into the corner, as Peter made his way to the end by clambering on top of her.

'I . . . can't . . . breathe . . .' she complained, but Peter wasn't listening.

'I'm going to get us out, don't you worry about that,' he was muttering, and Anna was surprised to hear a tinge of fear in his voice.

Then she heard a yelp of what sounded like terror and she shut her eyes tightly.

The next thing she knew, Anna was being pelted with dry mud, which found its way into her ears, her nose, her mouth, and, as soon as she opened them to try and make out what was happening, her eyes.

This was the end of everything, she thought to herself resolutely. This was what happened to Surpluses who thought they could break the rules. They were going to be buried alive.

But a moment later, Peter was scrabbling forwards and Anna felt his weight lifting from her. As she shook the mud from her face, she realised that he wasn't yelping in terror, but in delight.

'We're nearly there. The tunnel goes up from here. It's just blocked with mud from the Outside.'

Excitedly, Anna wriggled her arm free and felt the

mud for herself. She was touching the Outside, she thought to herself deliriously. It was so close she could actually feel it.

Peter hauled himself through the muddy opening above them and reported that the tunnel continued in the same direction above. Anna followed him, feeling happier now that Peter was in front. As she wriggled up the tunnel, she felt a welcome shiver of cold. It was wind, she realised. She could feel the wind.

The wind grew stronger as they continued along the passageway, turning from a welcome delivery of fresh air to an icy, biting squall that whistled down the tunnel, sounding like some kind of banshee. But Anna barely noticed the cold, or the wailing; she barely noticed the slime or the grazes on her knees, hands and elbows. Up in front of her, just beyond Peter, she could see something that made her feel strong enough to cope with anything. She could see the night sky. Just a fraction of it; mostly all she could see was a wall of some sort that jutted out in front of the tunnel's opening. But just there on the top right-hand corner, was the tiniest vision of a star, shining against a black sky, not hidden behind a grey blind, but right there in front of her. Anna had never seen anything quite so beautiful in her whole life.

Moments later, Peter disappeared, and within a few seconds she could see his grinning face at the mouth of the tunnel.

'We're here, Anna Covey. Give me your hand.'

With Peter's help, she scrambled out of the narrow

opening, and for a moment she couldn't even speak. Feeling the bitter cold air against her skin and listening to the distant hum of cars and the first, early morning sounds of birds singing, she found herself unable to take it all in. She'd thought she'd be unfazed. After all, she'd been Outside when she went to Mrs Sharpe's; had thought of herself as quite the worldly Surplus. But this was different.

The whole world was suddenly available to her, right there in front of her, waiting to be felt and heard and smelt. She had seen the moon before, of course, luminescent and bright, but only in stolen glimpses on cold evenings as she stared at it longingly through three thick panes of glass and imagined what it would be like to sleep outside underneath it. Now it felt like it was almost within reach, its perfect roundness unsettling her unperfect self and filling her with awe and something very close to ecstasy. She looked around wide-eyed and she didn't dare open her mouth in case she screamed or cried or laughed, or even all three all at once, because it was so beautiful and incredible and for this moment, at least, it was hers.

'OK,' Peter said, looking around quickly to get his bearings. 'We should be on the east side of the village. Which means . . .' He frowned in concentration. 'That we need to head in that direction.'

Anna nodded mutely and followed Peter down a small road. They looked awful, she realised, looking at his gaunt form in front of her. Their Grange Hall overalls were covered in grime, their faces muddy, and their hands and ankles were bloody.

'Everyone's going to know where we're from,' she said, 'in these overalls.'

Peter turned round. 'They're going to know where we're from anyway,' he said. 'Anna, there isn't anyone our age on the Outside. Not openly, anyway. There's the odd Legal, but you don't see them much.'

His eyes were flashing in anger, and for a moment Anna didn't know what to say. But then he shrugged. 'You're right, though. We need to find somewhere to hide, fast. But not too close to Grange Hall. The Catchers will be searching everywhere as soon as they know we're gone.'

Anna nodded again and hurried breathlessly after Peter, wishing she could be more help, but knowing that she knew nothing about this new, unfamiliar environment. Then she stopped.

In front of her was a wall, and on it there were several posters. One showed what looked like a computer screen with the outline of a man with a gun on it. Across the bottom was written 'Networks spread terrorism. Don't put your country at risk.' Another showed on one side a house with lights on in every room, and then a house that had crumbled to the ground on the other. Emblazoned across the top in large, red lettering were the words 'Protect Energy – keep Britain out of the Dark Ages'. But the poster that caught Anna's attention was the one that had a picture of a Small on it. The Small was chubby and it was eating, pushing food into its mouth with its little hands, and across the picture, in large black letters, was written 'Surpluses are Theft. Stay Alert. For more information on the Surplus Problem, visit www.thesurplusproblem.auth.uk'.

'Look,' she said. 'Surpluses are Theft. That's us, Peter.'

Peter frowned and stepped back so he could see the poster. Then he grabbed Anna's hand. 'One day there will be posters about the Longevity Problem,' he said angrily. 'That's the real theft. Stealing life from everyone else just so that Legals can live for ever.'

He stormed off down the road, dragging Anna behind him, ducking down behind walls and bushes whenever they heard the sound of a car or footsteps. Anna, who had longed to see the Outside, had longed to touch the grass and feel the night air on her face, was now very scared of this strange and hostile place. Peter was irritable too. It was getting late, he kept saying, and they should be further away by now. Much further away. The Catchers would be called any minute now.

At the mention of Catchers, Anna's heart skipped a beat, and she quickly caught up with Peter, forcing herself to look straight ahead instead of staring inquisitively at the houses they were passing.

And then she stopped abruptly.

'What is it now?' Peter said with a sigh.

'This house,' Anna said softly. 'I know this house. This is Mrs Sharpe's house.' The front garden outside the house was just as she remembered it from her internship as a housekeeper; whenever she'd had the chance, she'd sneaked a little peek out of one of Mrs Sharpe's windows to admire the green grass and perfect borders. And the front porch was unmistakable, with its bright red door and several wind-chimes, which had greeted Anna with a chorus of odd-sounding clanging every time she had taken out Mrs Sharpe's bin bags.

Peter looked at her uncertainly. 'Mrs Sharpe?'

'I told you, remember? I was her interim house-keeper. For three weeks. She was very kind.'

'A kind Legal?' Peter snorted.

'She was,' Anna said defensively. 'She was nice.'

'Fine, whatever. Come on, we've got to get going.'

They carried on walking furtively along the road, clinging to the bushes to the side of the pavement, when suddenly they heard a siren and saw lights flashing ahead. Peter pulled Anna back into the bushes, where they lay, hearts racing, in silence. A few moments later, the sirens were silenced and they looked at one another apprehensively.

'Come on,' Peter said hurriedly. He scrambled out of the foliage and pulled Anna to her feet. She emerged, scratched and trembling.

'Was that the . . .' she began to say, but was unable to finish the question.

'Maybe,' Peter said. 'Although the Catchers don't tend to advertise their presence like that. It was probably the police. Probably nothing to do with us.'

Anna nodded silently and followed Peter as he

started to walk again. But then she frowned.

'What's wrong with your leg?' she asked.

Peter shrugged. 'Nothing. Come on, we have to be quicker.'

He started to walk again, but Anna could see him wincing. Every time he stepped on his left leg, his body contorted slightly.

'You're hurt,' she said flatly. 'Peter, you're hurt.'

'So what if I am?' Peter snapped. 'Come on. We need to get out of the village. We can hide in the fields just outside. They're only a little bit further.'

He was sweating, Anna noticed, and his face was white. Quickly, she stopped him and pulled up his trouser leg. There was a large gash just above his ankle with blood encrusted in it.

'Peter,' she gasped. 'What happened?'

He sighed. 'The tunnel,' he muttered. 'I caught it on something.'

As she looked more closely, she realised that his lower leg was swelling up, and when she touched the surrounding skin, she felt Peter wince.

'You can't walk anywhere like this,' she whispered. 'You just can't.'

'I have to,' Peter said, gritting his teeth. 'There's no alternative.'

Anna bit her lip.

'There is one alternative.'

'What? Get caught?' Peter said, forcing himself to walk on a few steps, but obviously finding it increasingly difficult. 'Never. I'm not going back,

Anna, and nor are you.'

'We could go to Mrs Sharpe's. Hide there for a bit.'

Peter looked at her incredulously. 'Turn up on a Legal's doorstep and ask her to hide us? Have you gone mad?'

Anna blanched. 'I just thought –'

'Yeah, well don't, OK? I'll do the thinking,' Peter said angrily. He put his weight on his left leg and yelped as he did so.

Anna's eyes narrowed. She was tired and irritable. 'Fine. Because your thinking has worked perfectly so far,' she said sarcastically. 'Any moment now the Catchers will be after us. You can't walk, and we've got nowhere to go. Don't you think they'll find us, if we're hiding in a field somewhere?'

She folded her arms defensively. Peter turned to look at her and Anna thought she could see fear in his eyes.

'Anna, she'll turn us in. She's a Legal. Come on, there's got to be an alternative. And we have to find it before it gets light.'

'But it's already getting light,' Anna said urgently. 'Look.'

Peter looked up at the sky, which was gradually taking on a paler blue hue.

'We can't,' he said, sounding less certain. 'It's too risky.'

Anna thought quickly. 'She's got a summer house in her garden,' she said cautiously.

'A summer house?' Peter had stopped again.

'She used to tell me about it because her husband used it as a storeroom and she kept meaning to clear it out, but never got round to it,' Anna continued. 'I was going to help her, but then it was time for me to go back to Grange Hall.'

Peter looked around furtively.

'Do you think we could hide there? Just for today, I mean?' he asked, his voice now serious. 'Are you sure Mrs Sharpe never uses it?'

Anna shook her head, then nodded, then shook her head again. 'I don't know,' she said eventually. 'I don't think so, but it was a year ago.'

Peter sighed. 'Can we get to the summer house from out here?'

Anna nodded nervously, and they made their way back to Mrs Sharpe's house. Then she and Peter scurried to the tall wooden gate that separated Mrs Sharpe's front garden from her back garden, where Anna picked up a small rock from the ground.

'You're not going to smash something are you?' Peter sounded worried, but Anna shook her head.

'It isn't a rock,' she explained to Peter. 'It's for hiding the key. Mrs Sharpe showed me it. Look.'

Carefully, she opened the false rock and took out a key. Her fingers were trembling too much to put it in the lock, so Peter took over, opening the gate and locking it behind them when they were through.

Quickly they darted across Mrs Sharpe's beautifully manicured lawn, behind which lay the obligatory Allotment. There, at the bottom of the garden was the summer house, still full of furniture and boxes. And there, beside the door, was another false rock.

Two minutes later, they were both safely inside, hidden under a large double bed that was leaning up against the far wall. Using some heavy velvet curtains to wrap around themselves against the cold, they sat still and waited, the only sound their short, shallow breaths.

Chapter Sixteen

Maisie Wingfield didn't know what to do with herself. It had been her own stupid fault for going to check on the miserable little blighters, she realised, but how was she to have known what she'd find? Seeing as she was on night duty, she'd decided to give that Surplus a little warning before Mrs Pincent got back, a word in her ear that she better not let on about their run-in, else there'd be more trouble.

And now . . . well, now she was going to have to tell Mrs Pincent. Tell her that the horrors had got out. They were demons, that's what they were, Maisie thought to herself fretfully. Pulling themselves up the wall and into that little hole. Those Surpluses had no business existing, let alone running away like that.

'They never got out, did they?' Susan, another Domestic and Maisie's confidante, stared at her with her mouth open. 'You tellin' me that they've escaped?'

Maisie looked at her uncomfortably.

'It wasn't my fault,' she said firmly. 'Wasn't me what put them in Solitary. An' Surpluses ain't got no business being on the Smalls' floor either. Mrs Pincent's idea, that was. So it's her fault, really.'

Susan looked at her dubiously, and Maisie continued defiantly, 'Hasn't Mrs P always said that Surpluses isn't to go on Floor 3 on account of them getting a soft spot for the Smalls or worrying about them when they oughtn't to be worrying 'bout anything except doing what they's been told to do and feeling bad about even existing? That little cow Anna should've been given the belt, not put up there. That's what should've happened.'

'You goin' to tell her that?' Susan asked.

Maisie shivered. She'd thought Mrs Pincent was still away. She'd been going to leave her a note, just slip it under her door or something. But then she'd been on her way to do it, and Mrs Pincent had come in through the back door with a gentleman. They'd swept into her office, like it was the middle of the day not four o'clock in the morning, and Maisie had run back down the corridor towards the kitchen, which was where she was now.

'I'm goin' to go now,' she said hesitantly. 'Unless you want to tell her? Since you're on duty an' all?'

Susan shook her head incredulously. 'You can forget that idea right away,' she said immediately. 'I've got breakfasts to make, thank you very much. You just go and get it over and done with. And I'll make you a cup of tea for after.'

Maisie stood up.

'Right you are,' she said, trembling slightly. 'They

should put them Surpluses down,' she muttered to herself angrily. As she left the kitchen, she shot a last, panicky look at Susan, then made her way towards Mrs Pincent's office. 'Stop them getting Legal people like me into bother like this. It isn't right. It isn't right at all.'

She hesitated before approaching the door. Maisie didn't like trouble. Never had. As far as she was concerned, you did your job, you kept your head down and made sure you got paid, end of every week. So long as that pay cheque kept topping up her bank account, giving her enough funds to buy cream cakes, pints of cider at the local pub and comfortable shoes for her aching feet, she was happy. Grange Hall gave her all those things and a roof over her head to boot, and if that meant having to put up with those horrible screaming Surplus Smalls, well, that was a price she was willing to pay. She'd never asked for anything, never wanted more than she could provide for herself. She wasn't interested in promotion, or anything like that.

No, she was a simple sort of a person, really. Just a hard-working Legal, trying to make something of her life. And for a Surplus to get her into trouble – particularly a Surplus who spoke to her like she did, like she was the Legal, like she was *better* than her (Maisie grimaced at the thought) – well, she would have to make it clear to Mrs Pincent that she just wouldn't stand for it. Yes, she was going to speak her mind, tell her that it wasn't her fault Mrs Pincent couldn't keep them under control.

Arriving at the door, Maisie took a deep breath, knocked loudly and waited.

'Come in.'

Maisie tentatively opened the door and stepped into Mrs Pincent's office. It was a horrid, cold room, she thought to herself. The kind of room that sucked the soul out of you. Must've sucked the soul out of Mrs Pincent, that's for sure, because the woman didn't have one scrap of soul left. You could tell by looking at her eyes, if you ever dared, that was. They were black, beady, and lifeless. One peek was enough – you didn't want to go looking into eyes like that for too long.

Right now, they were worse than normal, she noticed apprehensively. They looked outraged and angry. Maisie supposed that whatever it was that Mrs Pincent had been doing at this time of night probably wasn't something she wanted people knowing about.

'What is it, Maisie?'

Maisie opened her mouth to speak, still trying to find the right words. The gentleman was staring at her too, like she'd caught them doing something they weren't supposed to. Maybe it was Mrs Pincent's husband, Maisie thought. People said she didn't have one any more, but maybe she did after all. Or maybe it wasn't her husband – maybe that's why they looked so uncomfortable.

She looked furtively at him to see what he was like. Short and bald. As Maisie flicked her eyes back towards Mrs Pincent, she started slightly. He was putting something in a box, and if she wasn't mistaken it looked like a syringe. She looked away quickly. If Maisie had learnt one thing in her life, it was that the less you knew, the less bother you got. She wanted to get out of that room just as soon as she could, and that's exactly what she was going to do.

'Well,' she began, searching for the right words. You had to say something like this quite delicately, she thought to herself. You couldn't just go announcing that two Surpluses had got out like you were announcing teatime, could you?

'It's about them Surpluses,' she said eventually. 'Them ones in Solitary.'

She saw Mrs Pincent's eyes narrow and dart over to the man, who was frowning. Maisie shrank back slightly.

'*That* Surplus,' Mrs Pincent corrected her, her voice agitated. 'There is only one Surplus in Solitary. What about him?'

Maisie took a deep breath. '*Them* Surpluses,' she continued, her forehead beginning to emit little beads of sweat, 'on account of there being two of them. Y'see, yesterday, while you was away, that other little tyke – I mean, Surplus, well, she was bothering us. Me and Mrs Larson, see. And it was her what said she should go to Solitary. Said she had it coming to her, what with her rudeness . . .'

Maisie couldn't help noticing that Mrs Pincent's

mood was blackening. Maisie's heart started to pound in her chest. She knew she was babbling, but there was nothing she could do about it; she felt barely able to string a proper sentence together. And the worst thing was she hadn't even got to the bad news yet.

'And anyway, the thing is Mrs Pincent, and I don't know how it happened, and I didn't even know there was a hole in the wall or nothing, but I went down there just now, and they ain't there any more, see? They've . . . they've gone, Mrs Pincent.'

She looked up imploringly and winced as the full power of Mrs Pincent's gaze fixed upon her.

'What do you mean, they've gone?' Mrs Pincent asked, her voice quiet, and her face thunderous.

'It wasn't my fault,' Maisie said immediately. 'I wasn't to know. You want to keep them Surpluses better behaved, that's what you want to do. How was I meant to know they'd escape? I thought it was impossible to get out. I thought –'

'Enough!'

Mrs Pincent stepped forward and grabbed Maisie fiercely by the shoulders.

'Now what exactly are you talking about?' she asked menacingly, and Maisie shuddered. Mrs Pincent's eyes were boring into her, and her nails were digging into her ample flesh. 'And who are *they*?'

'The boy and the girl,' Maisie whimpered. 'Anna and that boy what was down there already. The new Pending. They've escaped, see. Last night, so far as I can tell.'

'Impossible,' Mrs Pincent said angrily. 'There is no way of escaping from Grange Hall. You must be mistaken.'

Maisie was tempted to agree with Mrs Pincent and leave, but she knew she'd only get worse bother if she didn't stand her ground now.

'Seems there was a hole in the wall what we didn't know about,' she said, eyes lowered. *Like a blimmin' Surplus*, she thought crossly. *Mrs Pincent oughtn't to talk to me like that, not really.* 'I saw it, see, when I went to check on them at about quarter to four this morning, you know, just to check they was behaving themselves. But I couldn't see them anywhere. And then I saw the hole in the wall. And I thought to myself, well, that's where they must've gone, then . . .'

Maisie's voice trailed off, and Mrs Pincent tightened her grip on her shoulders.

'This was quarter to four?' she asked, her voice sounding strangled.

Maisie nodded meekly.

'And it is now quarter past four.'

Again, Maisie nodded.

'And why exactly did you wait so long to tell me?'

'Cause I knew you'd react like this, Maisie thought to herself defensively, but said nothing.

Mrs Pincent's face was now white, Maisie noticed, and the man was standing up, looking like he couldn't get out of there quick enough.

To Maisie's relief, Mrs Pincent let go then and grabbed the phone off her desk, dialling a number from memory.

'It's Margaret Pincent,' she barked down the phone. 'I need you here, now. No, immediately. We've had a breakout. They can't have got far. They must be caught immediately.'

Then she turned back to Maisie.

'Get out of here, you useless girl,' she spat. 'Get out of here now. Tell Mr Sargent to meet me in Solitary, and tell Mrs Larson to wait in reception for the Catchers. And you can tell the Surpluses that breakfast is cancelled today.'

With that, she pushed Maisie aside and, signalling to the man that he was free to leave, stormed off down the corridor.

Julia Sharpe stared at her reflection in the mirror listlessly. Her lines were definitely getting deeper, she realised. All that sunbathing was taking its toll on her complexion and if she wasn't careful she was going to look like one of those women who people stared at in the street. The walking dead, they called them. People who were already old when Longevity was discovered. They may be cured of dying, but they'd already hit old age; now they had an eternity of it.

Julia herself had a static age of fifty. It wasn't a bad age to stick at, really. Of course, she hadn't had a choice in the matter. Naturally, it would be a lot nicer to have an unlined face, but everyone had the same problem – even people who'd been taking Longevity from the age of sixteen still got wrinkles, even if they used the most expensive moisturisers. Longevity kept you young on the inside, but only regular facelifts could keep you truly young on the outside. And surgeons scared Julia rigid.

She sighed, and opened the bottle in front of her, taking out two capsules and swallowing them with a gulp of water.

Two little capsules, once a day, keeps the big bad wolf away, she thought with a little smile. But was keeping the big bad wolf away enough any more, she wondered. People said that the new Longevity drugs could do so much more. There was nothing you couldn't cure with the right stem cells, they said – and whilst state-approved drugs might give you the bare minimum, the new drugs gave you the whole works – self-renewing skin, lower fat levels and more. But that meant the black market, Julia thought with a sigh. And once you started down that path, you had no idea where it might lead you.

Julia didn't really understand the science of Longevity – it wasn't something she'd felt the need to know about; after all, what was important was *whether* it worked, not *how*. But her friends at the bridge club were adamant that their fresh complexions and firm figures were down to Longevity+. Apparently it was already available from select clinics in the USA, China and Japan, and was used widely by celebrities; the UK was only holding back because of the cost. But was any of that really true, she wondered? People did like to make up the most outrageous things. And then there was the question of where the stem cells came from. Traditional drugs used frozen umbilical cords, but rumour had it that Longevity+ required fresh, young stem cells. And where would such cells come from, she thought to herself, other than through very dubious means?

But maybe she was being too cynical. Just the night before, she'd been playing bridge with Barbara, Cindy and Claire, and she couldn't help noticing that Barbara's skin was looking rather . . . dewy. Yes, that was the word. Youthful.

She sighed and decided she would investigate further. You just never knew what they put in those bottles exchanged in dark alleyways for large sums of money. Never knew where they came from. But if they would cure her sagging jowls and lift the wrinkles around her eyes, maybe it would be worth it.

She was interrupted from her reverie by a loud knock at the door, and she looked up curiously. It was only seven o'clock in the morning. Who on earth could be calling at this time?

Wrapping her robe around her, she closed the bathroom cabinet and waited for her housekeeper to open the door. Then she heard another knock, and remembered that she'd lent her housekeeper to Cindy for the day to help her move house. Sighing with irritation, she made her way on to the landing, then down the stairs. Through the spyhole on her front door she could see uniforms, and it startled her slightly. Had there been a break-in on her street? Something worse?

She shuddered at the thought. Crime was so rare nowadays that even the smallest transgression was infrequent. Julia had often wondered whether crime had gone down now they had Longevity because people were satisfied with their lot and less interested in short-term gain – particularly when short-term was so very short-term. Or perhaps it was that crime was actually the domain of the young and that eradicating the youth was responsible for their safe streets. Her husband subscribed to the latter view, citing the Declaration as the panacea for all the world's ills, but Julia wasn't so sure. She rather suspected that every-one was simply too long in the tooth nowadays. No one had the imagination or energy to bother with crime any more.

She opened the door slightly, then frowned when she realised what the uniforms were. One of the men was in a police uniform, but the other two, if she wasn't very much mistaken, were Catchers.

Raising her eyebrows in curiosity, she allowed the men in.

Chapter Seventeen

Anna pulled the heavy curtains around her more closely and sneaked a little look at Peter, who was sitting beside her. He had matter-of-factly found the best position for them, a spot where they could not be seen, but from where they – or he, at least – had a full view of the garden, the door and the house. Once he had made sure Anna was warm enough, he had simply sat still, his forehead creased slightly in concentration, and said nothing.

Until now, that is.

'There are people in the house. It looks like Catchers.'

Peter spoke so quietly that Anna barely heard him, and yet the words felt like bullets firing into her chest. Catchers? How had they known they were here?

'Lie down and cover yourself with the curtain,' Peter whispered, and, trembling, Anna did as he asked. She could feel Peter's body was tense next to hers, like an animal on the hunt, and she tried to stop herself shaking with cold and fear.

She lay under the curtain for what felt like an eternity, but what was probably more like ten minutes, and then she felt Peter slither down under the curtain with her.

'They're coming down to the garden,' he whispered, and Anna could feel the warmth of his breath against her forehead. Without thinking, she reached out her hand and found his, squeezing it tightly. Then Peter pressed her head on to his shoulder and before she knew it they were wrapped around each other, arms clasped so tightly that they felt almost like one.

And then they heard someone trying the door. Anna froze, fully expecting them to walk right in and find them, but instead the door stayed firmly shut. Peter hugged her closer.

'You keep this door locked all the time?' It was a man's voice and Anna felt her muscles tighten.

'Of course. Well, my husband does, anyway. It's full of antiques, you see. Valuable, apparently, although I've never cared for them much. Still, each to their own, I suppose.'

Anna felt Peter's arms tighten around her as she heard the familiar tones of Mrs Sharpe.

'We've been instructed to search everywhere,' another man's voice said. 'Even if it's locked.'

'Very well.' Mrs Sharpe's voice was exasperated. 'I think the key's in here.'

Anna felt her heart thud in her chest. Mrs Sharpe would be looking for the key, which would no longer be where she left it. She would know that they had taken it. The Catchers would find them.

'Oh,' she heard Mrs Sharpe say. 'Well, that's funny . . .'

'The key's gone?'

There was a long pause. 'Ah, I remember,' Mrs Sharpe said suddenly. 'My husband took it. For safe keeping.'

'Perhaps we should break the door down,' one of the men suggested.

'You can try, but I don't think my husband would like it,' Mrs Sharpe said quickly. 'And I don't see how anyone could be in there anyway, if the door's locked. You may know my husband, actually. Anthony Sharpe? He's with the Interior Ministry.'

There was silence then for a few seconds, during which Anna barely dared to breathe.

'I know of Mr Sharpe, yes,' one of the men said. 'I didn't realise that you were . . . are . . . Well, we won't intrude any longer, will we men? Thank you, Mrs Sharpe, for your . . . assistance.'

And with that, Anna heard the most delicious sound she'd ever heard – the sound of the Catchers walking away.

Julia stood at her kitchen sink, her mind racing. The key could have been mislaid. It was possible.

But it was also unlikely. Things didn't tend to get lost in the Sharpe household.

Frowning slightly, she decided to turn on her computer. She'd been very energy efficient this month, because of the new solar panel installed on her roof, and she felt in need of some company, even if it was virtual.

As the screen flickered on, a newsreader appeared, talking seriously about the kidnapping of the Energy Minister by a Middle Eastern terrorist group claiming that the recently signed global agreement restricting the use of oil was an underhand plot to destabilise their economy. A personalised message appeared along the bottom of the screen reminding Julia that her Longevity prescription was ready to be picked up and that she had four energy coupons remaining this month; there was a second message at the top of the screen urging her to press the red button on her remote control to complete that day's brain agility activity. Ignoring the messages, Julia listened to the newscast for a few minutes, sighing and shaking her head. Poorer countries were taking desperate measures to convince the larger nations to allow them more energy. What the terrorists didn't seem to realise, Julia thought to herself, was that everyone was suffering. Hadn't China and the USA banned all air conditioning, forcing mass migration into cooler states? Hadn't South American countries been forced to halt their economic progression in order to protect the rainforests?

She remembered a time, when she was young, when energy was still plentiful and people thought that recycling was enough. Before islands started to be submerged by the sea, before the Gulf Stream changed Europe into the cold, grey place it was now, with short summers and long, freezing winters. Before politicians were driven to action because infinite life meant that they, not some future generation, would suffer if the world's climate wasn't protected.

But not all countries believed that they were being treated equally by the hastily convened world summit. And why should they? It wasn't exactly a secret that the richer countries were cheating. That banned energy sources were being used secretly, to provide electricity for essential services. That renewable energy was being imposed on poorer countries as the only available source, whilst corrupt countries traded secretly in oil, in coal. Britain itself had poured money and resources into the race to create a new, problem-free energy source that they could sell to other countries at a huge profit, re-establishing state-funded research departments that had been abandoned a century before along with the universities they'd been attached to, because there weren't any students any more.

But energy was not something that Julia could do much about; that was her husband Anthony's domain. Right now she had a rather more pressing problem to consider. There was nothing on the news about the Surplus escape, but that wasn't surprising – the news would only be reported once the Surpluses had been caught. No point upsetting people unnecessarily, Anthony would say.

She drummed her fingers on the kitchen counter,

trying to decide what to do, trying to work out why she hadn't let the Catchers break down the door to the summer house. Had it been to protect Anthony's furniture? Or had it been something else? Had it been the mention of the name Anna?

As she pondered that question, the phone rang and immediately she picked it up.

'Julia? Barbara. Have you heard the news?'

'The news?'

'The Surplus breakout. Surely the Catchers have visited you by now? They woke me up, you know. Terribly efficient, aren't they?'

Julia sat down. 'I suppose it's their job to be,' she said thoughtfully.

'Well, they told me there were two of them on the loose. So I've double-locked all my doors and windows. And I hope you'll do the same. You can't be too careful, Julia. I mean to say, who knows what damage they'd wreak given half a chance. Now perhaps people will take the Surplus Problem more seriously. Surplus Halls are a disaster waiting to happen. Keeping them there, using up all those resources. They're just a melting pot for young thugs, Julia. And so near the village too.'

'I don't think they're dangerous, Barbara,' Julia said, frowning slightly. 'And Surpluses are very well trained.'

She thought briefly of her own housekeeper, and of Anna, the one who had apparently escaped. They didn't wreak any damage. If anything, they seemed pitifully grateful for just a kind word.

'Well of course the Surpluses they *let out* aren't dangerous,' Barbara said darkly, 'but we only see the employable ones. The good ones. The rest are simply stealing from us, Julia. Stealing our food, our energy, our air.'

Julia sighed. Perhaps Barbara was right. Perhaps she'd been very wrong to let the Catchers leave without checking the summer house.

'And they're jealous,' Barbara continued. 'They dare to want what we have. But they don't have the right, Julia. Their parents didn't have the right. That's what I keep explaining to my Surplus, Mary. Very good, she is. Very hard-working. But the fact of the matter is, she shouldn't be alive, Julia. She just shouldn't. And now this escape. I tell you, this Surplus Problem is going to have to be dealt with. If you're too soft on them, people just won't be deterred from foisting more of them on us. Do you know how much of our tax goes towards the Surplus Problem? Do you?'

'No,' Julia said.

'Too much, that's how much,' Barbara replied ominously.

There was a pause, as Barbara drew breath. 'Anyway,' she said eventually, her tone becoming more business-like, 'the reason I'm calling is that I'm pulling a search party together. We have to protect ourselves, Julia. Have to find those blasphemers and deal with them. We're going to meet at my house this afternoon. I was sure that you'd want to be involved.'

'You don't think this is best left to the Catchers?' Julia asked tentatively.

'Julia,' Barbara said sharply, 'we cannot stand by and let two Surpluses threaten everything that Longevity has brought us. They could be anywhere, and we need to pitch in, to do our bit. If we let two Surpluses escape, where will it end, Julia? There's no room for them. They have to be stamped out.'

'Stamped out?' Julia couldn't hide the outrage in her voice.

'Dealt with, then,' Barbara conceded. 'Although I think stamping out a few of them really wouldn't be a bad idea. It would send a message out, don't you think?'

Julia took a deep breath and leant against the back of her chair.

'This afternoon,' she said eventually. 'I'll . . . well, I'll see you there.'

She put the phone down and sighed deeply. People were so scared of Surpluses, she thought to herself. Legal children, too, although you didn't see any of those around these days. It was as if everyone had completely forgotten about the good side of young people, had convinced themselves that anyone below the age of twenty-five was dangerous and subversive. Anyone under sixty, rather. That's how old the youngest person was now, apart from Surpluses and the odd Legal who slipped through the net after the Declaration. A world full of old people, Julia thought to herself, frowning. Old people who were convinced that they knew it all and that anything new or different could not be good – unless it related to Longevity drugs, of course.

Perhaps ironically, Surpluses were the only subject about which there still seemed to be some political debate, even if it was limited to a very small number of very vocal people. The liberal camp were calling for a more humane approach to the problem, more education to prevent Surpluses from being born in the first place, whilst Barbara and her fellow *Daily Record* readers thought that the parents of Surpluses should be locked up for life and their progeny put down. Not their own Surpluses, of course, not the ones who cooked their food, tended their gardens, worked on building sites or undertook any of the other tasks that no one else wanted to go near. No, not them; just the 'others', whoever they were.

No doubt the Authorities would conduct an opinion poll at some point, Julia thought to herself. Set up another working party. Give someone like her husband the job of overseeing it for twenty or so years until they had drawn some conclusions. And then . . . well, then they would implement the conclusions, she supposed. If anyone still cared enough about it.

The fact of the matter was, though, that Julia didn't have twenty years to form her opinion about the Surplus Problem. She didn't have twenty years to make her mind up about what to do. She wasn't certain the escapees were in her summer house, of course, but in her experience, two plus two usually made four.

Standing up and taking the spare key from the kitchen, she wrapped a coat around herself and put on wellington boots, then picked up some gardening tools for good measure. Just in case the neighbours were watching. Just in case anyone else was too.

She often wondered what drove the parents of Surpluses to defy the Declaration in the first place. Was it arrogance – a conviction that the Declaration didn't apply to them? Did they not realise that they'd never get away with it? She'd heard talk of a movement, a pro-new-life movement that believed that the Declaration was wrong, that people shouldn't live for ever, that youth was better than age. But no one took them seriously.

She'd suggested once to Anthony that Longevity drugs should contain birth control drugs, so there wouldn't be a Surplus problem. It had seemed so straightforward, so simple a solution. But Anthony said that it wasn't possible because the drugs were finely balanced and you couldn't overburden the formula; that birth control implants were better, safer, cheaper. Julia had pointed out they obviously weren't a hundred per cent effective. Anthony had told her that she simply didn't understand; that things were never that easy. But it seemed easy to her. She sometimes thought that the Authorities overly complicated things just to make sure they had enough to do.

Julia herself had been one of the lucky ones, of course. She'd had her children by the time Longevity came along. Never had to make the choice.

Well not children – child. But one was enough, she and Anthony had agreed. One was plenty. And Julia had been delighted when it turned out to be a girl. Someone to go shopping with, to have a bit of a gossip with, she'd thought happily.

Hadn't turned out like that, of course. Tracey had ended up moving to America when she was thirty-five. Had a career, she'd said, and that's where it was all 'happening'. That was seventy years ago now. It didn't seem that long, somehow, and yet sometimes it felt like a lifetime ago.

Tracey called from time to time, which was nice. And every so often, energy allowance permitting, Julia would fly over and see her, but her daughter was very busy and they hadn't managed to find a suitable date for the past ten years or so.

Still, she had her friends, Julia thought to herself, forcing a smile on to her face. She had the bridge club, didn't she? No, she was very happy, all things considered. And if she sometimes wondered what the point was of living for ever when you had no one to love, no one to love you, then she didn't dwell on it for long. She was one of the lucky ones, she would remind herself. She was really very happy indeed.

As she made her way towards the summer house, Julia wondered whether it was the same Anna. It had to be, didn't it? But what were she and the Surplus with her planning to do? Were they just hoping to enjoy a few days of freedom before their inevitable recapture, she wondered. Or were they more ambitious – did they actually think they'd be able to hide for ever? Except it wouldn't be for ever, would it, Julia reminded herself. They were Surplus. Their lives would be so desperately short it could hardly be worth the effort.

Quietly, she approached the small wooden building, and tapped lightly on the window.

'Anna,' she called softly. 'It's me, Mrs Sharpe. I'm fairly sure you're in there. The Catchers have gone now. Do you want to tell me what you're doing here, Anna? Are you going to let me in?'

'Don't say anything,' Peter whispered. 'It's probably a trick.' He was sweating; Anna wasn't sure whether it was pain or fear.

She nodded mutely, trying to resist the temptation to rush out and thank Mrs Sharpe for sending the Catchers away.

'Now listen to me, Anna. I need you to open the door. We'll need to be careful because you never know when the neighbours are looking, but no one can see me here unless they're in my house, and I can assure you, there's no one in my house. Not at the moment, anyway. But they might come back, so we probably need to get you out of here as quickly as we can. Does that sound reasonable? Anna?'

Anna looked at Peter. Under the curtains, all she

could make out were his eyes, and she could see that they were fearful.

'I trust Mrs Sharpe,' she said, squeezing him for good measure. 'And she didn't let the Catchers find us.'

Peter looked at her anxiously, then eventually he nodded, and bit by bit they peeled back the curtains. Peter got up and limped over to unlock the door, then shrank back towards Anna, his eyes darting around as if checking for an escape route if things turned sour.

Mrs Sharpe edged around the furniture and then manoeuvred herself so that she was beside the bed which was leaning up against the wall. Two pairs of wide dark eyes were fixed on her, one set looking at her cautiously, the other looking at her like a puppy dog, grateful to her for not drowning it.

'Oh, Anna,' she said, as she took in the state of them – the dirt and the bruises and the matted hair. 'Oh my dear girl, what have you got yourself into?'

Mrs Pincent narrowed her eyes at Frank, the lead Catcher assigned to the Grange Hall breakout.

'You will catch them,' she said. It was a statement, not a question.

Frank smiled. 'Always do,' he said comfortably. 'Of course, usually we're chasing hidden Surpluses. Acting on a tip-off. It's not often we're chasing escapees from Surplus Halls. Don't get that very often at all.'

He gave Mrs Pincent a meaningful look and she glowered at him.

'They got out,' she said, her voice angry, 'because the Authorities didn't think to mention to me that there was a tunnel out. I can assure you there has been no other breakout in my time at Grange Hall, and nor will there be another one.'

Frank shrugged. 'Don't matter either way. We'll get them back. Haven't got anywhere to go, have they?'

'What about the Underground?' Mrs Pincent asked, her face contorting with distaste as she spoke. 'I think the boy might have connections. He was new, you see. Too old to come to a Surplus Hall in my opinion, but there we are.'

Frank shrugged. 'The Underground?' he asked dismissively. 'Bunch of woolly liberals, that's all they are. All mouth and no trousers. They try to hide the odd Surplus once in a while, but we always sniff them out, don't you worry.'

Mrs Pincent nodded curtly. She knew all about woolly liberals. They wrote her letters from time to time, asking about the treatment of Surpluses. Sent in petitions, requesting that criminal parents be allowed to see their Surplus children on release from prison. Mrs Pincent hated liberals.

'What liberals don't understand,' she said, suspecting that in Frank she may have found someone who shared her views on Surpluses, 'is the price we must pay for Longevity. They live for ever in a world that is stable, prosperous and safe, and they conveniently forget what created this world for them.'

Frank nodded, and his eyes lit up. 'They're ignorant, that's all,' he agreed heartily. 'Poor Surpluses? Don't make me laugh. You and I are on the front line, Mrs Pincent. We're the ones who know the truth. If it wasn't for us, the world would be a very different place, you know.'

'Indeed,' Mrs Pincent said. 'Now, when you catch these Surpluses, they'll be brought back here, will they?'

Frank nodded. 'That's the normal procedure. If they're alive, of course. Sometimes, you'll understand, there are . . . complications.'

Mrs Pincent looked at him for a moment.

'Try to keep the girl alive,' she said, then stood up. 'The boy probably isn't much use, if you know what I mean.'

Frank grinned. 'I know exactly what you mean,' he said cheerfully.

'Good,' Mrs Pincent said, her eyes narrowing. 'Now, I had a little thought. Anna did some work for a woman in the village a year or so ago. Might be worth following up. I've got her name somewhere in the file.'

Sheila sat in Decorum, staring ahead at Mrs Larson and pretending to listen intently.

Anna's seat was bare, and no one else thought anything of it because she'd been sent to Solitary. But Sheila knew. Sheila knew what had really happened. She knew because she'd now read the whole of Anna's diary, had read about her plans. And she also knew because she'd been awake in the early hours of the morning when Maisie had shrieked in anger.

It had made Sheila very angry too, because Anna hadn't taken her with her. Of all the people in Grange Hall, she was the one who deserved to leave, she told herself fervently, not Anna. Anna liked it here. Anna was a Surplus. Whereas Sheila despised every moment spent behind these grey walls, wanted more than anything to see the Outside again, to see her home, her parents.

But still, Sheila was at least comforted by the fact that Anna wasn't as clever as she thought she was. Anna liked to think that she thought of everything, that she was the most Valuable Surplus ever to have lived. But would a Valuable Surplus have left her journal behind? Would a truly Valuable Surplus have allowed Sheila to delicately take the journal from her pocket as she was dragged through the training room by Mr Sargent, and to hide it in her own pocket, where it joined the beautiful pink knickers she'd appropriated during Laundry?

No, Sheila thought to herself. Anna had made a big mistake in not taking Sheila with her.

Thrusting her hand into her pocket to feel the soft suede against her fingers, she smiled, and looked up at Mrs Larson.

Chapter Eighteen

Julia looked from Anna to Peter, then nodded with satisfaction. They were clean, they were dressed, Peter's leg was bandaged up, and now they were eating, even if it had taken her for ever to get them to admit they were hungry. Their eyes kept looking up nervously, as if they expected a Catcher to walk in at any minute. They looked ridiculous, she thought to herself, with her and Anthony's clothes hanging off them, but what was the alternative? Leave them in those horrible overalls?

'You're going to hide in a lorry, you say?' she asked Peter and he nodded seriously.

'A lorry going to London. The Underground taught me how to break into one,' he said, and Julia thought that she could detect a hint of pride in his eyes.

'And what if you can't find a lorry going to London?' she asked.

'Then we'll walk,' Anna said, her voice quiet but insistent. 'Won't we, Peter?'

Peter nodded. 'We can't tell you any more,' he said

quietly. 'In case you're questioned. In case they torture you.'

'Torture me?' Julia smiled. 'Peter, they don't torture people in this country.'

Peter didn't smile back.

Julia looked at them, their faces so serious, and she didn't know whether to laugh or cry. She could see why the Catchers had referred to the boy as a trouble-maker; it was his eyes, so challenging and with a piercing look about them. They were eyes that trusted in nothing, and they made her uncomfortable around him, self-conscious.

But she also saw the way he looked at Anna – like he didn't know what to do with himself; the way he stiffened with pride when Julia said nice things about her; the way he hovered around her protectively, as if worried that she might at any moment disappear or be snatched away from him. She saw the way Anna looked up to him too. That girl had always looked like she willingly carried the weight of the world on her shoulders and still thought it wasn't enough of a burden. Julia didn't know how he'd done it – she had tried hard enough herself and got nowhere – but somehow Peter seemed to have managed to take some of the load from her. Somewhere in those dark, wide eyes, with Peter at her side, Anna might possibly have glimpsed just the smallest scrap of peace.

Not that she'd been particularly peaceful since getting changed. Anna had changed in Julia's bedroom, the curtains firmly closed, and had seemed happy, excited even, at first. But as soon as she'd taken off the overalls, something had changed in her. She'd gone through the pockets frantically, as though looking for something, even though she'd assured Julia that she wasn't. Then she'd run to the back of the house to look out of the window, even though Julia had told her it was dangerous. And now, she was looking like death, her face white, little beads of sweat on her forehead, her eyes dark and full of worry. It was probably the stress of escaping, Julia decided. Perhaps she was even having second thoughts.

'You're going to stick out like sore thumbs,' she said thoughtfully, leaning on the kitchen counter. But before either of them could reply, the phone started to ring, startling Julia and sending Anna and Peter scurrying for somewhere to hide.

Hoping it wasn't Barbara again, she picked up the receiver.

'Julia?' It wasn't Barbara.

'Oh, it's you,' she said.

'I wanted to check that you're all right. I heard about the breakout.'

Julia rolled her eyes. 'Anthony, I'm fine. It's two Surpluses on the loose, not two murderers.'

'Still. Don't like the thought of it. Catchers been to the house yet?'

'They came this morning.'

Julia eyed Anna and Peter cautiously and prayed that they didn't make a sound. Anthony simply wouldn't understand what she was doing, protecting escaped Surpluses. She wasn't entirely sure she did either.

'What's going to happen, do you think?' she asked.

'Happen? Well, they'll be caught, of course. Catchers won't let them get away, if that's what you're worried about.'

Julia was silent for a moment. 'And after that? What will happen to them then?'

'Happen to them?' Anthony's tone was incredulous. 'Well, they'll be punished. Locked up. If they make it, that is.'

Julia frowned. 'Make it?' she asked.

Anthony sighed. 'If they're still alive,' he said. 'Not officially condoned, of course, but Catchers do have leeway, if they're endangered themselves. You know the sort of thing. Apparently the boy's trouble.'

'But . . . but that's appalling,' Julia gasped, trying not to look at Peter as she spoke. 'They can't do that.'

'You wouldn't say that if you found him hiding in your house, Julia,' Anthony said tersely. 'You have to remember, these Surpluses have no right to life in the first place. No right at all. Each new person on this earth threatens our existence, steals resources that Legal people need to survive.'

'They're so young, though,' Julia said quietly. 'It seems so . . . inhumane.'

'Julia, they will be caught, and they will be punished or buried and either way I hope it's sooner rather than later,' Anthony said briskly. 'I don't like knowing that my wife is in danger, and nor should you.'

'You really think I'm in danger?' Julia asked curiously.

'I'm sure you'll be fine,' Anthony said quickly. 'You just keep the doors locked. Why don't you get one of your friends round for company?'

'And when will you be back home?'

Anthony sighed. 'I was hoping to be back this weekend, but I'm going to have to play it by ear, I'm afraid. You don't mind, do you, Julia?'

'No, no of course, not,' she said quietly. 'Well, keep me posted.'

'Right you are. Bye, then.'

'It's OK, you can come out,' she said, putting the phone down. 'Although we need to get you hidden again pretty quickly. Anna? Anna, are you all right?'

Anna looked up. She looked awful, Julia thought worriedly.

'I'm . . .' Anna said, then looked fearfully at Peter. 'I think I've lost. . . I mean, you haven't found anything, have you?'

Julia frowned. 'Found anything? What do you mean?'

Anna bit her lip and looked down at the table.

'Nothing. I . . . nothing.'

Peter frowned. 'Are you all right?' he asked concernedly, but his question only seemed to make Anna look worse. 'Have you lost something? What is it?'

Anna looked at Peter for a moment, and Julia thought she looked like she wanted to say something, like she wanted to unburden some terrible secret, but

213

after a brief hesitation, she just nodded.

'I'm fine,' she said weakly. 'Really, I'm fine.'

'Right,' Mrs Sharpe said seriously, 'well if you've had enough food, it's just gone nine, so I think you two need to go back to the summer house and wait there for me until it's dark. I've got . . . well, I've got some things to do.'

Anna nodded silently, and she and Peter stood up.

'Wait just a moment,' Mrs Sharpe said, 'while I check the coast is clear. The garden here isn't really overlooked, but you can never be too sure.'

She stepped out of the back door and had a look around.

'No, I think we're OK,' she said. 'Walk along the fence, though, not across the grass. And be quick. Look, take this bottle of water and this food.'

Peter took the water, and Anna smiled.

'Thank you, Mrs Sharpe. Thank you so much. I can't tell you how grateful we are,' she said quietly.

Mrs Sharpe shrugged. 'Just you stay hidden. Otherwise we'll all be in trouble.'

Nodding, Anna followed Peter out of the back door. They walked stealthily along the fence bordering Mrs Sharpe's garden, hugging the foliage until they reached the summer house. Then, silently, they slipped in, locking the door behind them and returning to their hide-out under the thick, heavy curtains that Mrs Sharpe had wanted to throw out fifty years ago.

Chapter Nineteen

Julia Sharpe didn't join the search party, feigning a headache. She supplied biscuits, though, and filled two Thermoses with sweet, milky tea, which she handed over guiltily, anxiously, before watching as her friends and neighbours set off. The plan, Barbara informed her, was to walk around the perimeter of the village, thrashing through fields and checking any disused buildings. They were carrying an odd assortment of rifles, spades, tennis rackets and croquet clubs, and Barbara was naturally in the lead, talking loudly about the need to stamp out the Surplus Problem, to show the world that they meant business. The others following her betrayed only a limited interest in Barbara's battle cry, Julia couldn't help but notice; most were discussing subjects closer to their hearts, such as new recipes, who was using Longevity+ and what they thought of the latest energy tariffs. Their voices were excitable and shrill, though, and Julia smiled to herself sadly. For most of her neighbours the search was, she realised, nothing more than an excuse to get together, an opportunity to convince themselves that they were doing something important.

And Julia couldn't begrudge them that. She'd have done the same, she knew that, if the circumstances were different. Life was good for the residents of her village. Life was comfortable. But sometimes they all craved a little bit of danger, of excitement, of meaning, even if only to reinforce how very comfortable and secure their lives really were.

Slowly, she walked back to her house, looking around as she did so. It was stupid to worry, she knew that. After all, no one would ever suspect someone like her. She was respected, well-connected, and even if someone found the Surpluses, she could always feign ignorance. But her eyes scanned the street, nonetheless, and her heart thudded in her chest, and adrenaline started to course through her veins, as she took out her keys to open her front door. Because without realising it, she had made a decision. Without allowing herself to dwell too much on the implications or the rights and wrongs of the situation, she had decided that she was going to help Anna and Peter get to London. They simply wouldn't make it on their own, and if they got caught, well, that was more than Julia could bear to think about. So she was going to take them. And she had just one afternoon to work out how she was going to do it.

Anna watched as Peter stared at Mrs Sharpe uncertainly, from his vantage point under the curtains in the summer house, his eyes narrow and untrusting. It was late afternoon, just getting dark, and her former employer was looking at them expectantly, having explained that she wanted to help them get away.

'Why?' he asked. 'Why would you?'

Anna looked from Peter to Mrs Sharpe nervously.

Mrs Sharpe bit her lip. 'To tell the truth, I'm not sure,' she said quietly. 'All I know is that it's not your fault you're Surpluses. And that as soon as you take one step into the village, someone will see you. You're so . . .' She frowned, looking for the right word, then she shrugged. 'So young. So slender.'

'But you'll get in trouble,' Anna said quickly, anxiously. 'Won't you?'

'Don't you worry about me. We'll have to be careful, but they're not going to be searching every car, are they? And they're certainly not going to search the car of Mrs Anthony Sharpe, I can tell you that for nothing.' Mrs Sharpe smiled, but Anna could see from the lines around her eyes and the way she kept picking at her clothes that she was scared too.

Peter looked at the ground, frowning intently. Then he looked back at Mrs Sharpe. 'The Underground Movement will be very grateful,' he said stiffly. 'If you can help.'

Mrs Sharpe raised an eyebrow. 'Underground Movement?' she asked archly. 'If you say so. But I want to make it very clear that I'm not doing this for any Movement. I'm doing this because you're too young to . . . to . . .'

She looked at Anna, then looked away again. 'Well, anyway,' she continued briskly, 'I'm going back to the house now in case anyone decides to pop in. They're . . . well, they're searching the village for you at the moment. The tricky thing is going to be getting you into the car with Catchers snooping around everywhere, but there's a petrol station not far from here – you can walk there from the back of the garden, once it's completely dark, hide there, and I'll meet you there with the car. I've got a friend in London, and there's no reason why I shouldn't pay her a visit this evening. What with everything going on . . .'

She ran through the details of her plan with them, then left the summer house again, and Anna turned to Peter. 'If they're searching the village, do you think they'll come back here?' she asked nervously.

Peter shook his head. 'No,' he said firmly, but Anna noticed that his brow was furrowed.

'Are . . . are you OK?' Anna asked tentatively. She didn't know how to talk to Peter at the moment; felt awkward saying the most straightforward thing.

'Yes,' Peter said abruptly. 'I'm fine. I just . . .' He sighed. 'I don't like depending on other people,' he said after a pause.

Anna nodded silently and crept back under the curtains.

They set off at 7 p.m., as soon as it had got properly dark and once Mrs Sharpe had discovered that the search party were safely back at Barbara's drinking sherry. She had bulked Anna and Peter up with jumpers so they didn't look so obviously thin, and had given them each a cap of her husband's to wear, pulled down over their faces. They skulked across the fields at the back of her garden and Anna had to force herself to walk silently next to Peter because the fresh air was intoxicating and the crunching sound of their feet on the frosty ground made her heart leap with exhilaration, even if it was also clenched with fear.

Finally, having sidled around the perimeter of an empty building site because of the bright lights shining everywhere, they arrived at the garage. They ducked down behind a wall and peered out on to the forecourt.

Mrs Sharpe's estate car was already there.

'Stay here,' Peter whispered, and inched around the wall, then he came back.

'She's seen us,' he said softly.

Anna heard an engine start, and a few moments later, she heard Mrs Sharpe's voice.

'No, thank you,' she was saying to someone. 'I'm just getting some air for my tyres.'

Anna waited for another agonising minute, and then Mrs Sharpe spoke again, this time to her and Peter.

'OK,' she said quietly. 'No one's looking. I'm going to open the boot and I want you to get in quickly and cover yourselves with the blankets. It might smell of dog, I'm afraid. I used the car to drive a friend's Labrador to the vet the other day.' Her voice was shrill, Anna noticed, as though she was trying to sound normal, but couldn't, because this wasn't normal, not at all.

Anna followed Peter silently into the boot of Mrs Sharpe's car, as Mrs Sharpe walked up towards the garage shop. A few minutes later, she returned to the car.

'No one even mentioned the escape,' she said. 'There's nothing to worry about at all.'

Anna wasn't sure whether she was talking to them or to herself. The whole car seemed to be filled with tension and fear, and even the engine sounded uncertain as it started up.

'You can put your head on my shoulder if you want,' Peter said softly.

Anna bit her lip, unsure what to say. She longed to put her head on his shoulder, to feel the warmth and security of having his arms around her. But she didn't think she deserved it. Ever since she'd discovered that her journal was no longer in her overall pocket, she had barely been able to look at Peter, hadn't been able to cope with his inevitable disappointment and anger.

Peter shrugged. 'It's just that there isn't much room,' he said casually, his eyes barely meeting hers. 'So it might be easier . . .'

Grateful for the logical argument, Anna nodded, and soon found herself happily nestling into his chest, wondering why it had suddenly got so hot in the car. And wrapped together like that, under the blankets, Peter's head resting on top of hers, his heartbeat the only sound in her ears, they continued their journey to London.

Eventually, the car came to a halt, and Mrs Sharpe turned round.

'There's something up ahead,' she said frowning. 'I think it's just a traffic jam.' Her voice was incredulous – traffic jams were unheard of now that energy coupons allowed only essential travel. Trams and coaches filled the roads and only the rich or well-connected could afford to drive on a regular basis.

Anna could hear Peter's heart beating loudly, and it both comforted and worried her. The car didn't move for ten or so minutes, and eventually, Mrs Sharpe opened her door.

'I'm going to see what's happening,' she said. 'Don't move.'

Neither of them dared say a word. Peter's arms encircled Anna slightly tighter, and she bit her lip so hard that she drew blood, but other than that, they lay absolutely still.

Eventually, Mrs Sharpe returned.

'They're searching lorries,' she said, her voice slightly tense. 'It's causing a big jam, I'm afraid.'

Peter lifted the blankets slightly. 'Searching for us?' he asked.

There was a pause. 'Yes, I believe so. Honestly, all this fuss is so unnecessary,' Mrs Sharpe said lightly, but Anna could sense the worry in her voice.

'Are they searching cars too?' Peter asked.

'I don't think so,' Mrs Sharpe said. 'At least, the man I spoke to didn't say anything about cars.'

'I think we should get out,' Peter said. 'I think we should go the rest of the way by foot.'

Anna's eyes widened.

Mrs Sharpe sighed. 'It's still such a long way. Ten miles at least,' she said, but she didn't sound like she was disagreeing with Peter.

'It'll be safer on foot,' Peter said firmly. 'For all of us.'

There was another pause. 'Yes, yes, I suppose you're right,' Mrs Sharpe said eventually. Her voice sounded defeated, disappointed. 'We're due east of London here,' she continued. 'This road takes you right into the centre. I don't suggest you walk along it, but the general direction is right. Are you . . . are you sure about this?'

'Yes,' Peter said tensely. 'How are we going to get out, though?'

'I'll turn off the road,' Mrs Sharpe said. There's an exit just ahead. I'll drop you around the corner and then I'll come back the way I came.'

Anna felt the car begin to move, and she clenched her fists and thought about her Decorum classes, about being brave and Focusing On The Task At Hand.

The car stopped again, and Mrs Sharpe got out and the door of the boot opened. Anna and Peter got out awkwardly, their limbs not working so well after being cramped up for so long.

And then it was time to say goodbye, but they had

to be quick, Mrs Sharpe said, they had to get themselves hidden. So Anna reached out her hand and took Mrs Sharpe's and she squeezed it, and she found that she had tears in her eyes, because Mrs Sharpe didn't have to help them at all, and Anna was sure that she didn't deserve such kindness. And then Peter pulled her away and into the shadows, and Mrs Sharpe pretended to be looking at her tyres.

'You look after yourself, Anna,' she whispered softly, staring intently at her car.

Anna didn't say anything, but stood very still with Peter, watching silently as Mrs Sharpe got back into her car and drove slowly off into the darkness.

'Right, we need to walk this way,' Peter said eventually, pointing up a grass verge when he'd made sure that they couldn't be seen by anyone. Then he looked over at Anna.

'Do you . . . do you want to hold my hand?' Peter asked, his voice and demeanour bashful and hesitant.

'I'd like that very much,' Anna replied, and, slipping her hand into his, they started to walk.

Chapter Twenty

Julia Sharpe was humming to the radio when she pulled into her driveway later that evening. She felt alive, she realised, more alive than she'd felt for years. She didn't know if the Surpluses would make it, of course, or what kind of life they'd be able to carve out for themselves even if they did. But for the first time in far too long, Julia hadn't felt like a spectator, hadn't felt detached and impotent as though she were watching her own life from the sidelines, never fully taking part.

As she switched off her engine, though, she frowned. Something wasn't quite right. The light in the kitchen – she hadn't left that on, had she? She never left lights on; no one did.

Taking the key out of the ignition, she turned to open her car door, but before she could do so, it opened for her. Surprised, she looked up, and then her face went white when she saw who it was.

'Ah, Mrs Sharpe. Back from a drive, I see. Identi-card, please.'

Julia silently dug her identity card out of her hand-bag and watched as it was scanned.

Then the man smiled icily. 'And would you mind telling me where it is you've been?'

It felt like they had walked all night.

They hadn't, though, Anna realised, looking at her wrist and discovering that it was only a quarter past midnight. It felt much later. And there was so much adrenaline pumping around her body that she felt vaguely unreal, as though it wasn't her hiding in the shadows, but someone else completely.

Every corner they turned could have a Catcher behind it. Every time someone looked at them, she was convinced that it was all over. Several times they thought they were being followed and had to duck into alleyways, or down steps into basements, not knowing if they would be cornered and captured, and even when there was no one there at all, Anna kept imagining that there was.

And all the while they didn't dare speak because they didn't want to draw attention to themselves and, anyway, there was nothing to say. Instead, Anna watched Peter in silent admiration as he worked out their direction of travel, choosing routes that enabled them to stay hidden, as invisible to the Legals walking around as Surpluses were expected to be in their employers' homes.

As they walked, Peter's eyes darted around madly, reminding Anna of the first time she'd seen him, back at Grange Hall a few weeks ago. It felt like months ago, years even.

Every so often, he would stop and check a road sign or some other pointer, would think for a moment, and then nod, as if agreeing with himself on something important, before motioning the way they would go and charging off. Anna could only follow, abandoning any desire for control, for knowledge, for security, and doing all she could to ignore her pounding head and aching feet as they traversed the outskirts of London.

As the city lights grew brighter and the roads more populated, they found a small area of green with bushes and trees, and hid for a couple of hours until once again the streets were almost deserted and they started to walk again, hugging closely to walls, heads cast downwards, like shadows, like the walking dead.

Then suddenly, when Anna had stopped even caring about her feet feeling like they were going to fall off, Peter stopped and turned to her.

'We're here.'

Anna looked up in shock. She'd been so deep in thought she'd barely noticed the last hour of walking, hadn't noticed Peter's pace picking up and his chin lifting as he realised how close to home they were.

Quickly, he pulled Anna into the shadows and she watched as he knocked on a window just below their feet. He knocked once, twice, then waited a few seconds and knocked again. Immediately a face appeared, then another, and then a door opened at the bottom of a flight of stone steps, similar to the ones they'd been ducking into on the way across London. In a matter of seconds, Anna found herself being bundled through it into a kitchen and arms closing around her. She could hear muffled cries of 'My baby, my baby!' and someone sobbing, and she could barely breathe, and it was all she could do to say Peter's name before her head rocked back and everything went suddenly black.

Julia tried to smile, but already she could feel her hands shaking. Breaking the law suddenly seemed a less attractive proposition than it had before.

The man blocking her way, was Mr Roper, the Chief Catcher. She'd seen him on the news before, but never in person.

Be calm, she told herself. *They've got nothing on you at all. They don't know a thing.*

'I went to see a friend in London,' she said quickly. 'Such a cold night isn't it? And I haven't used the car for so long . . . energy coupons, you know. I thought it might be a good idea to take it for a run.'

Her voice trailed off uncertainly.

'That's very interesting. I'll get my men to check that, shall I?'

Mr Roper's voice was silky smooth, and Julia swallowed nervously.

'I . . . I didn't make it in the end,' she said, trying to keep her voice level. After all, she had nothing to worry about, she told herself firmly. 'The traffic was so bad I gave up I'm afraid.'

'Yes,' Mr Roper said. 'I see. Shall we?' he continued, holding out his arm and making it clear that Julia was to go into her house.

'Yes, of course,' she said brightly, getting out of the car and locking the door. As she did so, another man appeared out of nowhere and took the key from her.

Julia opened her mouth to demand it back, but decided not to argue the point now. She'd get the key back, she thought to herself. It wouldn't do to be unduly rude. No doubt they'd ask her a few questions, and then they would leave. And if they didn't, she would simply call Anthony and he would sort things out.

'I imagine you'll know my husband,' she said, trying to keep her tone conversational. 'Anthony Sharpe?'

Mr Roper smiled. 'Indeed I do,' he said smoothly. 'Mr Sharpe was very concerned about the Surplus escape that occurred last night. Very concerned when he heard that we visited his house. He said to me that no wife of his would hide Surpluses.'

'Hide Surpluses?' Julia said indignantly. 'Well, he's absolutely right about that. The very idea! You know, we had a search in the village just this afternoon. These escapes can be very worrying.'

'Indeed, Mrs Sharpe, I'm sure they are. I'm sure you didn't mean to lie this morning when my colleagues visited you.'

Julia stared at him. 'I don't like your tone, Mr Roper. I don't like your behaviour much, either,' she said, crossing her arms. 'I have rights, and I think I would prefer it if you would come back tomorrow.'

Mr Roper shook his head. 'Impossible, I'm afraid, Mrs Sharpe. We need to talk to you now. About the calls we've had saying that young people were seen in your garden. I understand that the girl worked for you briefly. Seems likely that she would come to you, doesn't it?'

'Does it?' Julia asked stiffly, following him through her front door, which was shut behind her by a tall man in uniform. In her kitchen, she could see three more. 'Well, if she did, then I certainly didn't know anything about it.'

Mr Roper stared at her silently, and motioned for her to sit down.

'I hope that you won't be inconveniencing me for too long,' she continued curtly, as she sat down at her kitchen table. He was a slight man, she noticed, thinner than he looked in photographs, with pale blue eyes and dark blond hair. He'd be quite good-looking under different circumstances. Perhaps a bit of charm would be a good idea, she thought to herself. Maybe if she fluttered her eyelashes a bit?

But before she could launch her charm offensive, Mr Roper sat down across from her and grabbed her wrists.

'The men you see over there,' he said, pointing to the uniformed men standing around the sink area, 'are Catchers. Catchers, Mrs Sharpe, have very different codes to normal police. They have more . . . leeway, shall we say. More methods at their disposal. You are the wife of a senior official, and I would not like to hand you over to the Catchers because I am a civilised man, and prefer a civilised approach. But I cannot keep them off you for long. They want those Surpluses, and they will find them. Do you understand?'

He was leaning over the table and staring directly into Julia's eyes, making her blink nervously.

'But I'm a Legal,' she said hesitantly. 'You can't treat me like this.'

Mr Roper smiled. 'Mrs Sharpe,' he said, sitting back, his tone suddenly lighter, 'do you know what will happen if we arrest you for hiding Surpluses?'

Julia shook her head.

'You will be put in a cell,' Mr Roper continued, 'and you will be questioned. We can keep you for up to three months if we wish.'

'Three months?' Julia asked, her eyes wide. 'But I've done nothing wrong. This is . . . outrageous. It's just not acceptable!'

Mr Roper's eyes narrowed. 'Hiding Surpluses is outrageous, Mrs Sharpe. Defying the Authorities and the Declaration is not acceptable. I'm afraid that the normal rules and processes of the justice system don't apply to the harbouring of Surpluses. Too much at stake, Mrs Sharpe. You understand, I'm sure.'

He stared at her for a moment, then smiled. 'You know, of course, that Longevity can be withheld in prison. For the duration of your stay with us, if we deem it necessary.'

Julia stared at him incredulously. 'You can't do that,'

she said quickly. 'I want to have my solicitor contacted. Frankly, Mr Roper, I've had enough of this.'

'And frankly, Mrs Sharpe, we've only just begun,' Mr Roper said angrily.

Julia bit her lip nervously.

'Do you know what happens,' Mr Roper continued, 'when someone of your age stops taking Longevity?'

Mrs Sharpe shrugged. She didn't care, she told herself. These nasty men with their bully-boy tactics weren't going to scare her.

'After a month, all those signs of ageing that we've conveniently forgotten about start to return,' Mr Roper said, a thin smile on his lips. 'An aching back, knees that feel painful in the cold, lethargy, listlessness. After six weeks, your muscles will start to weaken, and your organs will start to fail. Two months and your hair will have thinned, your eyesight deteriorated along with your hearing, and your skeleton will begin to curve inwards. Up to six weeks, the situation is reversible. Two months, and you'll never go back to full health. At ten weeks, the ageing process really starts to kick in – your body will be susceptible to disease and rot, your muscles will have all but disappeared. Twelve weeks and . . . well, no one's made it past twelve weeks. They're usually glad to die at eleven, frankly. Can't move, can't think, can't do anything but wait for death to take away the pain of old age.'

'You wouldn't dare,' Julia said, her eyes narrowing. 'You're saying you'd let me die just because you suspect – and this is just a suspicion, let's be clear – that I may have hidden two Surpluses, two youngsters who managed to escape from that horrible Surplus Hall?'

Mr Roper looked Julia right in the eye. 'I'm so glad you understand,' he said.

'I want to call my husband,' Julia said firmly. 'I want to call him right away.'

Mr Roper nodded at one of the Catchers, who handed Julia the phone. She quickly jabbed at the numbers and listened as her husband's phone began to ring.

'Hello?'

'Anthony? It's me.'

He sounded tired, drained. 'Julia, thank God. What's going on down there? I'm being turfed out of my office, suspended. They seem to think you've got yourself involved with that Surplus breakout.'

'Suspended?' Julia felt herself going white.

'I told them it was preposterous. But one whiff of Surplus trouble and the rules change, I'm afraid. Just straighten things out, Julia, will you? I can't get an answer out of anyone at my end. They've even frozen the bank account. It's –'

One of the Catchers disconnected the phone.

'Like I said,' Mr Roper said smoothly, 'Surplus Management is not a game. If you cooperate fully, we can come to some arrangement. Your husband need not even learn of the truth. If you refuse, then I'm afraid, Mrs Sharpe, that you will be detained indefinitely under the Surplus Act 2098, and your husband's career will be over. It's really up to you.'

'You can't do this . . . you can't.'

'Oh, but we can, Mrs Sharpe. We can.'

As he spoke, another man emerged at the doorway. He was carrying Anna and Peter's overalls, which Julia had hidden in the summer house, unable to decide how to dispose of them. Her eyes widened, and she saw a little smile appear on Mr Roper's lips.

'What will it be?' he asked. 'I believe you don't have a choice, Mrs Sharpe. Not if you wish to live.'

Julia looked at Mr Roper for what felt like an eternity, then looked down at the kitchen table, her shoulders slumping, defeated.

She had done what she could, she told herself, her hands skating slightly. She didn't have a choice. There was simply no alternative to cooperating.

Forgive me, Anna, she said silently. *I'm sorry I'm not stronger. But I'm not ready to die – not yet. I've got too much to lose. It's all right for you – you're still young.*

Slowly, she looked back up at Mr Roper.

'I'll cooperate,' she said flatly. 'Just tell me what you want to know.'

Anna woke up to see a woman's face hovering over her, and she didn't know what to say, so she said, 'I'm sorry,' because she realised she must have fainted, and that wasn't the sort of thing Pendings did.

But instead of saying anything, the woman lifted

her hand to Anna's face and pushed some hair away from her forehead. Her hand was so soft, and the action so tender that Anna found herself covered in goosebumps, and she shivered. The woman leant down and kissed her on the forehead and said, 'Anna, my precious, precious child, you're safe now. You're home now.' Anna saw a solitary tear wending its way down her cheek, and suddenly Anna was crying too, and the woman pulled her towards her chest, and the two of them stayed like that for ages, just sobbing and holding each other, until Anna didn't think she had a single tear left and her arms were trembling. And then she fell asleep again.

An hour later, Mr Roper closed his notebook and smiled at Julia.

'You're sure they said Bunting?'

Julia nodded nervously. 'I only overheard them,' she said quickly, 'so I can't be absolutely sure, but he said that her parents had changed their name when they got out of prison. So she was Anna Covey, but they were . . . Bunting. Yes, I'm sure that's it.'

'Thank you,' Mr Roper said. 'And do send my best to Mr Sharpe.'

'Do you think you'll catch them?' she asked tentatively.

'Of course we'll catch them,' he replied. 'We always catch them. Every time.'

And with that, he and his colleagues left Mrs Sharpe, got into their car, and purred off down the street.

Chapter Twenty-one

Sheila sat silently in Central Feeding, methodically lowering her spoon into the grey soup in front of her, lifting it to her mouth and swallowing. Gradually, rumours about Anna and Peter's escape had started to circulate around Grange Hall. And Mrs Pincent said they'd been sent to a detention centre, but no one believed that. And for the time being, Sheila wasn't being bullied because she was considered someone who might have inside information on how they did it, even though that didn't stop Tania from taunting her. *Left you behind, did they? Can't say I'm surprised. Anna probably escaped just to get away from you.*

She snuck her left hand down the side of her overalls and into her pocket, where the silk knickers she'd stolen had taken up permanent residence, soft and indulgent, Sheila's only link with the world Outside from which she had been wrenched. The world where she knew she belonged.

Then, after draining her bowl of soup, she stood up. She had half an hour before she was due in

Laundry, and she planned to go to Female Bathroom 2, her new refuge from the brutal world of Grange Hall. She had replaced Anna's diary in its hiding place hours after Anna's disappearance, but it wasn't Anna's diary any more. Now it was Sheila's diary. She thought she might hide the knickers in the same place, build up a little treasure trove of beautiful things.

But as she made her way to the door out of Central Feeding, she found Surplus Charlie blocking her way.

'On your own, Sheila?' he asked softly, a mocking look in his eye. 'Got no friends now Anna's left without you? Not much of a friend, was she?'

Sheila glared at him.

'Get out of my way,' she said, her voice flat. 'Leave me alone.'

Charlie glanced around to check that no Instructors were nearby, then smiled superciliously at Sheila.

'Poor little Sheila,' he said, shaking his head. 'No Anna to protect you any more, is there? No one to protect you at all.'

He stuck his hand out and prodded her in the stomach menacingly.

Sheila felt herself tense up in fear, but stared at him defiantly.

'Leave me alone,' she hissed. 'Just go away.'

'You can't talk to me like that,' Charlie said, his eyes glinting. 'I'm a Prefect, and you have to do what I say.'

He had moved towards her now, bending down and coming so close that he was almost touching her, his chin at the level of her nose, his breath heavy on her forehead. Sheila could feel her legs trembling beneath her. She'd seen Charlie bully other Surpluses, had seen him taunt and hit them. But he'd never seemed to have noticed her before. Not before Anna left. Not before Anna deserted her.

'Charlie, Sheila, come here, please.'

They both turned immediately at the sound of Mrs Larson's voice, and walked towards her, heads bowed.

'And what were you talking about so secretively?' Mrs Larson asked crossly. 'Explain yourselves, please.'

'Charlie was . . .' Sheila started to say, then stopped.

'I was reprimanding her,' Charlie said smoothly. 'She left her bread, and I told her it was Wasteful. That Surpluses needed energy to be Useful.'

Mrs Larson raised an eyebrow. 'Is this true, Sheila? Did you waste your bread?'

Sheila felt herself flushing. 'Yes,' she said, hating Charlie with all her might and hating Anna even more for leaving her. 'Yes, I left my bread.'

She thrust her left hand in her overall pocket and felt the silk against it, comforting her, reminding her that she was better than this place, better than Surplus.

'Even though it's Wasteful?' Mrs Larson continued.

Sheila lowered her head. 'I wasn't hungry,' she said quietly.

'Very well,' Mrs Larson said, with a sigh. 'If you're not hungry, you can go without supper tonight too. Do you understand?'

Sheila nodded miserably, and she saw Charlie smirk. She shot him a look of hatred and turned to leave.

'Just one minute,' Mrs Larson said, as she reached for the door. 'What's that in your pocket, Sheila?'

Sheila felt the prickle of fear on her forehead.

'Nothing,' she said, taking out her hand and showing Mrs Larson. 'There's nothing in there.'

Charlie turned to stare at her. 'Yes there is,' he said. 'It's bulging.'

'No,' Sheila said desperately, 'it isn't.'

Mrs Larson frowned and came closer. Then she lifted Sheila's hand and thrust her own inside the pocket, gasping when she drew out the silk knickers.

'Oh, Sheila,' she said, shaking her head. 'Oh, Sheila, you will be beaten for this. Oh, dear me.'

Mrs Larson turned to Charlie.

'Charlie, get Mrs Pincent, please. Right this minute.'

Charlie looked at Sheila curiously for a second, then left silently.

'You stole these?' Mrs Larson continued, looking at Sheila with a mixture of outrage and pity. 'You actually stole these?'

Sheila bit her lip. Her heart was pounding and everything had taken on a slightly surreal sheen, as fear flooded through her veins.

Before she could reply, Charlie re-emerged. 'Mrs

Pincent said you should bring Sheila to her office,' he said breathlessly, 'right away.'

Mrs Larson nodded curtly and grabbed Sheila by the arm.

'Come on,' she said, pulling her roughly. 'Let's see what she has to say, shall we?'

Sheila felt the familiar feeling of nausea wash over her. Mrs Pincent's office represented Sheila's private hell, a room full of pain and despair. It was in Mrs Pincent's office that she had begged to be returned home all those years ago, that she had screamed for her mother, that she had cried desperate tears of remorse for whatever she had done that had resulted in her punishment.

And it was in Mrs Pincent's office that she had learnt, slowly but surely, that there was no way out. That this was not a punishment, but a life sentence.

Mrs Pincent closed the door and walked back to her desk.

'You know,' she said, 'in olden times, they would cut off a person's hand for stealing. A Legal person's hand too. What do you think they would consider a suitable punishment for a thieving Surplus?'

Sheila felt her lower lip begin to quiver, and she steeled herself.

'Your parents were so relieved, you know, when the Catchers finally found you,' Mrs Pincent continued. 'It was their idea, of course. They'd realised just what an evil, horrible child you were. Realised that no good could come from bringing up a Surplus to think it deserved a place in this world.'

'No,' Sheila cried wretchedly. 'My parents loved me. They said I wasn't a Surplus. They didn't sign the Declaration. They –'

Mrs Pincent laughed. 'They lied, Sheila, and that's the end of it. They brought you into this world illegally, and you have proved yourself to be the lowlife that all Surpluses are. Stealing. It's a Sin, Sheila. You do understand that, don't you?'

Sheila looked down at the floor, and clenched her fists as anger and resentment swelled through her.

It wasn't fair. None of this was fair, she thought to herself desperately.

Then, suddenly, she thought of something. Slowly, she allowed herself to look up at Mrs Pincent, who was staring at her beadily.

'Is stealing as much of a Sin as running away?' Sheila asked, her voice quiet.

Mrs Pincent's eyes narrowed. 'No one has run away, Sheila. No one runs away from Grange Hall. It's impossible. You know that!'

Sheila looked at Mrs Pincent blankly.

'Keeping a diary,' she continued. 'That's a Sin too, isn't it? For a Surplus, I mean. Keeping a diary and writing in it plans for escaping. That's surely a Sin?'

Mrs Pincent stood up.

'A diary?' she asked immediately, her eyes lighting up with curiosity. 'Did Anna keep a diary?'

Sheila looked down at the floor again.

'I'm an evil Surplus,' she said, her voice level. 'I don't know anything.'

'You insolent girl,' Mrs Pincent said angrily, her eyes flashing. She walked round her desk so that she was standing right in front of Sheila. 'If you know something, you must tell me.'

Sheila shrugged, and Mrs Pincent stared at her. Then she moved back so that she was leaning on the front of her desk.

'You know, Sheila,' she said thoughtfully, 'I might be able to overlook your stealing. If you were to help me, you understand. In fact, with Anna not with us any more, I need to appoint a new Prefect. A Prefect I can trust. A Prefect who tells me things that I need to know.'

Sheila looked up at her and smiled enigmatically. 'I think I'd be a good Prefect,' she said softly. 'Much better than Anna. Anna really wasn't a very good Prefect, Mrs Pincent. Not very good at all. She hid things, you see, Mrs Pincent. But I knew all about them. I notice things, you see.'

'I do see, Sheila,' Mrs Pincent said slowly. 'Now, as my new Prefect why don't you show me what you know?'

Sheila nodded gravely.

'Of course, House Matron. I'd be only too pleased.'

Anna woke in a cold sweat. She had slept fitfully, her head filled with nightmares and she was shaking. But she felt like she was floating on a cloud, so soft were the mattress and blankets surrounding her. The woman was still there, and there was a man at her side too now. He was handsome and had dark hair and he was looking at her like she was something very special, and Anna felt a bit embarrassed.

'I dreamt about Mrs Pincent coming to get me,' she said to the woman. 'And Sheila was calling after me and asking me to come back for her. And then there were Catchers, and . . .'

The man leant down to kiss her, then, and he held her to him, and he smelt like the Outside, so fresh and beautiful, and Anna found herself wrapping her arms around him like it was the most normal thing in the world.

'Do you know who we are?' he asked.

Anna shook her head, because she didn't want to get it wrong, because if they weren't who she thought they were then she'd feel stupid but also so disappointed she didn't think she could bear it.

And then the woman said, 'We're your parents. Anna, my darling, you're home now. And we're never going to let you go again. Not ever. So don't you worry about Mrs Pincent and the Catchers because you're safe. No one knows you're here, and we'll look after you, I promise.'

'And Peter?' Anna asked fearfully. 'He's still here?'

'He's asleep,' her father said, and just the fact that he was her father, that she'd allowed herself to even think the words 'my father', made her want to cry again. But she didn't because she was a Pending, and crying was a weakness, even on the Outside, even when you had parents.

'There's someone else we'd like you to meet, if you want to,' her mother said. And Anna sat up, because it seemed the right thing to do, and nodded and smoothed her hair down so she didn't look too much of a mess.

Her mother got up and left the room, and a few seconds later she came back in and she put a Small in Anna's arms. Anna didn't usually like Smalls, particularly young ones like this. The ones she'd glimpsed at Grange Hall from time to time looked dirty and smelly and all they did was scream. But this wasn't a normal Small. It was beautiful, with light downy hair on its head and the most wonderful smell, like heaven. And when she looked at it, it smiled at her and opened its mouth and gurgled something. Anna looked at it in amazement because she'd never known that a Small could be so intoxicating and precious.

'He's your brother,' her father said. 'And he's been so looking forward to meeting his big sister.'

Anna stroked him tenderly. She couldn't believe that such an incredible thing could be related to her.

'You must be hungry,' her mother said. Anna shrugged because she was – starving in fact – but she didn't want to let go of the Small.

'My brother,' she said out loud, enjoying the sound of the words coming out of her lips. 'My parents. My parents and my brother.'

And then the Small began to cry, and the noise cut

right through to Anna's heart and she would have done anything to make him happy again, and she worried that it was her fault and that her parents were going to be angry with her.

Fearfully, she looked at the woman.

'I'm sorry,' she said anxiously. 'What did I do wrong?'

But the woman, her mother, just laughed and took the Small in her arms and said, 'Well, he's hungry even if you're not.'

Anna's face flooded with relief, and she smiled and said, 'I am, really.'

Then her father smiled and got up, saying he'd bring her some food, and Anna thought to herself as he left the room that she had never known that such a wonderful place could exist with people who were so kind. It scared her, because she knew she didn't deserve it, and she knew she didn't deserve her brother either, or her parents, or Peter. And she knew that somewhere out there, the Catchers were searching, doing everything in their power to track her down.

Chapter Twenty-two

'So she drove us most of the way to London.'

'And can you trust her?'

'Yes. I mean, she would have told the Catchers when they were there, wouldn't she? If she wanted us to get caught?'

'I suppose. And you walked the rest of the way? And no one saw you? No one at all?'

Anna stood at the kitchen doorway hesitantly, not sure whether to go in. She'd been in bed for what felt like days. Apparently she'd had a fever, which meant that she had to 'get lots of rest'. Which had been absolutely fine by her – it was the most comfortable bed she'd ever been in, more comfortable even than the bed she had slept in at Mrs Sharpe's house when she worked there. It had a huge padded blanket on it, and two pillows, and every time she had tried to sit up and get up, she'd found herself sinking back down, not yet ready to face the world.

Her parents and Peter were talking seriously, sitting at a big wooden table in the kitchen.

Suddenly her mother looked up and saw her and

immediately got up.

'Anna, Peter was just telling us about your journey,' she said softly. 'Would you like some breakfast?'

Anna nodded. She felt sleepy still, which was stupid because she'd had more sleep than anyone could ever need. She stifled her yawn and tried to look more awake.

She was shown to a chair at the big wooden table, and food was put in front of her that she didn't recognise, but that she ate anyway, and it was the most delicious thing she'd ever eaten. She didn't say anything because she wanted them to keep talking about whether anyone saw them. If there was any information that would make her feel more secure and safe from the Catchers, she wanted to hear it. And if she wasn't safe, then she wanted to know that too.

'We've got a bit of time, I think,' her father said seriously, pouring her a cup of tea, which she'd only seen Legals drink and had never had herself before. It nearly burnt her mouth, but it was delicious and sweet, so she continued drinking even though it was too hot.

'We should lie low here for a few days,' he said. 'The last thing we want is to be out on the road when the Catchers are searching everywhere. Pip agrees we're safer here than anywhere else.'

'Barney says they're crawling all over the place,' her mother said, a hint of tension in her voice.

'Catchers are always crawling all over Barney.

That's nothing new.'

Anna kept quiet, her eyes cast downwards. She wanted to know who Pip and Barney were, wanted to know why the Catchers crawled all over Barney, but she didn't know whether questions were polite on the Outside, and she didn't want to appear rude.

Peter caught her eye and grinned at her.

'You OK?' he ventured. 'Got enough sleep now?'

He was laughing at her, she realised, and it made her smile.

'I suppose,' she said, pleased to see he didn't look at all worried about Catchers. Maybe they were safe here, after all.

Peter got up again to help himself to food, and Anna found herself turning to her mother. It was no good – she had to ask.

'Will . . . will you go to prison? If the Catchers find us? And will they take the Small away?'

Her mother looked at her, confused. 'The Small?'

Peter wandered back to the table. 'Ben. She means Ben.'

Her mother nodded. 'Of course.'

Then she looked at Anna and took her hand. 'No one's going to prison, Anna,' she said, then she sighed.

'I don't know what's going to happen,' she said softly, 'but I want you to remember this. We knew what we were doing when we had you, and we will gladly suffer the consequences. The important thing is that you are safe, and that Ben is safe and Peter too.

That's all that really matters. We're protected here – there are people all over London, all over the country, who think we're doing the right thing and who also have children, who are going to help us. They helped us before, when we got out of prison. So I don't want you to worry. And I don't want you to think that you've put us in danger either. We put ourselves in danger, and because of us you spent many years in Grange Hall, for which we will never forgive ourselves. But you're safe now. Because of Peter, you're back home. And home is exactly where you're going to stay.'

Anna nodded silently. She had so many questions, about Longevity drugs, about Opting Out, about Barney and Pip and the Catchers and Grange Hall and Peter. But she didn't know how to ask them without blurting them all out at once and sounding like a Pending who had finally been allowed to ask Mr Sargent a question and didn't know when to stop. So instead, she continued to eat, snatching little looks at Peter every so often, and feeling a huge wave of happiness wash over her when he caught her eye and grinned, then put his arm around her briefly to give her a squeeze.

'This is your home, Anna Covey,' he whispered. 'I told you it was worth it, didn't I?'

Anna smiled at him and nodded. But as she did so, the phone rang, and her parents looked at each other, their faces tense.

Her father picked it up, and he smiled and said,

'Pip,' and then his expression changed and a deep line appeared between his eyes. He nodded a few times, then said, 'Thanks,' and put the phone down.

'They're coming to Bloomsbury,' he said, in a low voice. 'They got a tip-off. It was the House Matron, apparently. But how could she have known? Nobody knows. Nobody at all.'

He sat down and looked at Anna's mother, who shrugged helplessly.

'Peter, you didn't tell anyone anything, did you?'

'Of course not,' Peter said hotly. 'Don't be ridiculous.'

'Well, then, I just don't know,' her father said, staring at the wall behind Anna. 'I don't know at all.'

Anna looked at him, terror rushing through her veins at the mention of Mrs Pincent and the Catchers. And then, suddenly, she knew how they'd found her. Knew that her First Sin had caught up with her, that her fate had been sealed the first time she broke the rules of Grange Hall, and that her transgressions were going to be the undoing not just of herself, but of everyone around her.

'It's my fault. I wrote a journal,' she said, her voice barely audible. 'About things that happened. Things that Peter told me. It was hidden in Female Bathroom 2, and then I put it in my pocket to escape, but when I got to Mrs Sharpe's it wasn't there.'

She swallowed uncomfortably. 'It might have fallen out in the tunnel. Or somewhere else. I . . . I'm not sure.'

Peter stared at her, and Anna felt her heart begin to beat faster as she saw her parents' expressions change, saw the muscles around their eyes and mouths tense. And then she found her own muscles tensing, and she braced herself, waiting to be beaten.

Chapter Twenty-three

Margaret Pincent sat at her desk, holding Anna's pink journal in her hand and smirking. The girl really was priceless, she thought to herself. It was as if she wanted to be found.

Well, whether she wanted to or not, she'd be back here soon enough, she thought, pleased with herself. The Catchers had been delighted with her suggestion that they hotfoot it to Bloomsbury. Had assured her that the Surpluses would be back in Grange Hall within twenty-four hours. It was the boy she really wanted to get hold of, though. And the parents. How dare they? How dare they think they could have what no one else could?

Of course, the real fault lay outside of Grange Hall, Margaret thought irritably. How could she not have known there was a tunnel, leading from the basement – the very place she sent Surpluses to be secure and out of the way? Why was she not told about it before? It was just so typical of the Authorities, think-ing that they didn't need to tell her anything. Thinking she wasn't important enough.

Well, she'd show them. She'd make sure the two Surpluses were caught and brought back to Grange Hall and then they'd see. She was the only one who'd be able to track them down – those Catchers might look scary with their black uniforms and little torture devices, but they didn't know how Surpluses thought. Not like she did. Had they thought of going to Julia Sharpe's house? No, of course they hadn't.

And when she caught them, assuming they were still alive, she would insist on punishing them herself. She knew that her cruelty would far outstrip those clumsy Catchers. By the time she'd finished with them, they wouldn't even remember their own names. They wouldn't want to. They wouldn't want to remember anything.

No one crossed Margaret Pincent, she thought bitterly. No one made her look a fool. Particularly not two Surpluses who should have been put down at birth, who had no right to even set one foot on this earth.

Not like her child.

Her child, who had had every right to live.

She sat back on her chair and allowed herself, just for a moment, to remember. Remember the son, the promise, the joy, and the anguish.

It had been the only thing she'd ever really wanted – to have a son, to make her father proud, to finally win his love. Impossible, of course; the daughter of the chairman of the biggest Longevity drug company could not Opt Out, not in a million years. But she hadn't given up hope. Back then, she'd had hope in spades.

She'd gone to university, but only half-heartedly, and had then worked for the civil service. Years she had spent filing reports and signing off papers, but all the time, she was busy researching, busy manoeuvring herself into position. Everything she did, she did for one reason only: to discover a way to have a child. A Legal child, all of her own.

And her diligence paid off. There were a handful of people, she discovered, who, because of their senior position, received special privileges. The privilege that Margaret was interested in was that of being allowed to sign the Declaration, take Longevity drugs *and* to have one child legally. Just five officials in the whole country were afforded this benefit, to reflect their contribution to the effective running of public services. And when she'd discovered that Stephen Fitz-Patrick, director general of her Department, was one of them, she'd known exactly what she had to do.

He'd been an odious man, she thought bitterly, and hard-up too; he earned good money, but spent more than he could afford, and he drank so much that his doctor was forced to up his Longevity intake just to enable his liver and heart to cope. But he was allowed one child. One child. Her child.

She did everything for him: listened to him, agreed with him, ran his life for him, until he told her that he didn't think he could live without her. She told him he needn't, not if he married her. And to her great delight, he agreed.

Not wanting to waste a single moment, she got pregnant a month after the wedding. And when the first scan revealed that it was a boy, she nearly wept with happiness. Her own little boy to love her. A boy who would win back the love of her own father, who had been severely disappointed when his own wife bore him a girl, a useless female. And who had been even more disappointed when Margaret had turned out to be mediocre at best in her lessons and sport. She was not even an attractive child, he would say. Her eyes were too beady, her brow too low, her hair too thin and straight. And within a few years, he lost interest in her completely.

Until the day she gave him the news of her pregnancy. He'd actually smiled at her then, perhaps for the first time. He'd shaken Stephen by the hand too, and welcomed him into the family – something he'd not found necessary to do at the wedding. And, as the final icing on the cake, Stephen had even agreed to allow the boy to take her family name, once her father had agreed to pay off Stephen's debts.

For several months, Margaret had walked on air. She ate nothing but the freshest food, took no exercise except brisk walking and avoided even the smallest glass of anything alcoholic. Her child was going to be perfect, she just knew it. He would be the happiest, most loved child that had ever lived. She would teach him and care for him, and everyone would stare at her enviously as she paraded him on the street. *I may not be as pretty or clever as you*, she would think to herself as she passed other women, *but I have Longevity* and *a child. And that is something you will never have.*

And then? And then . . .

Margaret felt the familiar feeling of bile rising up the back of the throat as she remembered the fateful day, seven months into her pregnancy, when she discovered the horrific truth. The truth that made her scream out, 'No! No, it can't be!' over and over again, unable to take it in, to comprehend it. The truth that had rendered her willing to kill. So willing, in fact, that she'd even bought a revolver for the very purpose, but she had been unable to use it, even on herself, because her husband had put her under twenty-four-hour surveillance. Nursing, he'd called it, but she'd recognised it for what it was. He was afraid of what she might do. And he was right to be afraid.

The horrible, desperate truth was that he'd had an affair. An affair that had started several months before their wedding and was still going strong a year later. An affair that had resulted in a pregnancy, two months before her own, and then the birth of a healthy baby boy who, arriving before Margaret's own son, snatched the Legal title for himself, rendering her own child a Surplus. The legality of her marriage did not protect her child, she discovered too late. One child, her husband was allowed, and no more.

It was too late to terminate the pregnancy. In some regions, no time was considered too late – long needles would be injected into swollen bellies to poison the unborn child, forcing the mother to give birth to her dead baby just hours later – but not here. Not in this civilised corner of the world. No, here, the baby would live long enough to be born and would then be packed off to a Surplus Hall to live a life of servitude.

But not *her* son, Margaret swore to herself. She wouldn't let them do it. As they took him away from her, just minutes after he was born, she cried out for someone to help her. He couldn't live as a slave. She wouldn't do that to her own son.

And finally, after the birth, her husband took pity on her and agreed to help. Perhaps it was guilt, or perhaps he shared her belief that death would be better than life as a Surplus, but he agreed to take care of the situation. The boy was still his son, he accepted, and he would let him die an honourable death rather than live a life of dishonour, of shame. He even let Margaret say goodbye, to clutch the baby to her chest one last time and feel the warmth of his skin against hers, before he was taken away for ever, leaving her cold, empty and bitter.

Now, Margaret felt nothing but contempt for Surpluses. Each new Surplus reminded her of what she had lost, of what her son had lost. They reminded her of what she had been forced to sacrifice because of her husband's mistress, that woman whom she hated to the bottom of her heart. What right did these Surpluses have to one moment's enjoyment, when her son lay in a grave somewhere? What right did any of their mothers have to bear a child? None, Margaret thought angrily. Surpluses had no right to anything but shame for their Parents' Sins. For everyone's Sins. And it was her mission in life to avenge her son's cruel fate by ensuring that each and every Surplus in Grange Hall endured a life that was not worth living. She would not tolerate any Surplus enjoying anything approaching a normal life when her own poor child had been denied it.

She thought she'd done such a good job with Anna too. The girl really did feel the shame of her parents' crimes. Until that Peter had come along.

Margaret's eyes narrowed as she thought about him. Evil boy. He would pay for this. They both would.

Slowly pulling herself back into the present, forcing herself to push all thoughts of her betrayed child from her head, she turned the pages of Anna's journal, shaking in outrage at the blasphemous thoughts that the Surplus had dared to commit to paper.

On the Outside I won't be a Prefect. I won't be set to be a Valuable Asset either. I don't know what I'll be on the Outside. Just an Illegal, I suppose. With a thudding heart Mrs Pincent continued down through the paragraphs, bristling with anger when Anna referred to the injections she'd given Peter, referred to her overheard telephone conversation. She'd have to make sure this journal never got into the wrong hands, she realised. The Authorities wouldn't understand that she'd only been planning to put him down for his own good – for everyone's good. Even if the escape had proved her right.

She continued reading, noting down that a neighbour had helped them by supplying floor plans to Grange Hall. Well, that neighbour would regret it. They couldn't be too hard to track down, and when they were, they'd see what a prison cell looked like from the inside, not just from a map.

Then her lip curled up in anger as she read *Peter's amazing*.

'Peter is a Surplus,' she muttered. 'A dirty, disgusting Surplus. He's . . .'

And then she frowned. Peter was adopted – she hadn't known that. It was odd, really. Who would want to adopt a Surplus? But that wasn't the bit in the journal that really drew her eye. It was the ring. The ring that he was supposedly found with as a baby. *A gold ring called a signet ring . . .*

Margaret's eyes widened briefly, then she shook herself. It was impossible.

But it was here, written in black and white: he was found with a ring. With the letters 'AF' on the inside. *With a flower engraved on the top of it.*

Slowly, she put the journal down, and turned to her computer, the only computer in the whole of Grange

Hall, turning it on and waiting for it to whirr into life. She went through the laborious password process, a rigmarole that was imposed on any Authority-owned system, and finally plugged Peter's name into the Surplus network. But to her annoyance, a small red flag appeared by his name. Access Denied.

Mrs Pincent frowned. Omnipotent in Grange Hall, controller of everything from the Surpluses' rations and treatment to their training and punishments, she resented any sign that her power did not extend outside its walls; any sign that the Authorities did not hold her in the esteem with which she held herself.

Irritably, she turned off the computer and picked up the phone.

'Central Administration,' she heard a woman say. 'Please state your business.'

'It's Margaret Pincent here from Grange Hall,' she said briskly. 'I need the file of Surplus Peter. The one who escaped.'

There was a pause as the woman on the other end of the line pressed some keys on her computer.

'I'm sorry,' she said eventually. 'That file is classified. Is there anything else I can help you with?'

Mrs Pincent frowned in anger.

'No, there isn't,' she snapped. 'And I don't care if it's classified – I need it. Do you realise who you are speaking to? This is Margaret Pincent. I am the House Matron of Grange Hall, and I want to know where he came from. I want to –'

'I'm sorry,' the woman said again, not sounding

sorry in the least. 'That file is classified, and you don't have access to it. If you would like special circumstances taken into account, we have an appeals procedure, which takes fourteen working days from receipt of form 4331b. Would you like me to send you a copy?'

Mrs Pincent pursed her lips. 'No, no, that's quite all right, thank you.'

Margaret put the phone receiver down. Would no one tell her anything? She needed to know where that Surplus scum came from. Needed to know how he came across a gold signet ring. If he was a thief as well as a Surplus, then she would kill him herself. She would torture him until he cried out for death, and she would enjoy every minute of it.

Then an idea came to her. Not a pleasant one, but one she hoped might work. Slowly she lifted the telephone receiver again and dialled a number from memory.

'Stephen, it's me,' she said, forcing herself to keep her voice steady and even. 'Yes, thank you, I'm well. I trust you are too. Stephen, I have some important information for you . . . No, I can't tell you over the phone. Can you come to Grange Hall right away? Good. That's very good. Thank you, Stephen . . .'

'That's all they've got – Bloomsbury? Do they know how big Bloomsbury is?'

Frank shrugged. 'That's all I've got here. Check every house, it says.'

'And these are the geezers who think they know it all? I thought they were called Intelligence. Doesn't sound like they're too intelligent to me.'

Frank sighed. 'Look, let's just get on with it, shall we?' he said, rolling his eyes at his colleague, Bill. 'When you've been a Catcher as long as I have, you stop worrying about the Intelligence, as you put it. Soon as we start showing some of the neighbours we're serious, we'll soon flush 'em out. You got the tools?'

Bill raised his eyebrows. 'When do I go anywhere without my little box of tricks?' He smiled maliciously.

'All right then, let's get to work,' Frank said. 'Nice houses around here, actually. Might grab ourselves a bob or two as well as the Surpluses. And people in nice houses don't half squeal quickly once they experience a little bit of pain. I reckon we'll be done here by the end of the day.'

Her parents hadn't hit her. No one had told her she was stupid, or useless, or unworthy.

But the truth was, she wished they had. Anna knew how to deal with beatings and harsh words. When she knew she deserved them, they felt almost like a release, like a penance that enabled her to keep living.

Anna had once heard Mrs Pincent say 'You can kill them with kindness, you know' to one of the Instructors, when she didn't know Anna was listening, and Anna hadn't known what she'd meant at the time, but she did now. She had never realised that kindness could be so painful, never known how agonising it was to be loved.

Instead of shouting at her, or punishing her because of the journal, her parents and Peter had just stopped talking for a moment or two, then quietly, kindly, asked her what she'd written in it. And then her mother had smiled brightly and said that she was sure it didn't matter, and that Anna shouldn't worry, but Anna did worry. She knew it did matter. She knew that everything mattered.

And now she and Peter were in the cellar, and her parents had said it was because it was comfortable down there and that everything would be fine, but Anna knew that they were hiding because before they knew about the journal, her parents had said that they didn't need to hide as the curtains were drawn and, anyway, no one would be looking for escaped Surpluses here. And she knew that her parents were worried because her father had a vein like Mr Sargent's, just above his right eye, and it was throbbing. And now they were going to the country that very evening, now that she'd told them about the journal, even though they hadn't been planning to go to the country until a few days later. Even though earlier, her father had said they'd be safer here.

The cellar was accessed through a trapdoor in the kitchen, which was hidden by a rug underneath the table. Peter told her that it used to be a coal cellar when people heated their houses using fires, but there wasn't any coal there now.

There was a sofa down there, which turned into a bed, and a big armchair which could also be made into a bed, but it took longer and it wasn't as comfortable. Peter had shown her everything when they'd first got down there, and it reminded Anna of his first days at Grange Hall, except that back then she'd been the one showing him the ropes. Peter said he'd hidden in the cellar before, and he almost looked excited when he said it, like this was an adventure or something, instead of a nightmare that was entirely her fault.

For a long time, she hadn't said much, because she didn't know what to say, so she'd just let Peter tell her all about the cellar, including the chairs and the tins of food and the bucket behind the curtain which you could use as a loo and the opening in the road where the coal used to be poured in, and where they could get out if the Catchers came, if the Catchers got into the house.

And that's when she started shaking.

'What will happen to us if they catch us?' she asked him, her voice small and hesitant. 'What will happen to the Small, and my parents?'

Peter looked away.

'They won't,' he said firmly, but Anna could tell he was scared too.

'You should have just left me there,' she said quietly. 'Then you'd all be safe and the Catchers wouldn't be coming. It's all my fault.'

Peter turned round to face her fully, and Anna saw that his eyes were flashing.

'It is not your fault,' he said. 'It's my fault. It was my escape plan, so I should have thought of everything.'

He turned away from Anna, then immediately turned back again, his eyes desperately seeking hers.

'You're the one that matters, Anna, not me. They're your parents, not mine. I'm just lucky they took me in. You might be a Surplus, but I'm a double Surplus because my own parents didn't even want me. I owe your parents everything, you have to see that. If anything goes wrong, it's my fault.'

Peter was blinking furiously, and as he saw her look at him, he dropped his eyes to the ground, and turned his body away from her slightly in embarrassment.

Anna frowned, deep in thought, then she took his hand tentatively, thinking as she did so about the boy who had come to rescue her, the orphan boy who had imagined their friendship before they'd even met. And she thought about his fighting Charlie, fighting the Instructors, fighting everyone and everything, for her, for her parents, for a chance to be loved, or liked, or just to be. And then she thought about all the time she'd spent at Grange Hall, trying to please Mrs Pincent, trying to be the best Surplus, the most Valuable Asset, just so that Mrs Pincent would like her and tell her that she wasn't completely unwanted after all. And she realised that she and Peter were the same, really. That without each other they were so alone it hurt. That they needed each other like flowers needed the sun. And she knew that she would follow him anywhere, that stories about angry roses and two-headed children didn't scare her any more, but that losing Peter did, more than anything.

'Peter, you didn't even know about my journal,' she said, her voice breaking slightly. 'And as a matter of fact, I owe *you* everything. More than everything, actually.'

She cleared her throat awkwardly and looked up at Peter. 'If it wasn't for you, I'd just be Surplus Anna. I'd be nothing. If it wasn't for you, I'd never have even known what it's like to have a friend . . .'

She trailed off, unable to express what she felt so strongly inside, unable to explain that her feelings for Peter had made her angry with the world because it had allowed him to grow up without love, made her angry with Longevity because no one deserved to live more than him.

So instead, she just looked at him unblinkingly, and allowed his eyes to sear through hers, to see her thoughts, her fears, her hopes.

They looked at each other for long, silent seconds until Anna's head was pounding because she'd never looked at anyone like that before, had never seen into someone's soul. And as she stared at him, Anna realised just why Surpluses were trained to keep their eyes cast downwards at all times, because she felt at that moment as if she knew everything there was to know.

Then, just as she was about to look away, Peter

opened his mouth to speak.

'I love you, Anna Covey,' he said, his voice barely audible. And slowly, clumsily, he leant forward, and his lips found hers, and as Anna felt him kiss her awkwardly, she knew that she wasn't a Surplus any more. And nor was Peter.

Surplus meant unnecessary. Not required.

You couldn't be a Surplus if you were needed by someone else. You couldn't be a Surplus if you were loved.

Chapter Twenty-four

Stephen looked as awful as he ever had, Margaret Pincent noted with some satisfaction. His flesh filled his shirt completely, and his trousers dug in to his belly painfully. His skin was red and blotchy, and his eyes were watery, as if swimming with the copious amounts of alcohol he consumed on a daily basis. She shuddered to think she was ever married to him.

'So, you have some information for us?' he said briskly. 'You know, it's very inconvenient for me to have to trek all the way out here. Couldn't you have come to London?'

Mrs Pincent stared at him.

'Sit down, Stephen,' she said calmly, closing the door behind him and locking it, just for good measure. She did not want any interruptions. Not today.

'I see your office is still a dump,' he was saying. 'Can't you get those Surpluses to clean it for you, maybe even give it a lick of paint?'

'I prefer it like this,' Mrs Pincent said, still staring at him, and sitting down at her desk, her seat of power. 'It creates an environment of fear.

Fresh paint can be too . . . welcoming.'

Stephen shrugged.

'So, the information,' he continued, 'I assume it's about these missing Surpluses?'

Mrs Pincent nodded.

'And you couldn't tell the Catchers direct? Margaret, I run a big Department, you know. I don't usually get involved in this level of detail.'

'Don't you?' Mrs Pincent's tone was sarcastic and Stephen looked at her curiously.

'You know I don't. I run the police force, the Catchers, immigration, the prisons . . . I don't have time for anything.'

'Really?' Mrs Pincent's eyes narrowed, and Stephen looked at her blankly. 'How very interesting.'

'Margaret, whatever it is, just tell me, and I'll be off. And perhaps you should take a holiday – you look dreadful. Do they give you holidays here?'

He smiled affably, but Mrs Pincent didn't return it. Slowly, she stood up.

'Stephen, what do you know about the boy?' she asked. 'The Pending boy who escaped. Peter.'

Stephen turned round immediately.

'Nothing. Nothing at all. Why?'

Mrs Pincent scrutinised his face, then walked towards the window behind her desk, which was covered with a thin grey blind, like every other window at Grange Hall. There was something he wasn't telling her, she just knew it. 'Do you know his background?' she asked.

'Of course I don't. You think I have time to worry about the background of Surpluses?'

'No, just this one. His file is classified.'

She turned round and saw that Stephen was looking at her irritably now. But she could also see that his eyes had fear in them. That she had asked a question he was afraid to answer.

He shook his head. 'The boy's file is nothing to do with me. I'm sorry, Margaret, but I do have to go now. Perhaps we could discuss this some other time.'

'He was found with a ring, apparently,' Mrs Pincent continued, her eyes now boring into Stephen's, which she noticed visibly widen as she spoke. 'A gold signet ring with a flower engraved on the top and "AF" engraved on the inside. Do you remember a ring like that, Stephen?'

Stephen's face went pale.

'There are lots of rings around, Margaret,' he said quickly, and stood up. 'I really think it's time for me to go.'

Mrs Pincent took a deep breath.

'Stephen, you are not going anywhere until I know the truth.'

'The truth?' Stephen asked, his face now reddening in anger. 'Don't talk to me like that. What does someone like you need with the truth?'

'My grandfather's initials were AF,' Mrs Pincent continued, her voice now tense. 'He had them engraved on a gold signet ring with a flower on it. A ring he gave to me, Stephen.'

Stephen said nothing.

Mrs Pincent turned back to the window, pulling back the blind slightly to view the grey landscape outside. It was a fitting place to live, she'd thought to herself when she first arrived at Grange Hall. A fitting place to live out a half-life, taking out her misery on the creatures she hated above all others.

'Stephen, I want to know the truth.'

Stephen stood up. 'There's nothing to say. I'm leaving now.'

He walked towards the door and grasped the handle, then shook it. He turned back angrily. 'Margaret, unlock the door,' he said. 'Unlock it right now.'

Mrs Pincent ignored him.

'Sit down, Stephen,' she said calmly. 'Our business is not yet finished.'

'Oh yes it is,' Stephen said angrily, marching over to Mrs Pincent and grabbing her arms. 'Our business was finished years ago. Give me the key or I will be forced to break this door down.'

'No!' Margaret spat. 'No. I will not give you the key. Why should I give you anything, Stephen? Why should I, when you took away the only thing that mattered to me in the whole wide world? When your slut, your treacherous mistress, killed *my* child.'

Stephen shook his head. 'Come on, Margaret. Enough now. It was the rules, you know that. There was nothing I could do. Now give me the key, will you?'

'Nothing you could do?' Margaret hissed, feeling the bile rising up the back of the throat. 'You and your slut stole my son's life.'

Stephen dropped Mrs Pincent's arms and slapped her around the face.

'I will not listen to this,' he shouted. 'I will not tolerate these words. You will give me the key, or . . . or . . .'

'Or what?' Mrs Pincent asked again. 'You'll kill me like you killed our son?'

Stephen went white and reached for the desk to steady his feet.

'Sit down, Stephen,' Mrs Pincent instructed. 'I want to know the truth, Stephen. I demand to know. So you can tell me the background of this Surplus Peter, or I can go to London and tell the Authorities about our son, the one you murdered. Which would you prefer?'

Stephen's face was white and haggard.

'Are you blackmailing me?' he asked, his face incredulous. 'You have as much to lose as I do.'

'I have nothing to lose,' Mrs Pincent said, in a low voice. 'I lost everything years ago.'

'This is hopeless. You know it's hopeless,' Stephen said, wiping the sweat from his forehead. 'Why can't you leave this alone?'

'Tell me why this Surplus was found with my ring. Tell me how some Surplus dirt came to have the Pincent ring with him. Did they dig up my child? Did they rob our son's grave? Tell me, Stephen. Who are his parents? I want them dead. I want them found, and . . . My son, Stephen. My . . .'

She started to weep. 'He knew, Stephen. Our son knew his fate before he was even born. He refused to turn, refused to let the midwife deliver him. He didn't want to be born, Stephen. And why would he, when the world no longer wanted him. When you no longer –'

'Pull yourself together, Margaret,' Stephen said angrily. 'This happened years ago. It's over.'

Feeling her chest constricting and her breaths shorten, Mrs Pincent wrapped her arms around her stomach, her eyes searching for the truth in her ex-husband's face.

'If someone has ransacked my son's grave, I will search them down and kill them. My son was denied legality and then life, and he will not be denied his heirloom.' She stared into Stephen's eyes. 'The Surplus boy, Stephen. Why did he have my ring? And where is it now? What happened to it?'

'Margaret, you're hysterical,' Stephen said, the tension showing in his voice. 'And I have no idea where the ring is. I can barely remember it.'

'The boy was found with a ring. My ring. And his file is classified. I want to know why, Stephen.' Mrs Pincent had moved to the front of her desk now, and was leaning forwards menacingly.

'I won't listen to this any more,' Stephen said, standing up hurriedly. 'I won't put up with this from you of all people. You are nothing, Margaret. You will not talk to me like that. What I did with our son or your ring is no longer your business. And if you tell a single soul, I will have you committed to a mental institution. Now, open this door, or I'll knock it down myself.'

'Tell me where my ring is,' Mrs Pincent said.

'I'll tell you nothing,' Stephen said bitterly and moved towards her. 'Now give me the key.'

Immediately, as if by reflex, Mrs Pincent opened her desk draw, took something out of it. 'Tell me, Stephen,' she screamed. 'You will tell me!'

Stephen's eyes widened and the look of irritation on his face was suddenly replaced with something much closer to fear.

'What are you doing, Margaret?' he asked incredulously, beads of sweat appearing on his forehead. 'What on earth are you doing with that?'

'Just tell me.' Mrs Pincent's voice was raw now. In her hands, aimed directly at Stephen's face, was a revolver. A revolver that she'd kept in her desk from her very first day at Grange Hall. Just in case it all got too much.

'You're insane,' Stephen stammered, but he sat back down.

'Just tell me what happened,' Mrs Pincent said, 'or I swear to you I'll pull the trigger.'

Anna was alone in the cellar, and she was making a plan. Peter had been called up to the house to help write some coded messages for her parents' Underground friends. She'd been given the Small – Ben – to look after until they were ready to leave.

Protectively, she held him to her, and smiled at him, feeling an incredible spark of love and exhilaration when he smiled back at her. He was the most perfect thing in the whole world, she thought. How could he be Surplus? Why would Mother Nature make something so beautiful if She didn't need it and want it? It didn't make any sense.

Having a plan made her feel better, like she was back in charge. Anna's plan was to get caught and sent back to Grange Hall. If she was caught, she reasoned, the Catchers wouldn't worry about chasing the others. The Authorities had only had Peter in Grange Hall for a few weeks, so they'd barely miss him, whereas she was going to be a Valuable Asset. If she went back, Peter would be safe. Ben would be safe.

She'd die before letting the Catchers take her brother away. She'd never known you could feel anything but disdain for Smalls, but now all she wanted was for Ben to grow up surrounded by love and affection, not the grey walls and discipline of Grange Hall.

As she tenderly stroked Ben's head, she heard the trapdoor open and saw Peter's face appear at it. He climbed down the ladder into the cellar, followed by her mother.

'This is for you,' he said proudly, offering her a yellow flower. 'It's a daffodil,' he continued, then leant down to whisper in her ear, 'when we're in the country, we'll have flowers everywhere. Flowers for my butterfly.'

Anna took the flower and gazed in wonderment at it – it was so bright, so fragrant. Then she took a deep breath.

'Actually,' she said, 'I was thinking that I wouldn't go. To the country.'

Peter frowned. 'Don't be stupid. You have to.'

'No, I don't,' Anna said seriously, standing up and looking at her mother and Peter pleadingly. 'You have to leave me here. Then you can all escape and they won't come after you, and you'll be safe. They'll never stop looking for me because I'm nearly a Valuable Asset, and if they find me, they'll find you, and Ben –'

'I'm not going anywhere without you,' Peter said hotly. 'Stop being stupid. If anyone should stay behind, it's me. This is your family, not mine.'

'I'm not being stupid,' Anna retorted. 'And it's my fault the Catchers are coming, not yours. I'm being sensible. I'm being –'

'Anna, sit down a moment, will you?' Her mother, who had been looking at them both sadly, came over to the sofa and sat down with Peter and Anna either side of her, taking their hands in hers.

'Let me tell you both a story,' she said, her voice soft and kind. 'This story is about a man and a woman who loved each other very much, and who wanted to have children, because, contrary to what you were taught at Grange Hall, Anna, Nature is not about preserving old things, but about creating new ones. New life. New ideas. Like your daffodil. It will die, eventually, but in its place will come new daffodils. That's the way things should be.

'Now, this man and woman went to the Authorities, and said that they would like to Opt Out of Longevity, so that they could have a child. But the Authorities said that they couldn't, because you had to Opt Out when you were sixteen, and if you didn't, you were deemed to have agreed to the Declaration. The man and woman said that they hadn't known they'd want to Opt Out when they were sixteen, that they'd been too young. But the Authorities told them that it was still impossible to Opt Out now, and that they couldn't have a child.

'So they were very sad, but then they started to meet other people who weren't allowed to have children. And they found out that not everyone thinks that Longevity drugs are a good thing after all, but that the drugs companies were so powerful that no one was allowed to question Longevity, and if they did, they ended up in prison. And so they joined something called the Underground Movement, and they decided to have a baby, even though they weren't allowed to, because they believed that if they didn't have children, the Authorities would have won, because if there weren't any children, people would forget about them, and everyone would have signed the Declaration, so there would never be any children again.

'So they had a child, and she was the most beautiful little girl, and she made them so happy they thought they would burst, even though they had to keep her a secret. They loved that little girl more than anything in the world, but they made a mistake. They met a woman, who said she wanted to join the Underground Movement, who said she and her husband wanted to have a baby. They trusted her, and they told her about their little girl, and a week later, the Catchers arrived and took their baby away, and put the man and the woman in prison, and they screamed and screamed for their little girl, but it was no use.

'A few years later, they were let out of prison, and they changed their names and joined the Underground Movement again, and the Movement gave them a new house to live in, here in Bloomsbury. And then one day, they were lucky enough to meet a boy called Peter, whom they loved very much and who agreed to live with them. And then they became even happier when they had another baby, this time a little boy. But all that time, they were still very sad, because they didn't have their little girl. They hadn't protected her. And now she was paying the price, locked away in Grange Hall.

'Now, Peter, here, was a very brave and wonderful boy, and he decided that he was going to save their little girl. The man and woman were worried for him, but he refused to take no for an answer, and they told him what their little girl looked like, that her name was Anna, and that she had a butterfly on her stomach, a little mark from Mother Nature to show the world that she should be free . . .'

Anna's mother squeezed her hand.

'You see, my darling,' she said, her voice catching slightly, 'none of this is your fault. And if you go back to Grange Hall, then everything will have been a waste. You and Peter and Ben are what matter. You are the future. You're what everyone in the Underground is fighting for – young people, new blood and new ideas. That's what Renewal should be about, not keeping old people alive.

'The Authorities don't want people to Opt Out, they don't want any new children, because that might change the balance of power. They like things the way they are, and they're afraid of change, so they suppress it. They kill it off at the roots. You are the revolution, Anna. You, Peter and now Ben. And you have to keep yourself safe because you have a responsibility to live, for all our sakes.'

Anna nodded seriously, and looked at Peter, whose eyes were flashing with determination.

'You see?' he said, his voice strangled. 'Now do you see?'

'I see,' Anna whispered, then she turned to face her mother.

'Do you still take Longevity?' she asked.

Her mother nodded.

'We take Longevity because we don't want to stand out. And because we didn't want to get ill, not whilst you were still locked away in Grange Hall. But now . . . well, now things are different. We don't need it any more. Not so long as you're safe with us.'

Anna bit her lip. 'Mrs Pincent told me my parents were selfish,' she said, feeling a lump appear in her throat. 'She said I should hate you. And I did . . .' She swallowed furiously. 'But now,' she continued, 'now I'm proud to be your daughter. I'm so proud. And I won't let you down. I promise.'

Her mother smiled, and Anna could see tears in her eyes.

'You could never let us down,' she whispered. 'None of you could. Now don't worry, my darlings. We'll get away, far away from here, and everything is going to be fine. Just wait and see.'

Chapter Twenty-five

Frank smiled as Bill held his knife over Mrs Parkinson's fingers.

'Now, Christopher,' he said to her husband. 'You don't mind me calling you Christopher, do you? Christopher, you know we don't want to hurt your wife. Don't want her mutilated, any more than we'd want our own wives mutilated. Fingers come in handy, Christopher, we know that. It's just that we've got a job to do here, same as anyone else, and we're not sure you're really telling us what we need to know. Look at it from our perspective. Here we are, trying to track down some Surpluses, some escaped Surpluses, in fact, and we know they're hiding with some neighbours of yours. Next door, for all we know. But you tell us you know nothing about it. And we find that hard to believe, Christopher. You see what I'm saying? Odd that you'd never have heard a single sound, or suspected anything at all . . .'

Slowly, Bill brought the knife down on Mrs Parkinson's little finger, and Mr Parkinson shouted out.

'No! Please, God, no! I think they might live at

number fifty-three. Or number fifty-five. One or the other. That's all I know – you hear rumours, that's all. Please, oh my God, what have you done?'

'There, that wasn't too hard, was it?' Frank said, beaming, as Bill put his knife away in a small leather box. 'You've been a pleasure to do business with, Christopher. We'll let ourselves out, shall we?'

Running to his wife's side to stem the blood that was pouring out of her hand, Mr Parkinson barely noticed them leave.

'I couldn't kill him. I couldn't kill the boy.'

Mrs Pincent reached behind her for her chair, all the time holding the gun straight at Stephen, all the time keeping her arms steady, even though the rest of her was shaking violently.

'You couldn't kill him?' she asked hoarsely. It was the conclusion she'd refused to draw, the truth she hadn't been able to face. Now that it had been uttered she felt as if she'd been punched in the stomach. Her son was alive. Her son was . . .

Mrs Pincent gasped as the awful truth hit her. Her son, alive. Her son, the Surplus, the boy with the eyes that bore into her with hatred. The boy she had . . . No, no, it couldn't be true. It couldn't be.

'I never agreed with you that we should kill the boy. A life is a life, Margaret, however it's lived,' Stephen was saying. 'But I couldn't stand him being a Surplus. So I left him outside a house known to have Underground sympathisers living in it. Faked a burial.

Margaret, I couldn't kill the boy . . .'

He was sobbing now, his large body juddering as he wept, his eyes seeking hers for what – forgiveness? Sympathy? He would get none from her.

'With the ring?' Somehow she managed to keep her voice steady, her mind too. She had to, she told herself. For her son. For everything she'd promised him and failed to deliver.

Stephen looked at her, then continued to weep.

'Did you leave the ring with him?' she asked again. She had to know for sure. 'Did you or not?'

'Yes.' His voice was pathetic. 'Yes I did.'

'And now? Where is it now?'

'It was sent to your father for safe keeping when the boy was apprehended.'

'My father? He knew? You both knew?' Margaret's head was throbbing and her body almost convulsing with the shock, the pain, but her mind was clear. Clearer than it had been for many years.

'You turned my child into a Surplus,' she said quietly, her eyes full of hatred as they rested on her ex-husband. 'Then you took him away, and you gave him to criminals to raise. My son . . .'

'I didn't think –'

'Quiet!' Mrs Pincent screamed. 'You do not talk to me unless I ask you to. You don't deserve to talk to me. You . . .'

She started to sob quietly, but immediately stiffened again. Stephen was sly and strong, and if he saw her weaken, he would take full advantage, she knew that.

The minute the gun was not trained at his head, this would be over.

'You took away my hope,' she said. 'Everything I ever wanted was wrapped up in that boy, our son. For the past fifteen years I have not lived, I have been a ghost. For the past fifteen years I have begged the cold ground to open up and take me, and even that is denied me. I have lived a half life, and it is all because of you. And now I discover that my son is alive. A Surplus. A Surplus who was brought to Grange Hall and who I nearly had put down. Stephen, I nearly killed my own child . . .'

She felt her stomach clench again and it was everything she could do to stop herself from collapsing on the ground and moaning. But she knew she had to stay strong. Knew she wouldn't give up now or all would be lost.

'What is it that the Declaration says?' she asked, blinking away the tears that were in her eyes, the tears which had not come for fifteen years, and which now threatened to pour out of her like an avalanche.

Stephen, who was sweating profusely now, shook his head.

'The Declaration?' he asked stupidly. 'I, um, well, you know . . .'

'A life for a life. Isn't that right?'

Stephen frowned. 'To Opt Out, you mean. Yes, that's how it's phrased, I think.'

'Not Opting Out,' Mrs Pincent said, her eyes now flashing. 'A life for a life. A Surplus will no longer be a Surplus if one or other of its parents dies. Is that not what it says?'

Stephen nodded, and his face went white as Margaret turned the gun on herself.

'You're not going to kill yourself?' he asked incredulously. 'Margaret, wait. Not here. Not . . .'

Then his face went even whiter as she trained the gun back on him.

'It never happens, of course,' she said thoughtfully. 'A life for a life, I mean. Who would have a child and willingly not be there to look after it? But our child doesn't need *looking after*, does he Stephen? Our child has rather proved himself capable of looking after himself, wouldn't you say?'

'Margaret, please, put the gun down,' Stephen begged. He was shaking violently, his mouth open, his eyes filled with fear.

'I would kill myself in a minute to save my son,' she continued. 'A *minute*. My life has been over for years – it would be a release to die. But then I'd never know he was safe, would I? I can't trust you, you see, Stephen. Can't trust you not to bury the paperwork, cover the whole thing up. Can't trust you not to betray our child for a second time.'

She walked around the desk.

'Margaret, no, no you can't. Margaret, you'll go to prison. You can't just . . . Margaret, please. Please, no . . .'

'You can give the boy in death what you weren't prepared to give him in life,' Mrs Pincent whispered.

'And prison doesn't scare me. I'm in prison now.'

And right then, she pulled the trigger, watching as the bullet unloaded into her ex-husband's head, forcing him backwards, his chair tipping over and depositing him on the floor in a pool of blood. Just where Surplus Sheila had lain earlier in the day, Mrs Pincent observed.

Slowly, she picked up the phone and dialled a number.

'Dad?' she said, her voice calm and still. 'I have some important information for you. Please listen carefully.'

Chapter Twenty-six

'You want a sip of this?' Frank offered his hip flask to Bill, who shook his head. Frank shrugged, and finished the rest himself.

He looked at his watch. 6.30 p.m.

'Ready Bill?'

Bill nodded, and, both taking a deep breath, they efficiently and effectively kicked the front door down.

Kate Covey looked at her husband Alan in alarm at the sound of the front door being forced.

She didn't dare say a word, didn't dare let on, even to a room empty but for him, that she might be more terrified of the Catchers than any other couple on this street. How had they got here so quickly, she wondered desperately. Why now, when they were ready to leave? They had just been waiting for darkness to fall completely; now it might be too late.

'Can I help you?' Alan had darted into the hallway to meet them, giving her time to prepare, she suspected. 'Do you people not knock any more?'

He sounded only mildly annoyed, but Kate knew it

was masking his abject terror. The Catchers could be going to everyone's house, and there was no reason to give the game away by appearing worried.

But Kate was more than worried. This could be it, and she knew it. The two of them could take prison again, but not the children. They'd promised them they'd be safe. They couldn't fail them again. Wouldn't fail them again.

She thought, frantically. Could Alan distract the Catchers whilst she got the children out? But it was useless – even now one of the Catchers was coming into the kitchen to find her. If she so much as glanced under the table, the trapdoor would be found. Her children would be found and taken away again, and she couldn't – wouldn't – take it.

'Mrs Bunting, I believe,' the Catcher asked her, and she nodded.

'So that's definitely Bunting and not Covey, then?'

Kate went white, and looked up to see Alan being frogmarched into the kitchen by a second Catcher.

'Only, we heard from our superiors that you might have changed your name,' the Catcher continued. 'Real name Covey, they said. Of course, they do get it wrong from time to time, our superiors. Think they know it all because they have computer screens and fancy offices. Whereas me and Bill, here, we're in uniform, but turns out that most of the time, we know more than they do. Funny, that, isn't it? So, what's it going to be – Bunting or Covey? Doesn't bother me either way, see.'

Kate met Alan's eyes and in them she saw the sign, the desperate message. As he passed her, his hand brushed hers and something was transferred, something small and pink, something that would dissolve on the tongue, that would bring about an ending and a beginning. And immediately, she knew what they were going to do, and she nodded, a move so slight that it was barely perceptible. But he saw. She knew that he'd seen it.

'Bunting,' he said calmly. 'Our name is Bunting.'

'Well, there we are,' the Catcher said, a little smile playing on his lips. 'So, Mr Bunting, let me tell you what's going to happen, shall I? What's going to happen is that you're going to tell us where the Surpluses are, we're going to collect them, and that will be the end of that. Except for you going to prison, of course. You can't get off that lightly, I'm afraid! Serious business, keeping Surpluses. But then you know that, don't you? Been caught before, haven't we?'

Kate could hardly breathe, hardly dare think about the children, hiding in the cellar.

'So that's what we'd like to happen,' the Catcher continued, his chirpy voice grating on and on. 'Now, if you want it to be more complicated, my friend Bill here has a box of tricks which he loves playing with. So if you don't want to tell us right away where the Surpluses are, if you've forgotten, say, then he'll be more than happy to take your wife here and cut her up a bit until you remember.'

As he spoke, the second Catcher, opened up the

black leather box in front of him and took out a knife.

Below them, Anna and Peter were staring at each other. They'd heard the door crashing in, and Anna had somehow managed to stop Ben from crying, but now they were rooted to the spot, too scared to move.

Escape was now impossible. Getting out involved crawling out of a hole in the street, where they would be seen, heard. Staying here, silent, was their only option. Staying here, silent, and waiting for their eventual capture.

Anna held Ben to her and rocked him gently. 'You are not Surplus,' she whispered to him, stroking his head gently and kissing him on the forehead. 'You will never be Surplus. Never.'

Gingerly, she and Peter sat down on the sofa, where they'd been a few minutes before until they had jumped up at the crash at the door.

'Are you scared?' Peter asked quietly, his face tense. Anna shook her head, unable to trust herself to speak.

'We'll escape again, if they catch us,' he whispered, clutching her hand in his so tightly she almost cried out from the pain.

'Of course we will,' she whispered back, trying her best to smile confidently. 'We'll run away with Ben and we'll find my parents and we'll all go to the country. And then we'll go to the desert, and it will be warm and sunny and we'll have a lovely big house with a big garden.'

'Of sand?' Peter asked, smiling now in spite of the fear in his eyes.

'Yes, of sand,' Anna whispered firmly. 'And there we won't be Surpluses, we'll just be people, and we'll be so happy.'

'And there'll be flowers,' Peter agreed. 'Lots of flowers, and books. And no Catchers.'

'No, definitely no Catchers,' Anna said softly.

She looked down at Ben and felt a rush of gratitude that he didn't know what was happening upstairs.

Please let him never know, she begged silently. *Please let him never need to know.*

As she stared at him, he opened his eyes and smiled, his perfect, angelic face breaking out into a toothless grin.

And then, with no warning at all, he started to cry. Not a timid, uncertain cry, but a loud howling, his mouth open wide and his previously cherubic features contorted into a bright red mass of distress.

Anna and Peter looked at each other in alarm. This was it. They were going to be discovered. They were not going to be saved.

Desperately, Anna tried to soothe him and coax him, putting the side of her finger to his mouth for him to chew on. But Ben spat it out in disgust and continued to howl. Peter put his arm around her. And then things seemed to go into slow motion. Anna could hear the table being moved upstairs, the trapdoor being opened. A Catcher's face appeared at the top and her parents were pushed down the ladder at knifepoint.

Then one of the Catchers held out his hands for Ben, and Anna screamed, 'No!' and the Catcher held out the knife and said he could do this the easy way or the hard way. Anna screamed that he would do it no way at all, that he would never take Ben away from his home. And then, suddenly, her father shouted, 'Now,' and Anna frowned, because she didn't know what he meant. Both her parents put their hands to their mouths, and looked like they were eating something, and then her mother smiled, like she was laughing, like she'd just been given something she'd wanted all her life.

And she turned to the Catcher, and she said, 'You can't touch them now,' and he frowned, and then her mother stumbled slightly, and she fell to the ground, followed by Anna's father. But they were both smiling, and their hands found each other.

'Anna,' her father said. 'Anna, you're free. You and Ben are free. A life for a life. It's in the Declaration. We've been waiting for this moment. Wanting it to come. Waiting to give you life again. A real life. A real future. We're so sorry, Anna. So sorry . . .'

He looked back at her mother, and Anna saw him holding her hand tightly, so tightly that it was going white. There were tears in her mother's eyes, and she mouthed, 'I love you,' to him. And then she looked back at Anna, and she smiled sadly, and she said, 'My Anna. My little Anna . . .'

Anna stared at her mother, and at her father, and as she watched them, she realised that she could see the life drifting out of them, each breath taking them further and further away. The Catchers were looking angry and confused, as if they weren't sure what to do. And then she saw her father looking at Peter and he looked distraught, and was shaking his head, and she didn't know why, and then she suddenly realised. Because if it was a life for a life, she and Ben were safe. But Peter wasn't. Peter, who had saved her, Peter who had rescued her from her prison, was going to be taken away from her, and she felt like it was her own life that was slowly fading away, not her parents'.

Anna's mother was looking at Peter too, and Anna could see her mouthing, 'Run, run, Peter,' but Peter was shaking his head. Anna wanted to scream, wanted to throw herself on top of Peter, a human shield, a barrier to protect him, to keep him with her. But instead, she clutched Ben to her and watched the people who loved her so much they were dying to save her, the people she'd been taught to hate above all others. She watched, unable to move, as the life ran out of her parents, like water, until there was nothing left but the sound of her brother crying.

Frank looked around the cellar and rolled his eyes.

Then he turned to Peter.

'Looks like it's just you coming along with us now,' he said, with a sigh. 'So you'll want to say goodbye to your little girlfriend.'

Anna stood up.

'You won't take him,' she said, her voice strong and

low. 'Take me instead. I'm more Useful.'

Peter pushed her aside angrily. 'It's me they want,' he said bitterly.

'They'll kill you,' Anna said desperately. She could see glimpses of tears in his eyes. 'I won't let them. I need you alive, Peter. I need you.'

The Catcher laughed. 'Touching little scene this, Bill, isn't it? Only, I'm afraid this isn't a game show – you don't get to choose who goes. So, Peter, is it? I think we'll just call you Surplus, if that's all right with you. And if it isn't, then we'll still call you Surplus. Right, follow Bill up the ladder.'

But before Bill could start climbing, another face appeared at the trapdoor. An unfamiliar face, attached to a pinstripe suit.

Slowly, he climbed down into the cellar, and his eyes widened when he took in the lifeless bodies of Anna's parents on the floor before him.

'Peter?' he asked.

Peter nodded cautiously.

'Peter, I'm your grandfather.'

The man looked at the Catchers, and handed them a piece of paper.

'He's coming with me,' he said, looking Peter up and down as if looking for clues for something. 'Peter, your father . . . died, today. Which means that you're Legal now. I'm Richard Pincent. We're . . . family, Peter, and I'd like to take you home.'

Anna watched wide-eyed as Peter stared at the man, then at the Catchers who were looking in fury at the piece of paper they'd been handed, and then at Anna herself.

'You're not my grandfather,' he said suspiciously. 'I was adopted. I don't have a grandfather.'

The man nodded sadly. 'I have something of yours,' he said then, holding out his hand to Peter. As he opened it to reveal a gold signet ring, Peter's eyes flashed.

Anna stared at the ring, trying to see if it had a flower engraved on it, wanting it to be Peter's ring and yet fearing desperately that if it was, it would take him away from her.

You can't go, she wanted to shout. *You belong here with me. You're my Peter*. But she didn't say a word. She was too weak for another battle. Too scared that he might want to leave.

Peter looked at her then, a look that penetrated deep inside of her. He looked scared, she realised, with a shock. Scared and helpless. And the man was just standing there, waiting, his hand outstretched. Anna squeezed Ben to her and just kept looking at Peter, wishing she knew what to say, and what to do.

Then Peter looked back at the man in the pinstripe suit, who smiled at him broadly and started to climb the steps. Peter looked back at Anna one last time, and then his eyes travelled to her parents' bodies, and the cellar that he'd lived in for so long. And then he turned back to the man and, silently, he followed him back up the stairs.

Chapter Twenty-seven

21 April, 2140

My name is Anna. Anna Covey.

I'm a Legal. That means I'm allowed to be here.

I have the certificate right here in front of me. I'm not a Burden on Mother Nature any more.

I can take Longevity drugs too, if I want to. The man from the Authorities who comes around once a week to see how we're Assimilating, says that it's very important I take them. That otherwise I'll get ill, and suffer from Old Age and Death.

But I don't want to. I'm not afraid of dying. I'm not afraid of anything any more.

We live in a house in Bloomsbury now – the one my parents lived in. The house is full of light from the sun, which shines through the front windows in the morning and the back windows in the afternoon because it's spring now, even if it's still very cold. All the walls are painted in warm colours, which I chose to remind me of Mrs Sharpe's house. There are reds and oranges and yellows, and we have thick carpet on the floor and big sofas that are soft and covered in cushions.

There's a picture of my parents too, on the mantelpiece, to remind us. Because they saved us. Because they died.

I used to think that my parents were Selfish, that they didn't care about me. But they did care – about me and Ben. They cared so much that they sacrificed themselves to make us Legal. They left us a letter, telling us that they died because they owed us a life, and they wanted to give it to us. They said they'd always planned it this way, that they'd hoped to have had a little more time with us, but that you can't always predict what's going to happen, and that at least they knew we were going to be safe. And they said that we should look for Peter, and try to rescue him. That they wished they could have saved him too. The letter said the pink pills were always their last resort, when they knew that there was no alternative, when they knew that all other hope was lost.

I wish they'd known about Peter's grandfather. I think that would have made them much happier . . .

'Anna? Where are you?'

Anna looked up to see Peter walking through the

sitting room door, and smiled.

'How was work?'

Peter grimaced. He worked in a local laboratory now, something that Anna found rather comical bearing in mind his lack of enthusiasm in Science and Nature. But he said it was better than working for his grandfather. His grandfather who made Longevity drugs. Peter hated his grandfather even more than he hated the Authorities. And nearly as much as he hated Mrs Pincent. Once Peter had found out what his grandfather did for a living, he had refused all contact.

'All right, I s'pose.' He bent down to pick up Ben, then looked at Anna and frowned.

'What's that?'

His eyes were on the soft, pink suede book that Anna was holding, and she reddened. It still felt slightly illicit, writing down her thoughts for anyone to see.

'I got my journal back,' Anna said awkwardly. 'They sent it to me. There's a letter for you too, from Mrs Pincent, from the prison. From your mother, I mean . . .'

She took out a piece of cream paper and handed it to Peter, who frowned and pushed it away.

'Not interested,' he said dismissively, then he looked at her curiously.

'Are you still writing in that thing?' he asked, his eyes taking in the pen Anna was holding.

Anna looked at him defensively. 'I was just writing

about the house,' she said, 'and Ben, and life on the Outside.'

Peter shook his head. 'Anna, you have to *live* life on the Outside, not write about it. Come on, I want to go for a walk, and I want you and Ben to come with me.'

Anna looked at him hesitantly. She loved going out – spent all her time out in their small garden, marvelling at the colour of the grass, at the flowers growing, thinking how beautiful and majestic Nature was, how lucky she was to be able to see the sky unhindered. She felt as if she could breathe in the entire sky. She loved pointing things out to Ben, like birds and clouds, knowing that he'd never be deprived of them. But then the garden was safe territory for Anna; walls and fences protected her. She'd physically left Grange Hall behind, but she still felt safest within boundaries, even self-imposed ones.

'People always stare at us,' she said quietly.

'Let them,' Peter said, with a shrug. 'In fact I like them staring. I hope we terrify them. Young people. Scary teenagers.'

He pulled a face, and Anna found herself laughing.

'You're not afraid of anyone, are you?' she said, looking at him in wonderment. 'Don't you mind people whispering behind our backs? Don't you mind that no one likes us?'

Peter raised his eyebrows. 'I don't like them either. Don't have time for people who think they deserve to live for ever. Anyway, people *do* like us. The Underground like us.'

Anna nodded awkwardly. Peter had already joined the Underground Movement. In spite of the danger, he spent most of his free time doing secret errands and sitting in on furtive meetings held in random places around London, which were only announced half an hour before. Peter relished the idea of a revolution, and when they were alone, he talked excitedly about the battle ahead, but it made Anna nervous. People always died in battles, and she didn't want to lose anyone else. Especially not Peter.

'So come on,' Peter said impatiently, his eyes darting around in their familiar manner but with excitement now, not trepidation. 'Let's go outside. Let's go scare the old people.'

He grinned encouragingly, and Anna, who could never resist Peter, put her journal down, smiling.

'Get Ben's coat,' she instructed Peter as he leant over to kiss her, then she started to put on her shoes.

But as Peter left the room, she picked up her journal again. Perhaps it *was* time to stop writing, she thought to herself as she flicked through the pages. Perhaps it was time to start living instead. But not before her journal was properly finished. The new fable of Anna and Peter had barely started, she knew that, but that didn't mean that her journal couldn't have its own ending.

Thoughtfully, she picked up her pen and turned to the back page, then started to write.

Life on the Outside is very different from Grange

Hall. Better different. Wonderful different.

There are no Rules, and no Instructors. There's no beating, or punishments, and I'm learning to cook with food from the maximarket and learning to plant vegetables in the Allotment.

We have a computer in our house, and it tells us the news and we can talk to people with it. Peter's teaching me to type, and he says I'm going to be very Valuable to the Underground because of my 'inside knowledge' of Surplus Halls. He told me that the Underground say all of us are Valuable because we're 'young, and the young are the future'.

Being Valuable is different from being a Valuable Asset, though. No one owns me any more, they said. I can do what I want with my life. All of us can.

I don't know what I want to do with my life yet. Peter wants to fight for the Underground – he's always talking about 'war' and 'revolution', and he insists that they're going to stop Longevity, and that afterwards there won't be Surpluses any more.

I worry more about the Surpluses now, though. About Sheila, and Tania and Charlotte and even Charlie. Because they're still at Grange Hall, still in that cold, grey prison, working to pay for their Parents' Sins, working to be Valuable just because Legal people got here first.

I don't know what's going to happen to them. And

when I ask Peter, he frowns and talks about the 'bigger picture' and needing to focus on the cause, not just the effect.

I don't know about that. But I do know that the world is the most beautiful place to be and that we're very lucky to be here. I know that we have to live each moment because we won't be here for ever, and that I wouldn't want to be anyway, because knowing something's going to end makes you appreciate it more, makes you want to savour every moment.

And I know that I won't sign the Declaration, even if it makes me different, even if it makes me suspicious. Because no one needs to live for ever.

I think that sometimes you can outstay your welcome.

I also know that I'm not Surplus Anna any more.

I am Anna Covey: Opt Out.

pledged—even if it seemed to him that the class was histori- cally doomed. He shared what he called a "double allegiance to the class I am part of, and to the Great Change I believe in." Unable to reconcile these two loyalties, he developed in his work an attitude toward Marxism that was neither em- brace nor rejection. . . .

Marxism and Class Loyalty

Edmund Wilson asks if it might be possible to hold Marxist political views and yet "not depict our middle class republic as a place where no birds sing, no flowers bloom and where the very air is almost unbreathable." Fitzgerald accomplishes some- thing very close to this. He depicts lovingly the charm and grace of capitalism's upper classes, yet consistently states his conviction, born of personal resentment and a sense of his- torical necessity, that they are doomed. Not entirely enthusias- tic about this prospect, and with "no faith in the future of my [k]ind in the supposedly classless society," Fitzgerald creates in [hi]s art a strategy of literary debate that permits him to deal [wi]th his ambivalence.

[ ]Fitzgerald's Marxist tendencies are more expressive of capi- [talis]t culture's disillusion with itself than of hopes for a new [comm]unist order. The appeal of Marxism for him comes not [from] any vision of a new social order, different from and be- [yond b]ourgeois society, but from a "socialism" that embodies [the hig]hest ideals of bourgeois society. . . .

[An] idealist reading of Marxism remained consistent with [Fitzgerald] over his career. In a letter of 1920, he listed Marx, [wit]h [Jean-Jacques] Rousseau and [Leo] Tolstoi, as a [th]ought, an impractical man, an "idealist" who has [fre]e to decide the food you eat and the things you [ ]all the millions of Roosevelts and Rockefellers that [ ] years." And in a late letter to his daughter from [ ]he writes that "poetry is either something that [ ]ou—like music to the musician or Marxism to

Wealth and Desire

It is commonplace to cite chapter, verse, and semicolon to support the view that Fitzgerald's tragedy was that he had not been born to wealth. . . . Yet to say that Fitzgerald wanted money, and to stop there, seems to me to say nothing. What did he seek that money could, he thought, provide? Or, per- haps more accurately, what did he think the rich possessed, because of their money, that he wanted so badly? . . .

The list which Gatsby's father shows to Nick Carraway is not so important for what the old man thinks it represents, that his son "was bound to get ahead," though this is a part of the Carraway theme. Rather, in its boyish effort to reduce the world to terms in the Chaucerian sense of "boundaries," the "schedule" imposes on the haphazard circumstances of life a purpose and a discipline, just as Fitzgerald the man attempts in his novel the same sort of thing.

Many elements now seem to fall into place. The conversa- tion about carelessness between Jordan Baker and Nick as- sumes a different stature, and in the thin red circle which Gatsby's blood traces in his swimming pool "like the leg of transit" we can see a meaning: the end-and-beginning within which lies, at least, something else than *khaos*, the mother of all disaster. "It is not what Gatsby was," a student of mine once wrote, "but what had hold of him that was his downfall." "What had hold of him"—and of F. Scott Fitzgerald himself— was the dream that all share who seek to impose some kind of order on a cluttered universe. The meaning Gatsby sought— the "order," if you will—was Daisy; when the betrayal came, his dream disintegrated. . . .

Lionel Trilling thinks that Jay Gatsby "is to be thought of as standing for America itself." Perhaps; everyone is Everyman, in a sense, and Gatsby can stand for America as conveniently as he can stand for himself. But it seems to me that the true significance of *The Great Gatsby* is both more personal and more specific. The "spiritual horror" which Mr. Trilling finds in the novel he ascribes to "the evocation of New York in the heat of summer, the party in the Washington Heights flat, the terrible 'valley of ashes' seen like a corner of the Inferno from the Long Island Railroad ... Gatsby's tremendous, incoherent parties ... the huge, sordid and ever-observant eyes of the oculist's advertising sign." This we may accept; but summer heat and ashes and oculists' signs are horrible not per se but *per causam.* The cause of the horror is, in *The Great Gatsby,* the terrifying contrast between the Buchanans, Jordan Baker, the obscene barflies who descend in formless swarms on Gatsby's house, all symbolized by the gritty disorganized ash heaps with their crumbling men, and the solid ordered structure so paradoxically built on sand (or ashes) which Gatsby's great dream lends to his life. And over it all brood the eyes of Dr. Eckleburg, symbols—of what? Of the eyes of God, as Wilson, whose own world disintegrates with the death of Myrtle, calls them? As a symbol of Gatsby's dream, which like the eyes is pretty shabby after all and scarcely founded on the "hard rocks" Carraway admires? Or—and I think this most likely—do not the eyes in spite of everything they survey, perhaps even because of it, serve both as a focus and an undeviating base, a single point of reference in the midst of monstrous disorder? ...

Here Fitzgerald nearly calls his turn—yet he misses again. For Tom and Daisy retreat "back into their money *or* their vast carelessness." And in the implication of the phrase we see that Fitzgerald was himself unready to give up his old, warm world; that Jay Gatsby was not the only one to pay a high price for living too long with a single dream.

Daisy or Marx?

Ronald J. Gervais

Ronald J. Gervais is a scholar of American literature and a professor of English at San Diego State University.

Fitzgerald, like many intellectuals in the early twentieth century, felt a strong attraction to Communist and socialist ideals. However, his most famous works—including The Great Gatsby—*evoke an intense loyalty to the class system that Marxism said would inevitably be overthrown. Fitzgerald was more interest[ed] in Marxism in theory than in practice. After thorough dis[cus]sion, the author concluded that he could not embrace a po[litical] and social theory so at odds with his romantic individua[lism.]*

In major works written during the "Red Scare" World War I and during the "Red Decade" of Scott Fitzgerald cast his responses to Marxism of ambivalent literary debates in which the op as much attraction for the other side as they their own. His biography and correspond periods also reveal his two-mindedness to For on this subject, too, Fitzgerald cultiv vision, his ability, as he describes it, ideas in the mind, at the same time, to function." Fitzgerald uses Marxis als and frustrations; his qualified his most extreme protest agains the *haute bourgeois* class whi and judges so scathingly, a

Ronald J. Gervais, "The Socialist a[nd...] giance," *Mosaic: A Journal for the* [...] 1982, pp. 80–91. Copyright © 198[...] is herewith made.

the Communist—or else it is nothing, an empty, formalized bore". However materialistic were the ends of Marxism, its origins, as Fitzgerald saw it, were ideal, and not unrelated to bourgeois idealism.

Finally, Fitzgerald could suspend his ambivalences in 1935 only by saying that even though he had been "a Marxist socialist since [he] started thinking," his "writer's instinct" held him back from going all the way.

The separateness of that "writer's instinct" from ideological commitment is made clear in "The Crack-Up" (1936), in which Fitzgerald feels that someone should have helped him to keep his shop open, though "it wasn't Lenin and it wasn't God". And lest any ideologist try to explain too quickly the immolation Fitzgerald sees around him in men of honor and industry, he cautions: "I heard you, but that's too easy—there were Marxians among those men". Fitzgerald decides in the essay to give up his old dream of becoming a Bourgeois Superman, "a sort of combination of J.P. Morgan, Topham Beauclerk and St. Francis of Assisi," and to become "a writer only". Such a concept of the writer as complete individualist and as reduced from total man to the writing function only, immediately drew the fire of John Dos Passos, who in a letter of October 1936 remonstrated with Fitzgerald in the vein of the committed author: "Christ, man, how do you find time in the middle of the general conflagration to worry about all that stuff. . . . We're living in one of the damnedest tragic moments in history—if you want to go to pieces I think it's absolutely o.k.". If cracking up is in question, to the Marxist sympathizer Dos Passos it is the cracking up of a whole world that matters, not of an individual self. Dos Passos could not see that the artist was fulfilling his role by proceeding in Fitzgerald's manner—that is, by looking inward, by exploring his own inner consciousness.

For Fitzgerald, despite his recognition of forces at work in society and the world, it was his own deepest feeling of self

and his hero-worship of other exceptional selves—both lega-
cies from bourgeois individualism—that gave him whatever
sense of orientation he had as a writer. What finally mattered
to him was not the just society but the exalted individual,
though he tried to manage both. . . .

[H]e praised John Reed, the American radical and author
of *Ten Days that Shook the World*, not as a keen observer of
social revolution but as a talented and rebellious young man
of action, such as Fitzgerald himself yearned to be. Despite
whatever radical leanings he professed, Fitzgerald was ultimately less interested in investigating social problems than in
illuminating his own experience and feeling.

Yet part of Fitzgerald did seek a social viewpoint founded
on a practical observation of the facts. He told Malcolm Cowley in 1932, for example, that his "peasant" mother, Molly Mc-
Quillan, was "as realistic as Karl Marx," because she kept telling him, "All this, family is a lot of shit. You have to know
where the money is coming from." But he then proceeds to
tell Cowley how he is descended from Francis Scott Key, to
whom there is a statue in Baltimore. Fitzgerald wonders, at
first jokingly, if they would put up a statue to him, "because
[he] died for communism." But then, more soberly, he imag-
ines a statue to "the author of *The Great Gatsby*!" This mixture of detached social observation and starry-eyed personal
aspiration is Fitzgerald's special gift. It is, Cowley observed, as
if he were describing a big dance to which he had taken the
prettiest girl, and at the same time was wondering how much
the tickets cost and who payed for the music. Fitzgerald knew
as well as any Marxist "where the milk is watered and the
sugar sanded, the rhinestone passed for diamond and the
stucco for stone", but was nevertheless committed to the possibilities of romantic wonder offered by his time and place
and social class. . . .

Romance Above Socialism

Fitzgerald's love for the romantic possibilities of individualism, against any concept of collectivism, puts him ambivalently on the side of the most individualistic of all socioeconomic systems, even when he sees that its freedom has become ruinous. His description of Nicole's shopping trip in *Tender Is the Night* is both an indictment of the moneyed aristocracy and a wonder-song to the glittering life-style open to them. Nicole buys from a great list and buys the things in the windows besides; everything she could not possibly use herself, she buys as a present: beach cushions, love birds, rubber alligator, chamois leather jackets and much more. Then Fitzgerald offers his poetic version of Marxist social analysis, penetrating the veil of appearances to discover the sub-stratum of crude human relations and degradations that private property masks. . . .

Despite its impending doom, the way of life open to the rich is infinitely charming. Its "feverish bloom" and "grace" are insidiously beguiling. . . .

Fitzgerald's own humorous attitude toward Marxism cautions us not to accept his sympathies for it without extreme qualifications. The writer who complains in his *Notebooks* that "in thirty-four and thirty-five the party line crept into everything except the Sears Roebuck catalogue," and who intones with tongue-in-cheek solemnity that, "To bring on the revolution it may be necessary to work inside the communist party," clearly writing from ironic detachment rather than commitment. And if we look at his professions of sympathy throughout his career, we see that they are usually qualified by support for a counterideology which espouses the concept of the superior or autonomous individual. In 1924, for example, he proclaimed himself "a communist." . . . If a proletarian Superman sounds paradoxical, his Jeffersonian communism of 1931 is at least explainable in terms of the Communist Party effort in the 1930s to stress the "revolutionary" and "original democratic" impulses of the Founding Fathers and their documents. In the 1931 interview with a Montgomery, Alabama newspaper, Fitzgerald said he was "a Jeffersonian democrat at heart and somewhat of a Communist in ideals." . . .

Fitzgerald seems to have hoped to the end that individual freedom he knew as a bourgeois artist could somehow be reconciled with the socio-economic critique and concern for justice that he admired in Marxism. If the plight of two friends who had managed their resources wisely, yet had been dragged down in the terrible reverses of 1932 could drive Fitzgerald "more and more toward the red flag about which I have been may-poling at a distance all through the decade," the fact is that he consistently maintained that critical distance. The combination of enthusiasm and skepticism implied in the metaphor is characteristic of his double-vision; he could incorporate Marxism into the moral standpoint from which he examined and condemned his American plutocrats, and yet not be blinded by its ideology from seeing and wondering at their beauty and heroism.

Social Issues
in Literature

Chapter 3

Contemporary
Perspectives on
Class Conflict

The Rich Are Different

Richard Conniff

Richard Conniff is a prolific writer on a wide variety of subjects, ranging from natural history to economics. His books include The Energy People: A History of PSE&G *(with James C.G. Conniff);* Irish Walls *(with Allen MacWheeney);* Spineless Wonders, *and* The Ape in the Office.

Fitzgerald once wrote that "The rich are different from you and me." In 2007, with corporate salaries reaching into the hundreds of millions annually while many make less than four dollars an hour, this statement is as true as it was when the author composed it. In the following excerpt from his book The Natural History of the Rich, *Richard Conniff attempts to explore the differences of the rich by applying animal studies to human beings. When members of a certain species (such as apes) acquire more food, they begin to behave differently than others of their kind, and others act differently around them. So do humans, Conniff concludes. In* The Great Gatsby, *we can see this kind of behavior modification in the relationship between the Buchanans and the Wilsons.*

L et's begin with an embarrassing admission. Unlike certain pioneering works in the field of evolutionary psychology, this book did not have its origins on the rock-solid foundation of an attitudinal survey. Nor did it, like many great studies in animal behavior, emerge as a result of ten thousand hours of careful fieldwork watching spiders spin webs. It started with a tip from a stockbroker. I was visiting Monaco on an unlikely assignment for *National Geographic*, and it felt as if I had entered another universe, where even the most casual conversation was liable to veer off at any moment into the surreal. One day, for instance, I was having a friendly drink with two young women seeking starter husbands when one of them asked the other, "Does he still have the Jaguar with the matching dog?" . . .

As a natural history writer, I've always assumed that all individual animals, from the Australian bulldog ant on up to [media executive] Rupert Murdoch, conform, more or less, to the rules of their species. They fit into basic patterns of physiology, territoriality, social hierarchy, reproductive behavior, parental care, and so on, and the ones that don't fit generally get eaten.

So I began to wonder if it wasn't possible to think of the rich in a new light—as animals, that is. . . .

Second, we all hope to be rich ourselves. We are descended almost by definition from people who liked food and sex. From them we have inherited deeply embedded biological drives for status, for waterfront real estate, for landscapes of the English country house variety (derived ultimately from the African savanna), and for a variety of other attractive features often associated with the rich and famous. Moreover, all our disclaimers to the contrary, we long to be like them. We pay attention to the rich as slavishly as a troop of gorillas following the lead of its dominant silverback. We mimic them as aptly as a viceroy butterfly mimics the coloration of a monarch. As in any dominance hierarchy, we also fear the rich. They can use their power to hurt us in ways we hardly recognize. . . .

Moreover, life at the top can be in some ways exceedingly unpleasant. I recently heard a trust fund beneficiary rattle off a list of woes associated with inherited wealth, including social isolation, resentment from peers, rich-bashing from society, betrayal or exploitation by friends, unrealistic expectations from family and society, unequal financial status in marriage, and an absence of all the usual factors (like worrying about the rent) that cause the rest of us to drag ourselves out of bed most mornings in search of bread and a modicum of self-worth. He might also have added that the rich get no sympathy. When you are worth millions of dollars, there is a presumption that you should shut up and bear it. . . .

If men come from Mars and women from Venus, where on earth do rich people come from? Are they, as ordinary people often suspect, an alien life form? Is their blood the color of money? Do they have special antennae, as their press people like to suggest, for picking up distant intimations of profit and loss? Can they see around corners? Is life on Canis Major, the big dog star, really light years apart from the bow-wow world of ordinary runts like you and me? The truth is that rich people are not even a different species from us. They are more like a different subspecies.

The rich themselves often say that they just want to be normal people, leading normal lives. "I just want to be middle class," was a familiar refrain among dazzled Internet millionaires in the late 1990s. Then, to their horror, they got what they wished. This ambivalence about wealth is perhaps sincere, but it's also a little disingenuous. Jeff Bezos of Amazon.com made himself a folk hero of the era as a billionaire who drove a beat-up Honda and celebrated frugality. "I don't think wealth actually changes people," he declared. But at the time he was moving out of his 900-square-foot rental in downtown Seattle to a $10 million waterfront house in the leafy suburb of Medina, where his new neighbors included Microsoft billionaires Bill Gates, Jon Shirley, and Nathan Myhrvold. Then, 7,000 square feet perhaps seeming relatively frugal in this context, he decided to expand the place. Wealth is like that. . . .

A Numbers Game

One afternoon in Aspen, I had coffee with a local craftsman. He was the second person that day to let me know early in the conversation that he didn't need to work for a living. He'd married into a prominent family, and when the name failed to produce a satisfactory response, he said, "They owned General Dynamics," a manufacturer of some of the deadliest weapon systems on Earth. "They owned the Empire State building," he said. "Do you have the *Forbes* 400 list?" he asked. It turned out that they are currently worth about $3 billion. . . .

He was scathing about wannabes. Maybe it was because he was himself a relative newcomer in this world. "You can't pretend to have the speed of a cheetah, when you're really a mule," he said. A new country club in town especially irked him. It created "a different level of Aspen citizen, those who belonged, and those who didn't. It was really terribly exclusive in a way a lot of us resented." He'd signed on as a charter member, just to get in a quick round of golf. But the other members turned out to be, on average, sixty-four years old. Mules, not cheetahs. They needed five-and-a-half hours to complete a round. So having bought his membership at $60,000, he sold out at $175,000 and could savor his righteousness. . . .

Money Doesn't Interest Me

What do they all have in common? Almost all in one form or another expressed the idea that money by itself didn't interest them that much. In the beginning, this sounded like the fourth biggest lie, along with "the check is in the mail," and so on. If so, it was a lie with a great tradition. In the library at The Breakers, their seventy-room cottage in Newport, Rhode Island, for instance, Cornelius and Alice Gwynne Vanderbilt had a white marble mantel bearing the venerable French inscription, "Little do I care for riches, and do not miss them, since only cleverness prevails in the end." Biographer Barbara Goldsmith writes that the Vanderbilts saw no irony in purchasing this mantel, which had been pried off the fireplace of a 400-year-old château in Burgundy. Presumably the builder of the

Billionaire Paul Allen's yacht, the Octopus, *is seen here anchored off Rio de Janiero, Brazil, in 2004. Reported to have cost over $200 million to build, the 126-meter-long yacht is one of the largest in the world.* Vanderlei Almeida/AFP/Getty Images.

château also saw no irony in putting the mantel there in the first place. Rich people have always believed it is their cleverness, their wit, their taste, their athletic ability—anything but their money—that makes them special.

And yet they often acted as if money was the only thing that interested them. They practiced the dull art of price-tag parlor talk: "The trouble with Arnie is that he'll only spend $150,000 for a pilot, when he could get a damned good one for $250,000." They applied price tags with wild, domineering abandon even to the most delicate questions of marriage and family life. A photographer friend who was making portraits of two gorgeous younger wives not long ago overheard one of them discussing a sex act proposed by her aging husband. For better and for worse, the details of this sex act are unknown, except that she refused to participate. So he offered her $100,000 and then $200,000. "I'm not doing it," she said, to which he replied, "$350,000, and that's my final offer." She thought about this for a moment, perhaps contemplating what her mother once told her about the spirit of give-and-take in marriage. Or maybe she was just thinking about the price of a Russian sable fur coat. Then she said, "I'll do it for that." . . .

Pecking Orders

Dominance is an astonishingly new idea in biology, first put forward early in the twentieth century by an obscure Norwegian researcher studying the behavior of chickens. Thorleif Schjelderup-Ebbe coined the term "pecking order" and defined the idea of the dominance hierarchy. For his efforts, he was thoroughly crushed by the Scandinavian biological hierarchy and never gained academic employment. But his ideas caught on. In the 1930s, other researchers coined the term "alpha male" to describe the leader of a wolf pack. Biologists began to see dominance hierarchies almost everywhere.

Unfortunately—and this is the first caveat—they have never come remotely close to agreeing on just what dominance means. Different researchers looking at the same group of animals may identify the dominant individual by any of four common definitions: It's the one who can beat up everybody else but doesn't necessarily need to (the Warren Buffett 800-pound gorilla style of dominance). Or it's the one who displays the most aggression (the school of competition exemplified by Larry Ellison of Oracle, who once quoted Genghis Khan: "It is not sufficient that I succeed; everyone else must fail"). Or it's the one to whom other members of the group pay the most attention (the Richard Branson "Look at me in a wedding dress" paradigm). Or it's the one who gets the first pass at resources like food, sex, or a nice place to sleep (King Fahd of Saudi Arabia has bedrooms reserved for his pleasure in the palaces and yachts of Saudi princes around the world, the equivalent of several dozen $2,500-a-night hotel suites, on call every night, all year long, year after year, though he will almost certainly never visit them).

The obvious problem with these four definitions is that the same animal can easily turn up as the alpha in one study and the beta in another. Researchers who regard control of resources as the defining factor, for instance, tend to believe the dominant individual in a group is *least likely* to display aggression. Everybody else is too scared to challenge his status, except at great intervals. Aggression is more typical, they say, of middle-rank individuals jockeying for position in the hope of an eventual bid for the top. . . .

An Elaborate Code

So how do we read the rest of the unwritten code of social dominance? An alpha wolf establishes his authority by biting a rival on the neck and pinning him to the ground. Rich humans are seldom quite that direct. On the Mexican border one time, I met a beautiful, fast-talking, finger-snapping young woman in spangled earrings and a short skirt. She let me know unabashedly and at every turn the power of her family's money. "I mean, we don't own *everything*," she said. "But we own things that you guys need. That humans need. We own the gas company. We own the industrial park. We own the print shop. We have a construction company. Nobody has anything against us," she said, and then she explained: "*We'll cut off your gas.*"

The better class of rich people tend to frown on such crass expressions of power. Well, they frown on them and yearn for them at the same time. People expect Oracle and Microsoft to work out their differences like grownups, in the courtroom, with antitrust lawyers as intermediaries. But how delicious it is when the rivalry surfaces in a personal context. A couple of summers ago, Oracle's stock was soaring and Larry Ellison briefly passed Microsoft cofounder Paul Allen to become the world's second-richest person. Ellison was celebrating aboard his 243-foot yacht off Capri. Then he spotted a 200-foot yacht heading out on a twilight cruise to the village of Positano. It was Paul Allen's *Meduse*, the sort of thing rich people make a point of knowing. When they land the Gulfstream V at Aspen airport, they check out the tail number on the Gulfstream V next door to see how the pecking order stands. So Ellison ordered his captain to crank his yacht's three engines to full speed. He overtook Allen's yacht at forty miles an hour, throwing up a huge wake that sent Allen and his guests staggering. "It was an adolescent prank," Ellison told *The Washington Post* afterward. "I highly recommend it." It was of course also an expression of social dominance. (Foul weather warning: Allen has since moved back up to number three on the *Forbes* 400, while Ellison has fallen behind to number four, and both men now go down to the sea in much bigger ships.)

Twenty-First-Century Flappers

Gloria Goodale

Gloria Goodale is a staff writer of the Christian Science Monitor.

The flappers of The Great Gatsby's *Jazz Age, with all their talentless, coarse but endless publicity, are alive and well in the first decade of the twenty-first century. The most notorious is Paris Hilton, whose chief advantage is being one of the heirs to the multibillion-dollar Hilton fortune. Like Fitzgerald's flappers, Paris enjoys the publicity that her fame and fortune, as well as her behavior, has brought her. Appearing on reality TV, Paris and other young heirs have shown the working class what it is like to be young, famous, and very wealthy. Because of this insight into the lives of the rich and famous, the lower class has developed the habit of being in constant pursuit of wealth. People desire a life of luxury, much like the characters of* The Great Gatsby.

There is a moment in the coming Fox reality show, "The Simple Life," in which hotel heiress Paris Hilton, who has been transported to work on a dairy farm in rural America, asks her host family what a Wal-Mart is. "Do they sell walls there, or something?"

Reality TV Gold

For producers, this is reality-TV gold, because of course, the entertainment value of the show lies in displaying the clueless rich girl as she flaunts her ignorance about the way simple folk live.

The problem with this scenario is that it's not true. Ms. Hilton was tweaking the family—and the producers—for her own fun. "I was joking," she says simply. "I was, like, playing dumb."

As the show unfolds, the girls (Ms. Hilton is joined by her best friend, Nicole Richie [daughter of singer Lionel Richie]), play with our preconceptions about the pampered rich. Perhaps because both the girls and the family turn out to be unexpectedly endearing, the show is delicious fun.

When "The Simple Life" debuts Dec. 2 [2003], it will join two others already on the air—"Born Rich" on HBO, and "Rich Girls" on MTV—that deal with the lives and attitudes of some of our country's most well-known wealthy offspring. Providing entertainment by tweaking the rich is as old as the Greeks. But, say observers, in targeting privileged progeny, these shows actually reveal an important sea change in our attitudes about money and its role in that most basic of American pastimes, the pursuit of happiness.

Making Money Is Most Important

"If you look at studies of what college kids ranked most important back in 1967, contributing to society ranked very high," says Elayne Rapping, media studies professor at State University of New York at Buffalo. "Becoming wealthy was much lower. Today, it's just the opposite."

Several participants in the "Born Rich" film say their parents never mentioned the possibility that their life goals might include anything other than making money.

"[We have] affiliations that don't favor charitable actions," says S.I. Newhouse IV, heir to the *Condé Nast* publishing fortune.

Pursuit of Money Has Become "An Illness"

Many of the young heirs in these various programs, Dr. Rapping points out, were born during the go-go Reagan years, in which greed was considered good in some quarters. They came of age during the stock-market explosion of the 1990s. Today, she adds, "we are living in a world in which the pursuit of money has become what I would dub an illness."

These shows are like giant Rorschach tests, says Paul Schervish, director of the Social Welfare Research Institute in Chestnut Hill, Mass. "The commentaries that we make around the water coolers and living rooms in dealing with the subject of wealth are as much about ourselves as they are about the object of our attention," he says, adding that we look for in others that which we aspire to ourselves.

As we examine the young adults in these various shows, we are taking stock of what Mr. Schervish calls our own moral biographies.

"We are tempted in our views to either adulate or attack the wealthy; to be at their throat or at their feet," he says, primarily because we expect more of them. "We look to the wealthy to have somehow not only greater capacity, but greater character," he says. When they do, we admire them. When they appear to fail on the character front, we feel justified in excoriating them.

Examination of the Wealthy

College student Ivanka Trump [daughter of American business executive Donald Trump] who appears in "Born Rich," knows something about being watched. "As I go into life," she says, "people look at me sometimes in a different way and expect me—or sadly, sometimes want me—to fail in certain ways."

This examination of the wealthy for clues about our own motivations has taken on particular power in today's hyperdeveloped consumer culture.

For the first time in history, observes Schervish, it is possible for middle-class families to taste the kind of life only the rich could afford just a generation ago.

Paris (r) and Nicky Hilton pose for photos at a pre-Oscar event in 2004. AP Images.

"You can buy that Lexus or go on that cruise and be on the same boat with the rich," he says, adding that this shift means more and more choices are no longer dictated by the wallet but by values.

Breeding a Society of Discontent

"Luxuries have become necessities," agrees Diane Wood, executive director of the Center for a New American Dream in Takoma Park, Md. This means that "we are breeding a society of discontent."

While confessing that she herself would not be able to survive without her money (she recently purchased a $1,500 dog carrier for her pet), Hilton herself has a thing or two to say about money and happiness following her experience "roughing it" in middle America.

"I met some people there, and they're so much happier than people I see in L.A., who have so much money. People who didn't have anything were, like, more happy than people I've met out here because it's just all about your family," she says. "And I think it would be a great place to, like, raise kids, instead of raising them in L.A."

The Criminal Class

Gene Mustain and Jerry Capeci

Jerry Capeci and Gene Mustain are specialists in the study of gangsterism. Both are former New York Daily News *reporters. Their books include* Murder Machine *(1992). Capeci is also author of* The Idiot's Guide to the Mafia.

One of the most intriguing characters in The Great Gatsby *is Gatsby's business associate Meyer Wolfsheim, an influential mobster. Fitzgerald suggests that Gatsby's association with Wolfsheim brought him the wealth he spends so freely, and that this wealth was based on smuggling and selling alcohol into the United States during Prohibition (1919–1933). By the middle of the twentieth century, organized crime figures had moved on from smuggling alcohol to infiltrating unions, hijacking trucks, and extorting money from businessmen. John Gotti, who died early in the twenty-first century, was one of the most formidable mob bosses. Gotti and Gatsby share some characteristics in common: they were both reared in poor households, they both aspired to high station, and they both enjoyed lavish lifestyles.*

The day after John Gotti became a grandfather in 1984, he won $55,000 playing "the numbers"—the widely patronized though illegal Family [mafia, or organized crime] lottery. He celebrated by buying his grandson a $10,000 bond, worth $20,000 at maturity.

"Second day of his life, the kid has twenty thousand dollars," John told Dominick Lofaro. "Me, I had two . . . cents."

The Humble Beginnings of a Wealthy Gangster

John Joseph Gotti Jr., born October 27, 1940, in the Bronx, also had a dozen brothers and sisters. He was the fifth child of a construction worker and his wife, Fannie. Two brothers and twin sisters, all less than 5 years old, preceded him. And over the next 11 years they were joined by four more boys and two girls. Two other siblings died during childhood.

John Joseph Gotti Sr. was a hard-working but low-earning man of Neapolitan origin. With 13 kids in 16 years, he was barely able to provide. When the namesake son's freedom was at stake in Brooklyn more than four decades later, his lawyer painted a portrait of a proud man whose fastidious appearance lay in the fact that he overcame a childhood of severe deprivation.

"He doesn't apologize for growing up poor," Bruce Cutler would say. . . .

The same forces that affected Italian Harlem caused John's family to move away from the Bronx during the middle of his fourth year at P.S. [public school] 113. They moved into a two-story wood-frame house on East Thirteenth Street in Sheepshead Bay, a tranquil community in the far southeastern corner of Brooklyn, near the Atlantic Ocean.

John enrolled in P.S. 209; classmates included kids whose parents had achieved more prosperity than the Gotti clan. John began to see that in some minds a kid's status was unfairly tied to his parents' status, which was measured by income. It wasn't his fault he was poor; a little river of resentment began to flow through John, and occasionally it bubbled up as a cocky strut and a sharp tongue. . . .

Teens at Franklin K. Lane High School had many competing street gangs to choose from. John joined the Fulton-Rockaway Boys. Brother Peter already was a member; brothers Richard and Gene signed up later. Another member was Angelo Ruggiero, a pudgy-faced, pigeon-toed kid who was called "Quack Quack" and became John's pal. As was the custom, the Fulton-Rockaway Boys, whose name came from a street intersection a few blocks from school, adopted special colors; theirs were black and purple, the color of bruises. In such gangs, poor teenagers found self-esteem and group identity. The year John joined the Fulton-Rockaway Boys, Marlon Brando starred as Johnny, the rebel hero of *The Wild One*, a popular film about a gang taking over a town. . . .

Youth Gangs of New York

In 1952, the future crime boss completed the sixth grade. This was the year 12-year-old Johnny Gotti, according to Bruce Cutler's trial portrait, went off "on his own"—and the year the Gotti clan was forced to move again after their house was sold.

John's parents had few housing options. They finally moved to the Brownsville-East New York area of Brooklyn, a neglected working-class community that was home to thousands of southern Italian immigrants and Eastern European Jews who had abandoned stacked Manhattan ghettos. . . .

The Rockaway Boys also feuded with the Ridgewood Saints, a particularly violent gang, according to Matthew Traynor, an ex-Saints gang leader who went on to bank robbery and other crimes. In one fight, a Rockaway bled to death after he was stabbed and tossed through a window. Another incident involving a Rockaway landed Traynor in jail. . . .

Eventually, the neighborhood's older gang members, who called their gang a Family, heard about this boy who talked like a politician and wasn't afraid. Pivotally, two of these adult-gang members were Carmine and Daniel Fatico, who, the boy-gang members knew, were connected to a large Family led by Albert Anastasia, who was so important his name was only whispered.

The Fatico brothers operated out of a storefront they called The Club and were active in hijacking, extortion, gambling, and loan-sharking. They killed only when necessary, the boys thought. Carmine was older and cagey; he had been pinched more than a dozen times but had hardly spent any time in jail.

New York City mob boss John Gotti appears in court. AP/Wide World Photos.

Besides the Fatico brothers, plenty more of the wrong role models lived close by. Two of them, Wilfred "Willie Boy" Johnson and William Battista, would become important members of John's crew in Ozone Park. Willie Boy was a sausage stuffer by day, a bookmaker by night, a part-time boxer, and part American Indian. He had a violent and justifiably tough reputation, having fatally stabbed his brother-in-law and survived a bullet to the head fired by the dead man's friend.

Battista was a gambler, too, but his early fame was based on a truck hijacking he had staged using inside information from a secretary who lived on Bergen Street, around the corner from John. Battista waited until the truck driver took his coffee break at the time and place the girl indicated, and then just hot-wired the rig and drove off with $75,000 worth of new clothes. . . .

En route to the majors, John made rookie mistakes. At 17, he was arrested for burglary after he and a few confederates were caught in the act of stealing copper from a construction firm. He pleaded guilty and was placed on probation.

The terms of his probation required him to shun unsavory places and characters—a nearly impossible burden for anyone in Brownsville-East New York. Now a committed juvenile delinquent, John continued to hang out in poolrooms, bars, bookie joints, and racetracks.

In 1959, he was arrested for the first time as an adult. The charge was unlawful assembly; he had been caught in a raid on a gambling location. Theoretically, he had violated his probation and could have been jailed immediately. Instead, he was allowed to remain free. Nearly a year later, after he had been arrested again and fined $200 for disorderly conduct, the unlawful assembly charge came up on the court calendar. . . .

The Adult Gangster Class

He wasn't making much money, however. Between the family and the car and the hanging out, he was always broke. And he and [wife] Victoria kept having kids: three in three years. Angela was followed by another girl, Victoria, and a son, who was named John. Money woes and his nocturnal touring of pool halls, gambling dens, and honky-tonks caused the young parents to fight; they separated several times.

Some separations were forced. In 1963, John went behind bars for the first time—20 days in a city jail after he and Salvatore Ruggiero, Angelo's brother, were arrested in a car reported stolen from the Avis rent-a-car company. Salvatore was a bright boy who would go far in crime, too, but not as a Family man. Sal would become a very rich drug dealer. . . .

He was acquitted of the January charges, but pleaded guilty to the attempted theft and was jailed for several months in 1966. This cost him his job with the Barnes Express Company and a lot of goodwill with his wife. Struggling to support three small children whose father was a jailbird caused her to seek public relief from the New York City Department of Welfare and to file support petitions against him in Domestic Relations Court in Brooklyn.

Any reluctance to completely embrace crime as a way of life melted away in the wake of these humiliations. In the next year, John would not find another job; he would become a professional hijacker.

John was only 26, not too old to seek the education or training which might have opened a legitimate door of opportunity. But he was too impatient and too scornful. He had a wife, three kids, and expensive appetites. He had them *now*. What could he be? A store manager? An insurance salesman? *Forget about it.*

When John thought of successful men, he thought of Carmine and Daniel Fatico. They wore fine clothes and drove big cars. At the track, they could lose with cheer as opposed to despair. They were respected, maybe not by the wider world, but by the young men of John's world.

The Club and Class

Mike Morris

Mike Morris, editor-in-chief of The DePauw, *the oldest student newspaper in Indiana, broke the story of the Delta Zeta scandal a week before the* New York Times *and other national newspapers picked it up. Morris went on to win a prize for in-depth reporting from the Granville, Ohio, Sentinel.*

F. Scott Fitzgerald recognized the importance of what a later generation would call "networking" in The Great Gatsby. *The influence of a fine college and the reputation of its clubs and fraternities were well known in the 1920s, and the exclusiveness of these social organizations was felt to be crucial to one's social status in adult life. It was commonplace for members of fraternities, sororities, and other social organizations to remain close for the rest of their lives, and to help each other in advancing their careers. These facts stayed with Fitzgerald throughout his career.*

Class consciousness in fraternal organizations remains an issue at the beginning of the twenty-first century. In 2007, the Delta Zeta sorority at DePauw University expelled twenty-three members, giving as its reason that the women did not meet standards of attractiveness. Some of the expelled members later indicated that they felt they were also targeted because of their ethnicities.

Twenty-three members of Delta Zeta sorority—half of the chapter—were asked in early December to leave the house in a move national organizers say will strengthen the house by its centennial at DePauw in 2009. Six others have since chosen to leave.

Trouble started last August, when junior Sarah Carlson, a former officer, said national representatives gave the officers

Mike Morris, "DZ 'Reorganizes,' Loses 29 Women," *The DePauw*, vol. 155, February 2, 2007, pp. 1, 3. Reproduced by permission.

two options: improve recruitment or choose not to participate in rush. Too small a pledge class or a vote not to participate in rush would result in the closing of the house.

The officers brought the matter before their sisters, and after one deadlocked vote, the women chose not to participate in rush.

Carlson, who was asked to leave, attributed the vote to a sense of disillusionment with recruitment.

"We were just tired of fighting all year," Carlson said. "We were tired of trying to fight the system. . . . We just wanted to enjoy the year together."

But everything changed Sept. 12, when two Delta Zeta national representatives met with Greek Life Director Tom Hansen and Dean of Students Cynthia Babington. Closing the chapter, Hansen said, would not guarantee Delta Zeta a place on campus when it came time to reopen—their proposal to start a new chapter would be one of many.

The sorority's national Executive Director Cindy Menges was surprised by the news.

Complex Politic of the Greek System

"Wow, OK," she said. "What do we do now?"

Of the alternatives Hansen presented to Menges and the sorority's national Vice President Kathi Heatherly, the two chose to conduct a membership review to identify the women willing to commit to recruitment.

For years, DZ has been DePauw's smallest sorority. Menges said the chapter's struggle with recruitment was caused by the perception of the chapter as being unsuccessful.

"Delta Zeta was the odd man out because we just didn't have as many numbers as the other groups," she said.

Senior Morgan Murphy, who is one of six women staying in the chapter, sees overcoming these perceptions as the task awaiting those women who remain.

"I've seen a lot of girls go through Delta Zeta's recruitment process and seem like they're having a great time . . . and everybody thinks they're going to go there, but when it comes right down to it, they won't go there," she said. "And it's not because of the women, it's because of the stigma of being a Delta Zeta. . . . We're trying to move beyond the stigma."

Two consultants from headquarters are now living in the house and have spearheaded a marketing push to distinguish the Delta Zeta of last semester from the house they're attempting to build. The effort has included the posting of flyers around campus and the delivery of letters and even desserts to other greek chapters.

One of the consultants, Liz Urso, said the chapter has participated in formal recruitment this week but is focusing on a more informational approach.

The move, termed a "reorganization," sent a ripple through the campus community.

"I do not think it's fair to disrupt a chapter and the lives of women who thought they were going to live in that house for a year to tell them in the middle of the year they have to move," said University President Robert G. Bottoms in a mid-December interview. "I also do not think matters were handled in a very sensitive manner. Even if you're justified in taking the actions that they took, why in the world would you do it the week before finals?"

Communication Breakdown

DZ women said things first got fuzzy at the Sept. 12 meeting. They said the national representatives told them things—particularly about the membership review conducted in mid-November—that would turn out to be false. Uncomfortable with the situation, four women took alumnae status even before the review began.

Menges said Delta Zeta as a national organization does not typically conduct member reviews.

"We're not saying that we're free of mistakes," Menges said, admitting the process could have been clearer.

Sophomore Lindsey Kinker, who was asked to leave, remembers being told that women uncomfortable with the plan could take alumnae status voluntarily. Carlson and sophomore Joanna Kieschnick, who was invited to stay but chose to leave, recalled Heatherly saying similar things.

Heatherly said even if she can't recall her exact words Sept. 12, she knows her intentions were good.

"What they thought we meant wasn't what we meant, and we're sorry for that," Heatherly said. "We're certainly willing to say that we're sorry."

At the same time, Heatherly said, the women may have "heard what they wanted to hear" at the meeting.

Menges said if the women recommended for alumnae status had fought to remain in the sorority, they could have circumvented the recommendation. No one has done so, she said.

During the membership review, however, Kieschnick and Carlson each recalled asking their interviewer whether they could remain active members if they were recommended for alumnae status.

"We were told that if we were recommended for alumnae status we would have no say in the matter," Carlson said. "If we tried to challenge it they would deactivate us."

Kieschnick said she received the same response.

Party More but Losing Out

Junior Rachel Pappas, the chapter's former secretary, took unofficial notes at the Sept. 12 meeting. Her notes showed Heatherly suggesting the women bend the rules and perhaps party more.

"I am a . . . national vice president, and if you think that I'm going to go out to a chapter and tell them to bend our national rules and risk my 25 years of service in Delta Zeta . . . then I'm sorry, but I would not do that," Heatherly said, but added: "There is a social climate to the DePauw greek community . . . I'm not talking about drinking, I'm talking about socializing and getting out and meeting people and making friends."

To Carlson, the whole process seemed wrong. She said she thought things had been finalized when the women voted not to participate in rush Aug. 20.

"We thought that we had made the decision for them, and they couldn't change what we decided," she said.

The Aftermath

Each woman interviewed received a letter Dec. 2 informing them of nationals' decision.

There are competing theories as to why some women were asked to stay and others to leave. Senior Cindy Geiger, who was asked to stay but chose to leave, said she thought it was social networks: if the interviewers liked someone, they'd identify her closest friends and invite them to stay.

Menges said the choices were based solely on the member's ability to commit to recruitment.

"During that membership review, if someone tells you that they love Delta Zeta . . . but I really don't have the time you're asking me for, we said that's part of what our problem is, ladies. We've got to have the commitment," Menges said.

Kinker said her life is less stressful without the time commitment of greek life, but that she was willing to help the plan succeed.

"I told them it was hard for me to live in a house on this campus, but I was willing to do whatever it was to participate and be a part of this organization," she said.

Geiger said she knew even before opening her letter she wouldn't stay.

"I just didn't like the idea that they could ask active, dedicated members who did nothing wrong . . . to leave their own chapter," she said.

Sisterhood Not Enough

Ultimately, the process has embittered women on all sides. As it stands, the women who accepted alumnae status were paid $300 to cover the difference between room and board at DZ and University housing. Most have moved into Bloomington Street Hall or North Quad.

But the business-like attitude of this process did not appeal to Geiger.

"I wish that nationals could have found a way to market what we had with the sisterhood and market that to make it appealing," she said.

Making matters worse, senior Crystal Drummond said a few days after she received the letter asking her to take alumnae status she received another letter asking her to donate money to the Delta Zeta Foundation. She declined.

Murphy took a broader view.

"Greek life is about image and popularity and numbers and those are all areas where Delta Zeta lacked, despite the fact that we had amazing sisterhood," she said. "Obviously, on DePauw's campus, sisterhood alone isn't enough to keep a sorority alive."

For Further Discussion

1. Identify two of the writers included in this volume who hold different views of Gatsby. Evaluate their positions.

2. Drawing on the articles and your own reading of *The Great Gatsby*, examine Fitzgerald's feelings toward the upper class in the novel and compare them to those of today's society. (See Bewley, Millgate, and Morris.)

3. Write a paper on the portrait of the lower class in the novel. Is it negative or sympathetic? (See Bewley.)

4. Examine Gatsby's character. Is he primarily sympathetic or unsympathetic? Does he ever see the upper classes for what they are? (See Cowley, Meredith, Curnutt, and Dyson.)

5. Describe Fitzgerald's portraits of upper-, middle-, and lower-class women. Compare them with the current views of the early twenty-first century. (See Sanderson and Goodale.)

6. Examine Fitzgerald's social view of class. Is he a traditionalist or a leftist? (See Millgate, Burnam, Gervais, and Conniff.)

For Further Reading

Theodore Dreiser *An American Tragedy*. New York: Boni and Liverright, 1925.

F. Scott Fitzgerald *The Beautiful and the Damned*. New York: C. Scribner's Sons, 1922.

F. Scott Fitzgerald *Flappers and Philosophers*. New York: C. Scribner's Sons, 1920.

F. Scott Fitzgerald *Tender Is the Night*. New York: C. Scribner's Sons, 1934.

F. Scott Fitzgerald *This Side of Paradise*. New York: C. Scribner's Sons, 1920.

William Dean Howells *The Rise of Silas Lapham*. Boston: Ticknor, 1885.

Henry James *The American*. London: Ward Lock and Co., 1877.

Henry James *The Wings of the Dove*. New York: C. Scribner's Sons, 1902.

Sinclair Lewis *Babbitt*. New York: Harcourt Brace and Co., 1922.

Edith Wharton *The Age of Innocence*. New York: D. Appleton and Co., 1920.

Bibliography

Books

Frederick Lewis Allen — *Only Yesterday: An Informal History of the 1920s.* New York: Harper and Row, 1931.

Herbert Asbury — *The Great Illusion: An Informal History of Prohibition.* New York: Doubleday, 1950.

Matthew Bruccoli — *Profile of F. Scott Fitzgerald.* Columbus, OH: Charles E. Merrill, 1971.

Kenneth F. Eble — *Scott Fitzgerald.* New York: Twayne, 1977.

William Fahey — *F. Scott Fitzgerald and the American Dream.* New York: Crowell, 1973.

Frederick J. Hoffman. Ed. — *"The Great Gatsby": A Study.* New York: Charles Scribner's, 1962.

Alfred Kazin. Ed. — *F. Scott Fitzgerald: The Man and His Work.* New York: Collier Books, 1967.

Christopher Lasch — *The Revolt of the Elites.* New York: W.W. Norton, 1995.

Page Smith — *Redeeming the Time: A People's History of the 1920s and the New Deal.* New York: McGraw-Hill, 1987.

Brian Way — *F. Scott Fitzgerald and the Art of Social Fiction.* London: St Martin's Press, 1980.

Periodicals

E.C. Bufkin   "A Pattern of Parallels and Doubles: The Function of Myrtle in *The Great Gatsby*." *Modern Fiction Studies*. Vol. 15 (winter 1969–1970): 517–524.

Jeffrey Louis Decker   "Gatsby's Pristine Dream: The Diminishment of the Self-Made Man in the Tribal Twenties." *Novel*. Vol. 28 (fall 1994): 52–71.

Barbara Ehrenreich   "The Rich Are Making the Poor Poorer." Alternet. http://www.alternet.org/workplace/53962/. June 13, 2007.

Martin Kallich   "F. Scott Fitzgerald: Money and Morals." *University of Kansas City Review*. Vol. 15 (summer 1949): 271–280.

Kenneth S. Knodt   "The Gathering Darkness: A Study of the Effects of Technology in *The Great Gatsby*." *Fitzgerald/Hemingway Annual*. Vol. 8 (1976): 130–138.

Alberta Lena   "Deceitful Traces of Power: An Analysis of the Decadence of Tom Buchanan in *The Great Gatsby*." *Canadian Review of American Studies*. Vol. 28 (1998): 19–41.

Michael Millgate   "Scott Fitzgerald as Social Novelist." *English Studies*. Vol. 43 (February 1962): 29–34.

Kermit W. Moyer   *"The Great Gatsby*: Fitzgerald's Meditation on American History."
Fitzgerald/Hemingway Annual. Vol. 4 (1972): 43–57.

Robert Ornstein   "Scott Fitzgerald's Fable of East and West." *College English*. Vol. 18 (December 1956): 139–143.

Alan Reynolds   "Class Struggle?" The Cato Institute. May 19, 2005.

Joseph N. Riddel   "F. Scott Fitzgerald, the Jamesian Inheritance, and the Morality of Fiction," *Modern Fiction Studies*. Vol. II (Winter 1965–1966): 331–350.

Michael Santoli   "Rich America, Poor America." *Smart Money*. January 23, 2007.

Gary Scharnhorst   "Scribbling Upward: Fitzgerald's Debt to Horatio Alger, Jr." *Fitzgerald/Hemingway Annual*. Vol. 10 (1978).

Silicon Valley Blogger   "Does Achieving Wealth Make You 'Upper Class'? Facts about Class." *The Digerati Life*. July 12, 2007.

Jim Webb   "Class Struggle: American Workers Have a Chance to Be Heard." *Opinion Journal*. November 15, 2006.

Index